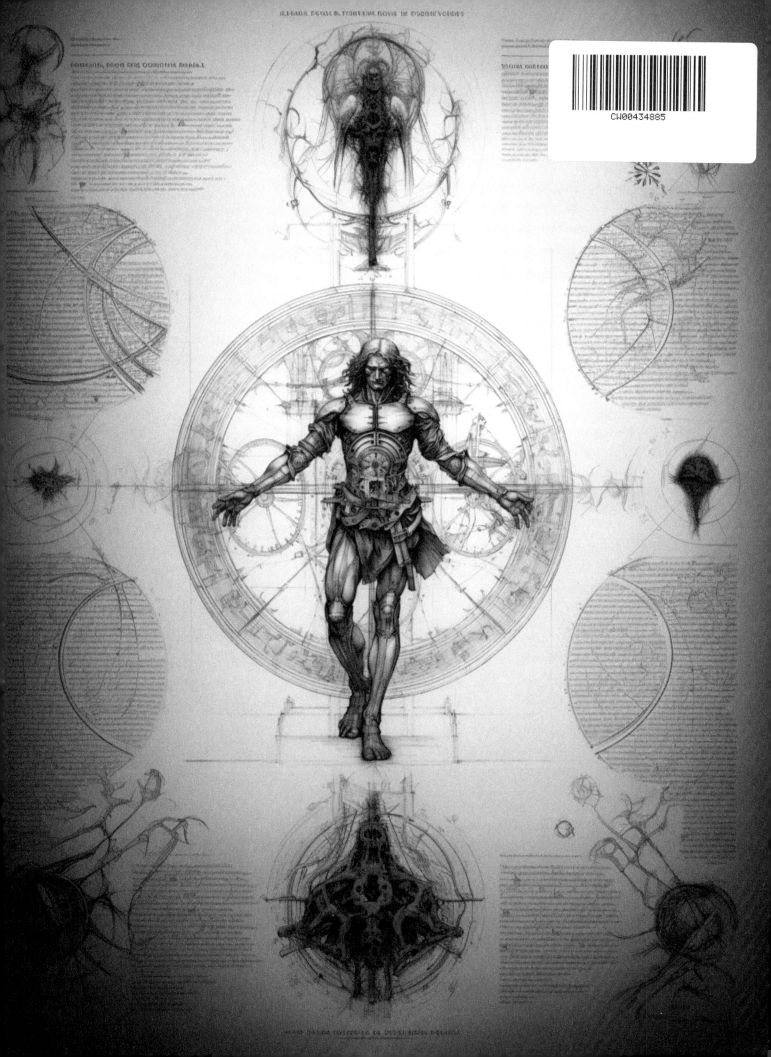

da Vinculum
The Lost Language and Arcane Arts of Leonardo da Vinci
Book 1 of Artes Arcani

© Copyright 2023 Cineris Multifacet

by Vannevar Mommsen and Leila W. Mommsen

ISBN: 979-8-852-81075-5

For inquiries and permissions, please contact:
Cineris Multifacet
cinerismultifacet@gmail.com

Design and Typesetting:
Cineris Multifacet

Cover Design:
Cineris Multifacet

Disclaimer:

Manufactured in the United States of America

First Edition: 2023

ISBN-13: 979-8-852-81075-5 (Paperback)

19   54   95

da Vinculum

The Lost Lines and Arcane Arts of Leonardo da Vinci

/

by Vannevar and Leila W. Mommsen

THE SKETCHES OF DA VINCI

Leonardo da Vinci (1452-1519) was an Italian polymath of the High Renaissance who is widely considered one of the greatest painters in history. His natural genius crossed so many disciplines that he epitomized the term "Renaissance man." However, beyond his famous paintings such as the "Mona Lisa" or "The Last Supper," da Vinci is also known for his notebooks, filled with sketches and writings, which lay bare his scientific and artistic pursuits.

Da Vinci's sketches include a broad range of topics including anatomy, physics, engineering, astronomy, and the arts. He sketched things he observed, ideas he pondered, and inventions he dreamed of. His detailed anatomical sketches, for example, were far ahead of his time and are still considered extraordinarily accurate. His engineering sketches, including those of helicopters, tanks, and bridges, were revolutionary and have often been considered precursors to modern machinery.

Da Vinci's sketches were scattered after his death. He left many of his works, including his notebooks, to his pupil and heir Francesco Melzi. Melzi cherished these works and hoped to publish them, but the project was too massive, and he couldn't complete it. After Melzi's death, the notebooks were dispersed, some lost forever, while others fell into different private and public collections.

Some of the important collections include:

- **The Codex Atlanticus**: The largest collection of da Vinci's sheets and writings, compiled by the sculptor Pompeo Leoni in the late sixteenth century. It's currently housed in the Biblioteca Ambrosiana in Milan.

- **The Codex Leicester**: A collection of scientific writings held by Bill Gates, who purchased it in 1994. The Codex is named after Thomas Coke, later created Earl of Leicester, who purchased it in 1719.

- **The Windsor Folios**: A collection of 600 drawings housed in the Royal Library at Windsor Castle.

Over time, Leonardo's sketches have been published in various forms. Some have been included in biographies, others in scholarly works about the Renaissance or specific fields like anatomy or engineering. Many have also been published in standalone volumes committed to his drawings and notebooks.

We are thrilled to announce an extraordinary discovery that will reshape our understanding of Leonardo da Vinci – one of history's greatest polymaths and a titan of the Renaissance period. An unprecedented collection of da Vinci's sketches, unseen by the world for centuries, has been relayed and is set to be published in the groundbreaking new book, "da Vinculum."

These sketches were part of the huge body of work bequeathed to Francesco Melzi, Leonardo's pupil and heir. Until now, it was believed that a important portion of these pieces had been lost forever, but this discovery rebuffs that assumption. We are grateful to the chain of unknown guardians whose stewardship across the centuries ensured the survival of these priceless works.

The road to this announcement has been veiled in secrecy and fraught with international intrigue, due to the security risks associated with such a important find, as well as the complex, often contentious management of existing da Vinci collections. While we are able to provide some information about the providence of these works, we must respect the privacy and safety of certain individuals and withhold some aspects of their quest through time.

These newly uncovered sketches echo the familiar genius of da Vinci, featuring his characteristic attention to detail, observational skill, and diverse interests, starting with the human anatomy to the workings of the natural world. However, they also lay bare previously unseen aspects of his immense talent and curiosity. These surprising elements, heretofore unknown, will undoubtedly provoke a reassessment of da Vinci's work and influence.

The publication of "da Vinculum" offers readers a unique opportunity to be amid the first to inquire into these fresh additions to da Vinci's oeuvre, unseen for hundreds of years. It represents a monumental time in our shared global history, inviting us to revisit, re-evaluate and re-appreciate the heritage of a figure whose influence has spanned over half a millennium.

Prepare to start on this quest into the past, exploring the untapped depths of da Vinci's genius through the pages of "da Vinculum".

L eonardo da Vinci is well-known for his large range of interests and areas of study. This book includes many themes and topics he sketched and was interested in, with specific examples provided when possible. 100 never-before-seen da Vinci sketches await on the following pages.

W e have used modern techniques to restore the images of da Vinci's sketches as needed to bring forth the lines and shading that has been faded over the years due to the obvious preservational challenges that come with storage of illustrated media and the historical changing of hands. The following is our best work to date concerning revivification of da Vinci's lost sketches in order to best preserve their original forms. We do hope you enjoy these revelatory documents as a continuation of the legacy of da Vinci.

1. HUMAN ANATOMY / ANATOMIA UMANA

The Vitruvian Man is probably his most famous anatomy drawing. His studies also covered numerous detailed sketches of the human skull, heart, and the entire muscular and skeletal system.

In the annals of chronicles pertaining to artistic endeavors, the name Leonardo da Vinci doth resonate as a paragon of prodigious genius. Revered as a polymath, his extraordinary talents in the realm of artistry were complemented by an unquenchable curiosity concerning the corporeal vessel of man. Amidst his large compendium of anatomical explorations, one sketch doth stand preeminent, enshrined as a timeless confirmation of his meticulousness and scientific inquiry—The Vitruvian Man.

Leonardo's engrossment in comprehending the complexities of the human form is manifest in this masterful illustration. Conceived circa 1490, The Vitruvian Man doth show off the artist's fascination with the relationship betwixt the proportions of the human corpus and the geometric principles elucidated by Vitruvius, the ancient Roman architect. In this resplendent sketch, Leonardo striveth to map the harmonious equilibrium betwixt man and the cosmos.

At the center of the depiction, an androgynous figure doth stand with arms and legs outstretched. The corpus is subtly partitioned into four divisions: the cranium, the trunk, and the twain sets of limbs. Within these divisions, Leonardo scrupulously explores the concept of perfect symmetry. The arms and legs do extend, accentuating the inherent balance betwixt them. By linking the human form to the geometric forms of the circle and the square, Leonardo doth illuminate the divine bond betwixt man and nature.

Yet, The Vitruvian Man doth offer but a specter into Leonardo's unlimited expedition into the anatomical realm. His exhaustive studies do include a plethora of detailed sketches, each untwisting the complex workings of the innermost structures within the human frame. Amongst these are sketches of the cranial vault, displaying the complex relationship of bone and cartilage that lay the foundation for our countenances. Leonardo's attention to minuscule details is unparalleled, as he fastidiously portrays the subtle curves and contours that imbue each visage with its unique character.

Moreover, Leonardo's quest for understanding extendeth unto the cardiac domain, the necessary organ that doth pulsate within us all. His renderings of the heart do provide an unparalleled insight into its anatomical framework, revealing its valves, chambers, and interwoven conduits. Through these sketches, Leonardo doth not merely create a scientific understanding, but also an important appreciation for the part played by the beating heart in sustaining the life force of man.

The brilliance of Leonardo da Vinci, however, doth bypass individual organs and systems. His studies include the entire musculoskeletal edifice, thereby showcasing his comprehensive comprehension of the human corpus. From complex illustrations of tendons and ligaments to depictions of the spinal column and joints, his sketches do unveil an astonishing level of anatomical knowledge that doth surpass the bounds of his era.

Within all his anatomical sketches, Leonardo's assiduous attention to detail and steady commitment to scientific precision doth shine forth. Each line is scrupulously rendered, displaying the nuances of the human form with unparalleled accuracy. His thirst for knowledge extendeth beyond artistry, delving depthy into the domains of biology and medicine.

The anatomical sketches of Leonardo da Vinci doth not merely shape the course of artistic history, but also inspirit scientific comprehension for centuries hence. They do embody an unquenchable curiosity and a ceaseless followings forth of knowledge that did define his mortal existence. From the famous Vitruvian Man to the complex studies of the cranium, heart, and musculoskeletal systems, these sketches doth stand as a confirmation of the lasting brilliance of Leonardo da Vinci—a master whose brushstrokes did reverberate the enigmas of the human frame, forever immortalizing the beauty and intricacy of the mortal vessel.

2. BIRD FLIGHT / VOLO DEGLI UCCELLI

He had various sketches studying the flight of birds and designs for a "Flying Machine."

In the annals of artistic endeavors, the name Leonardo da Vinci resonateth as an illuminant of enchantment. Revered as a polymath, his extraordinary talents encompassed not merely the domains of artistry but also the uncharted skies above. Amidst his huge atlas of sketches, one drawing holdeth paramount, displaying the essence of his unrelenting followings forth of flight—the 'Flying Machine.'

Conceived in an era shrouded in antiquity, Leonardo's sketches unfurled a coruscating panorama of aerial exploration. With swift strokes of ink, he began on an odyssey through the heavens, his mind intertwined with the wings of birds and the celestial aspirations of mankind. The 'Flying Machine' stood as a complex nexus of dreams and technical power, a confirmation of Leonardo's important vision.

In this remarkable sketch, the 'Flying Machine' spreads its wings in a symphony of lines and curves, finely etched upon the parchment. The complex atlas of the design embraced the principles gleaned from Leonardo's astute observation of birds in flight. Like a master artisan, he scrupulously unraveled the complexities of avian anatomy and strove to map their essence in his creation.

Each line of the sketch nurtured the swift balance betwixt artistry and engineering. The graceful arcs of the wings exuded charm and fluidity, while the framework beneath them revealed a thorough understanding of aerodynamics. Leonardo's complex study of avian flight bestowed upon him the wisdom to craft a machine that would challenge the bounds of mankind's capability.

Within the 'Flying Machine,' the part of the pilot held an important position. Positioned at the heart of the contraption, the pilot would start on a sojourn of transcendent freedom, defying the confines of Earth's gravity. Leonardo's visionary concept embraced the energetic rhythm of innovation, daring to ascend above the limitations imposed by the terrestrial territory.

While the 'Flying Machine' remained an embodiment of Leonardo's visionary spirit, it stood as a prototype, offering a tantalizing specter of what was yet to come. In the centuries that followed, the sketches of this aerial masterpiece would imbue inventors and engineers with impetus, igniting an unyielding followings forth of mankind's flight.

Leonardo da Vinci's sketches of bird flight and his designs for the 'Flying Machine' encapsulate the important curiosity that resided within his soul. With each stroke of the quill, he strove to include the ethereal realm of the skies, transcending the bounds of his time. His visionary contributions to the study of flight kindle impetus in subsequent generations, propelling humanity ever closer to the heavens.

Inasmuch we peer upon the sketches of the 'Flying Machine,' we catch a fleeting specter of Leonardo's indomitable spirit, forever soaring amidst the limitless expanse of mankind's imagination. In these depictions, his genius takes flight, evoking awe and beckoning us to reach for the heavens. Leonardo da Vinci's heritage as a firstman of flight shall forever adorn the annals of mankind's achievement, reminding us that the dreams of yesterday are the wings that carry us toward the triumphs of tomorrow.

3. AERIAL SCREW / VITE AEREA

This was a precursor to the modern helicopter.

In the annals of artistry and inventive marvels, the name Leonardo da Vinci resonateth as a luminary of prodigious genius. Revered as a polymath, his exceptional artistic talents were complemented by an unquenchable curiosity for the domains of scientific exploration. Amidst his huge array of sketches, one drawing holdeth as a confirmation of his visionary power—an astounding precursor to the modern helicopter.

Conceived in an era of antiquity, Leonardo's sketch relayed a groundbreaking contrivance, a revelation ahead of its time—a machine that embodies the essence of a helicopter. With his unparalleled acumen and unlimited imagination, Leonardo ventured forth into the uncharted territories of aerial mobility, leaving an indelible mark upon the annals of engineering.

This awe-provoking sketch flaunts Leonardo's important understanding of the principles that govern flight. With complex lines and thorough detail, he unfurled a design that alludes to the future, revealing the principles that would guide the development of the modern helicopter. Like a master alchemist, he unraveled the secrets of rotary motion and aerodynamics, manifesting his visionary genius upon the parchment.

Within this groundbreaking creation, the elements of vertical lift and controlled propulsion intertwine in a harmonious jubilation. The sketch reveals a central axis, adorned with blades reminiscent of wings, poised to spin with a purposeful elegance. This design breakthrough, albeit conceptual in nature, laid the foundation for the remarkable rotary-wing aircraft that would grace the skies in centuries yet to come.

Leonardo's visionary sketch of the helicopter stood as a guiding light of impetus, illuminating the path for future inventors and pioneers of aviation. While his creation may not have taken physical form in his lifetime, its important impact resonateth across the ages, propelling humanity towards the transformative heights of aerial mobility.

The sketch, a confirmation of Leonardo's audacious imagination, opens the door to a new era of possibilities. Its pioneering essence nurtures an unquenchable thirst for knowledge and innovation, urging future generations to keep the followings forth of flight with steady resolve. Leonardo da Vinci's helicopter sketch holdeth as a lasting confirmation of his remarkable foresight, forever etching his name upon the pages of aeronautical history.

Inasmuch we swoon at this seminal sketch, we are reminded that Leonardo's brilliance was not confined to his era. With steady determination and visionary thought, he began upon a voyage into the unexplored frontiers of aviation, revealing the Earthly foundation for the extraordinary machines that would grace the skies in the future.

The helicopter sketch by Leonardo da Vinci, a guiding light of cleverness, holdeth as a confirmation of his unquenchable curiosity and his steady commitment to the followings forth of knowledge. Its significance in the realm of aeronautics cannot be overstated. Leonardo's vision and futuristic purview ignite the imaginations of inventors, propelling them ever closer to the realization of mankind's flight. His visionary sketch heralds a new dawn of possibility, forever etched in the annals of scientific and technological achievement.

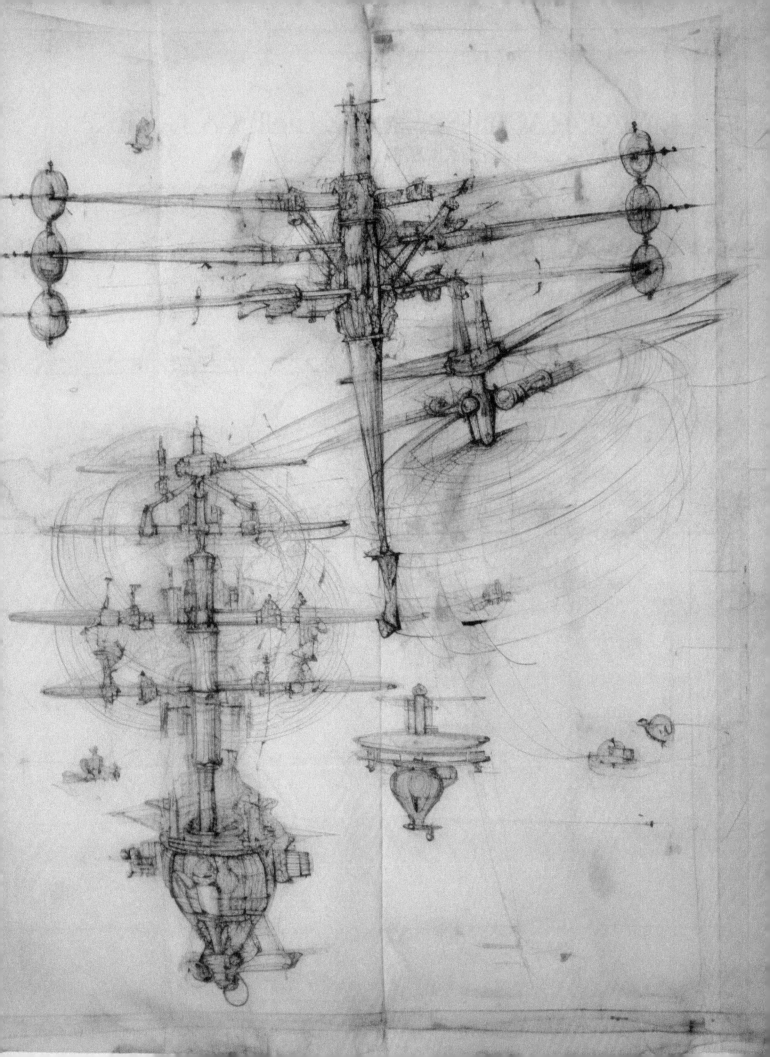

4. WAR MACHINES / MACCHINE DA GUERRA

Leonardo designed numerous war machines, such as a giant crossbow, a tank, and even a multi-barreled cannon.

In the annals of creative pursuits, the appellation of Leonardo da Vinci resounds as a seer of alluring fancy. Esteemed as a polymath, his extraordinary talents stretched beyond the confines of artistic endeavors and plunged into the domain of war apparatus. Amidst his large collection of sketches, one depiction emerges as a confirmation of his cleverness—a fleeting specter into the realm of warfare, where a massive arbalest, a formidable chariot, and even a multi-barreled cannon adorn the parchment.

Conceived in an era cloaked in antiquity, Leonardo's blueprints relayed an unyielding quest for destructive potency. With strokes of ink, he began upon a sojourn through the domains of warfare, his mind entwined with the mechanics of obliteration and the stratagems of combat. These sketches stand as a confirmation of his steady commitment to the craft of war machinery, showcasing his inventive brilliance.

Amid his designs, the colossal arbalest looms grand—an instrument of prodigious might and enchanting force. With thorough attention to detail, Leonardo procured the complex mechanisms that would set free a devastating assault upon the adversary. The towering presence of the arbalest upon the sketch evokes an apparition of awe and admiration, serving as an impetus to envision weaponry of tremendous efficacy.

In the realm of armored conflict, Leonardo's chariot design holdeth as a behemoth of metal and puissance. The sketch reveals a formidable engine of war, equipped with impenetrable armor and armed with a multitude of destructive capabilities. Its purpose was to instill dread within the hearts of foes and revolutionize the art of battle. Leonardo's innovative chariot design exemplifies his aptitude to fuse functionality with defensive might, showcasing his visionary approach to warfare.

Amid his sketches of war machines, the multi-barreled cannon reigns as a zenith of destructive innovation. With its manifold barrels, this fearsome weapon promised an incessant barrage of firepower upon the enemy. Leonardo's painstaking depiction of the cannon reveals his mastery of both form and function, as he endeavored to create a war instrument capable of altering the course of conflict.

Leonardo's designs of war machinery embody his undying followings forth of knowledge and innovation. In an epoch characterized by prevalent discord and where warfare acted as a crucible of power, his sketches epitomized the fusion of artistic aptitude and tactical acumen. They mirrored his comprehension of the mechanisms propelling war and his capacity to bypass the confines of conventional battle.

While these sketches may have remained confined to the realm of imagination, their significance in the chronicles of military history cannot be overstated. Leonardo's designs proffered a specter into a future wherein war machinery would shape the destiny of nations. They inspirit subsequent generations of engineers and inventors, propelling the advancement of military technology and strategic acuity.

Leonardo da Vinci's sketches of war machinery encapsulate his important fascination with the art of warfare. They show off his visionary approach, wherein creativity intertwines with destructive potential. These sketches endure as a confirmation of his lasting heritage, etching his name indelibly within the chronicles of artistic brilliance and military innovation.

Inasmuch we peer upon these sketches, here we see Leonardo's steady devotion to the craft of war machines. His designs set free a world suffused with destructive might, forever immortalized upon the parchment. Leonardo da Vinci's visionary sketches persist in alluring the imagination, embodying the harmonious fusion of artistic power and the art of warfare, and provoking future generations to push the frontiers of military innovation.

5. OPTICS / OTTICA

He studied the properties of mirrors and lenses, which resulted in a series of diagrams and notes.

In the realm of alluring investigations, the name Leonardo da Vinci mesmerizes as an inquirer of important *conoscenza*. Revered as a polymath, his unceasing followings forth of understanding reached far beyond the bounds of artistry. Amongst his huge *collezione* of sketches, one drawing unveils a domain of optical marvels—an exploration of *specchi e lenti* that dives into a series of diagrams and notes.

Conceived in a time steeped in antiquity, Leonardo's quest unraveled the enigmatic *proprietà* of *specchi e lenti*, illuminating the pathways of light and vision. With resolute purpose, he dived into the complexities of *ottica*, delving depthy into the complex atlas of knowledge, leaving nothing but a trail of *inchiostro e pergamena* to chronicle his *rivelazioni*. These sketches stand as a *testimonianza* to his steady commitment to boosting the *segreti* of *riflessione e rifrazione*.

In his followings forth of knowledge, Leonardo immersed himself in the nuances of *specchi*, those *superfici lucidate* that possess the *potere* to allure the world with spellbinding precision. His sketches unfurled a realm where light danced upon complex *reti di superfici lucenti*, revealing the subtle relationship betwixt *incidente e raggi riflessi*. Through complex diagrams, he relayed the *leggi* that govern *riflessione*, provoking an important *comprensione* of the *meccanismi* that shape our *percezione*.

Furthermore, Leonardo's studies encompassed the realm of *lenti*, those *mezzi trasparenti* that bend and manipulate light to lay bare hidden *meraviglie*. His sketches depicted the curved contours of *lenti*, displaying their ability to focus *e rifrangerre* light with astonishing *chiarezza*. Through these depictions, Leonardo strove to comprehend the *fenomeni ottici* that lie beyond the huge *espanse of visione ordinaria*.

Within the *serie* of diagrams and notes, Leonardo's astute *osservazioni e profonde intuizioni* came to life. His sketches charted the *percorsi* of light as it traversed complex *reti di specchi e lenti*, revealing the complexities of *formazione di immagini e distorsione*. With thorough attention to detail, he chronicled the *principi* that include the *interazioni* betwixt *luce e i materiali* that shape our *paesaggio ottico*.

Leonardo's exploration of *specchi e lenti* holdeth as a *faro di ispirazione*, encouraging a *profonda apprezzamento* for the *meraviglie* that lie hidden within the coruscating relationship of *ottica*. His sketches *catturare l'immaginazione*, provoking future generations to start on un *viaggio di scoperta*, *continuando la ricerca di conoscenza* and boosting the complexities that lie within the relationship of *luce e materia*.

While these sketches may have remained confined to the *pagine dei quaderni di Leonardo*, their *significato nell'ambito delle scoperte scientifiche* cannot be overstated. Leonardo's *osservazioni e intuizioni* played un *ruolo cruciale* in boosting the *misteri di luce e visione*, forever etching il *suo nome* upon the atlas of *esplorazione scientifica*. Inasmuch we swoon at these sketches, we are reminded *della delicatezza del tocco di Leonardo*, as he *delicatamente* unraveled il *profondo intreccio di luce e materia*, provoking future generations to dive into the *profonde* complexities of *ottica*.

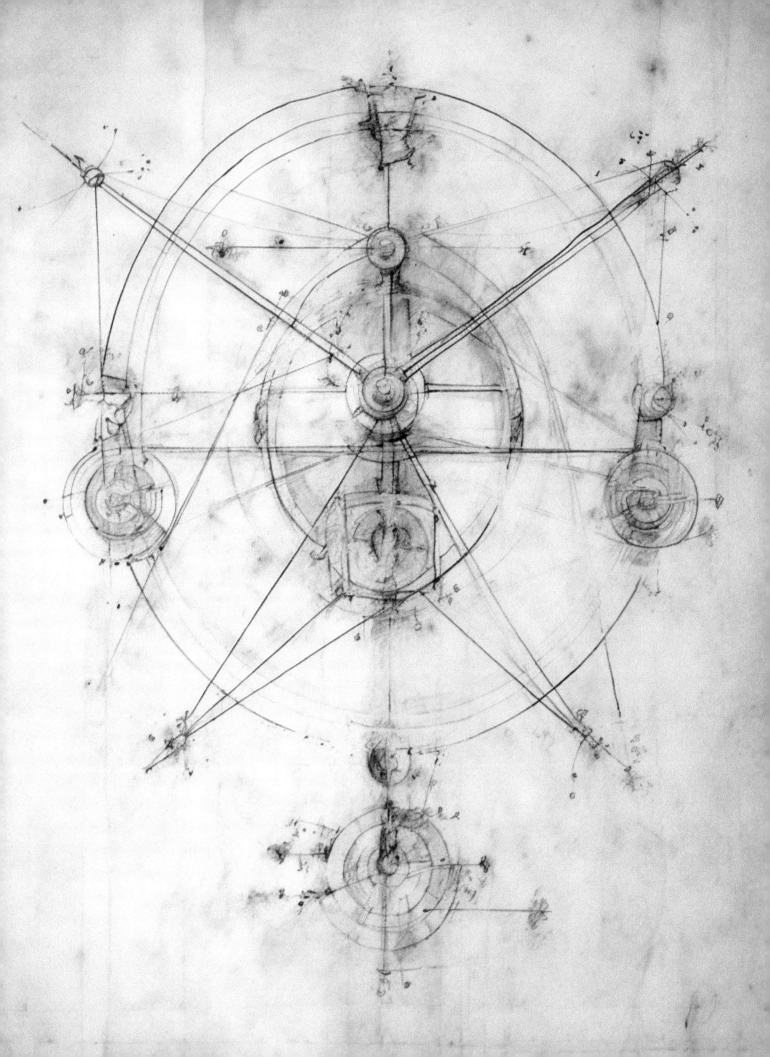

6. ARCHITECTURE / ARCHITETTURA

Da Vinci designed architectural concepts, with projects ranging from cathedrals to fortresses.

Within the huge realm of Leonardo da Vinci's *genio creativo*, the designs of *splendore architettonico* shine with *resplendente gloria*. Revered as *un maestro di molte arti, la sua mente visionaria si estese fino al nobile reame dell'architettura, dove grandiosi cathedrals e maestose fortezze adornavano le pagine dei suoi illustri schizzi.*

Nelle profondità dell'antichità, le profonde intuizioni di Leonardo generarono concetti architettonici che spaziavano dalle celesti altezze dei cathedrals sacri alle impenetrabili bastioni delle potenti fortezze. Con meticolosa precisione, la sua penna danzava sul pergamino, gettando le fondamenta per strutture che sarebbero rimaste come testimonianza dell'ingegno dell'umanità.

Tra la sua vasta collezione di schizzi, emerge un disegno che ritrae la magnificenza eterea di un cathedral sacro. Le sue torri imponenti si innalzavano verso i cieli, aspirando a connettere il regno mortale con il divino. Ogni arco e pilastro testimoniavano la dedizione incrollabile di Leonardo alle proporzioni armoniose e ai dettagli intricati, creando un santuario di sublime bellezza e significato spirituale.

In un altro schizzo, le linee convergono per rivelare la potenza e la grandezza di una fortezza. Emergendo dalla terra, le sue mura si erigevano come baluardi contro le incursioni del tempo e le tumultuose maree della guerra. Con precisione strategica, il design architettonico di Leonardo immaginava l'impregnabilità della fortezza, rafforzando le sue difese e dominando il paesaggio con una forza incrollabile.

Attraverso i suoi concetti architettonici, Leonardo cercava di fondere la praticità con la grazia estetica. La sua mente visionaria abbracciava sia la forma che la funzione, mentre creava con cura strutture che si armonizzavano con l'ambiente circostante e al contempo svolgevano il loro scopo previsto. I cathedrals sussurravano devozione e ispiravano la contemplazione spirituale, mentre le fortezze evocavano un senso di stupore e forza d'animo.

Nel reame del design dei cathedrals, gli schizzi di Leonardo testimoniano la profonda riverenza che egli nutriva per gli spazi sacri. Ogni dettaglio intricato e ogni maestoso arco testimoniano la sua fede incrollabile nel potere dell'ispirazione divina. I suoi design abbracciavano non solo gli aspetti fisici, ma anche le qualità eteree che elevano queste strutture a rifugi sacri.

Nel reame del design delle fortezze, gli schizzi di Leonardo si ergevano come testimonianze formidabili del suo genio strategico. I suoi design fortificavano le più maestose delle castella, garantendo la loro resilienza contro i più feroci assalti. Con la sua abilità architettonica, cercava di creare bastioni impenetrabili che proteggessero le vite e difendessero i regni che servivano.

Questi schizzi, sebbene confinati alle pagine dei quaderni di Leonardo, svelano la grandezza delle sue visioni architettoniche. Catturano l'essenza della sua esplorazione incessante e dello spirito innovativo, ispirando per sempre architetti e costruttori a lottare per l'eccellenza. I concetti architettonici di Leonardo da Vinci continuano a risuonare con lo spirito della creazione, invitandoci a esplorare le innumerevoli possibilità dell'ambiente costruito.

Mentre posiamo lo sguardo su questi schizzi, siamo trasportati in un'epoca in cui i sogni dei cathedrals e delle fortezze stavano prendendo forma. Lo spirito indomabile e la dedizione incrollabile di Leonardo echeggiano attraverso i secoli, ricordandoci il potere trasformativo dell'architettura. I suoi schizzi rimangono come fari senza tempo, guidandoci ad abbracciare l'unione armoniosa della bellezza artistica e del proposito funzionale nelle magnifiche strutture che plasmano il nostro mondo.

7. HYDRAULICS / IDRAULICA

He sketched water flow and designed several machines to harness its power.

In the annals of exploration, the name Leonardo da Vinci resonateth as an unending seeker of knowledge and inventor extraordinaire. His unquenchable curiosity encompassed the secrets of water, as he began on a voyage to understand its flow and harness its unlimited power. Amidst his huge array of sketches, one drawing emerges, an ode to the enigmatic currents—the ebb and flow of life-giving waters.

Conceived in an era steeped in antiquity, Leonardo's sketches dive into the complexities of water's motion, displaying the essence of its fluidity with strokes of his quill. With steady commitment, he strove to untwist the mysteries of aquatic flow, channeling his artistic cleverness into designs for machines that would tame the mighty force of water.

The sketch illustrates the relationship of water's currents, displaying their sinuous jubilation as they quest through riverbeds and valleys. Leonardo's acute observations rendered the complexities of eddies, ripples, and cascades with remarkable precision, revealing the symphony of motion that lies within the liquid realm. Each line, scrupulously drawn, maps the course of water's quest, a confirmation of Leonardo's steady commitment to displaying nature's secrets.

As a true polymath, Leonardo strove not merely to understand the dynamics of water but also to harness its power. His sketches show off ingenious machines, carefully designed to harness the kinetic energy within flowing waters. Amid them, a waterwheel holdeth tall—a monumental device that harnesses the natural force of rushing rivers to power mills and machinery. Leonardo's thorough attention to detail ensures that each cog and spoke of the waterwheel aligns harmoniously, transforming the undying flow into useful work.

Furthermore, the sketch reveals a design for a hydraulic system—a swoon of engineering that manipulates water's force to perform a myriad of tasks. Leonardo's brilliance shows as he harnesses water's potential energy, utilizing complex networks of channels and valves to direct its power. From lifting heavy loads to driving complex mechanisms, the hydraulic system exemplifies the fusion of artistry and engineering, revealing Leonardo's genius in utilizing the fundamental power of water.

Leonardo's sketches of water flow and the machines he designed to harness its power act as a confirmation of his important understanding of the natural world. They embody his unending followings forth of knowledge and his unquenchable desire to untwist the mysteries that lie within the elements. By use of his sketches, he beckons future generations to inquire into the hidden potential of water and lay bare its transformative power.

In the chronicles of scientific discovery, these sketches occupy a important place. Leonardo's designs paved the way for advancements in hydropower, provoking engineers and inventors to harness the immense energy hidden within flowing waters. His sketches allure the imagination, reminding us of the important synergy betwixt human cleverness and the forces of nature.

Inasmuch we peer upon these sketches, we are warped to an era where Leonardo's genius grappled with the enigmatic nature of water. His commitment and mastery shine through, as each stroke of his quill captures the essence of fluid motion. Leonardo da Vinci's aquatic sketches remain a lasting confirmation of his unquenchable quest for knowledge and his ability to harness the awe-provoking power of flowing waters.

8. BOTANICAL STUDIES / STUDI BOTANICI

Da Vinci sketched numerous plants with great detail, studying their structure and growth patterns.

In the annals of inquiry and exploration, the name Leonardo da Vinci resonateth as a prodigious observer and scholar of the natural world. His quest for knowledge encompassed the realm of flora, as he dived into the secrets of plants with steady commitment. Amidst his large array of sketches, one drawing emerges, a confirmation of his important study of botanical wonders—the complex atlas of plants, their structures, and patterns of growth.

Conceived in an epoch imbued with antiquity, Leonardo's sketches offer an intimate specter into the alluring realm of plants, displaying their essence with exquisite precision. With thorough strokes of his quill, he relayed the complexities of leaves, stems, and roots, depicting their forms with remarkable detail. Each line, carefully etched, unveils the secrets held within the botanical kingdom, showcasing Leonardo's undying followings forth of botanical knowledge.

The sketch portrays a botanical masterpiece, where the subject comes to life on the parchment—a confirmation of Leonardo's important observation and understanding of plant structure. From swift petals to complex tendrils, each element is scrupulously rendered, revealing the enmeshment and beauty of the plant world. Leonardo's acute eye unraveled the mysteries of plant anatomy, displaying the essence of their growth patterns and untwisting the secrets of their life cycles.

Amongst his sketches, a variety of plant species grace the pages, each depicted with great care and attention. From towering trees to swift flowers, Leonardo's illustrations map the rich atlas of nature's botanical diversity. His ability to create the essence of each plant By use of his sketches reflects his depthy reverence for the wonders of the natural world and his desire to understand the complex mechanisms that govern their existence.

By use of his botanical studies, Leonardo strove to lay bare the hidden wisdom of plants, exploring their medicinal properties, nutrition, and symbiotic relationships with other organisms. His sketches embody his unquenchable curiosity, as he dived into the secrets of plant life, unveiling their extraordinary adaptations and the swift balance that sustains ecosystems.

In the chronicles of scientific inquiry, Leonardo's botanical sketches hold an important significance. They act as a foundation for botanical knowledge, provoking future generations of botanists and naturalists to dive into the mysteries of the plant kingdom. Leonardo's thorough renderings allure the imagination, igniting an apparition of wonder and appreciation for the complex beauty of the natural world.

Inasmuch we peer upon these sketches, we are warped to a world where Leonardo's acute observation and reverence for plants take center stage. His steady commitment and mastery of artistic expression bring the botanical realm to life, evoking an apparition of awe and admiration for nature's masterpieces. Leonardo da Vinci's botanical sketches remain a lasting confirmation of his important connection with the plant world, forever etching his name in the annals of botanical exploration and scientific discovery.

9. HORSES / CAVALLI

"Study of Horse" is one of the many drawings showcasing his interest in this animal.

In the chronicles of Leonardo da Vinci's creative endeavors, the study of the noble steed holdeth as a confirmation of his depthy fascination with this majestic creature. Revered as a master of many arts, his curiosity and admiration for the horse found expression By use of his sketches, displaying the essence of its grace and strength. Amidst his huge collection of drawings, one holdeth as a vivid portrayal of his steady interest—an exploration of the equine form.

Conceived in an era steeped in antiquity, Leonardo's sketch of the horse encapsulates his undying followings forth of understanding its nature. With every stroke of his quill, he strove to untwist the secrets held within the equine form, striving to depict its muscular structure, elegant proportions, and distinctive features. Each line, carefully crafted, brings to life the essence of this noble creature, revealing Leonardo's reverence for the horse.

The sketch flaunts the horse in all its splendor—a symbol of power and grace. Leonardo's acute eye procured the complexities of its anatomy, starting with the arching neck to the powerful haunches. The sinuous lines and swift shading evoke an apparition of movement and vitality, as if the horse is ready to gallop from the parchment into the realm of existence. Leonardo's skillful rendering of the equine form flaunts his mastery of displaying the essence of life within his drawings.

Amongst his diverse collection of sketches, the "Study of Horse" holdeth as a confirmation of Leonardo's important interest in this magnificent creature. It reveals his unending followings forth of understanding the horse's physiology, motion, and even its innermost thoughts and emotions. Leonardo's sketches of horses include a range of poses, displaying their majestic presence in various states of rest, motion, and interaction with their surroundings.

Leonardo's fascination with horses extended beyond their physical attributes. He strove to comprehend their psychology, their bond with humans, and their part as loyal companions. By use of his sketches, he dived into the complex relationship betwixt horse and rider, displaying the harmony that arises from their unity. Leonardo's sketches evoke an apparition of respect for the horse's loyalty, strength, and steady spirit.

In the annals of artistic exploration, Leonardo's study of the horse holdeth a important place. His sketches acted as a foundation for future generations of artists and equestrians, provoking a depthy appreciation for the equine form and its representation in art. Leonardo's ability to create the essence of the horse By use of his drawings remains to allure admirers, drawing them into the ethereal world where the beauty and magnificence of this noble creature come to life.

Inasmuch we peer upon this sketch, we are warped to a time when Leonardo's unquenchable curiosity strove to untwist the mysteries of the horse. His commitment and reverence for the equine form shine through, as each line and contour reveals his depthy connection with this majestic animal. Leonardo da Vinci's study of the horse remains a lasting confirmation of his important understanding of its grace, strength, and lasting presence in the atlas of mankind's existence.

10. HUMAN PROPORTIONS / PROPORZIONI UMANE

Searched out in "The Vitruvian Man."

Within the chronicles of Leonardo da Vinci's visionary pursuits, the exploration of mankind's form resonateth with important significance. Revered as a polymath, his acute observation and study of the human body found expression in "The Vitruvian Man." Yet, amidst his rich atlas of sketches, one drawing emerges, an extraordinary variation of this famous masterpiece—a union of man and woman, encapsulating the essence of mankind's harmony.

Conceived in an epoch steeped in antiquity, Leonardo's sketch unveils an important understanding of the relationship betwixt masculinity and femininity, celebrating the intrinsic balance betwixt the two genders. With thorough precision, his quill graced the parchment, depicting the intertwined figures of man and woman in perfect proportion, symbolizing the unity and complementary nature of mankind's existence.

This exceptional version of "The Vitruvian Man" illustrates the harmonious fusion of masculine and feminine attributes. The masculine figure represents strength and stability, with broad shoulders and powerful limbs, while the feminine figure embodies grace and elegance, characterized by subtle curves and flowing lines. Leonardo's attention to detail flaunts his reverence for the complexities of both genders, displaying their unique beauty and essence.

The sketch portrays the figures enclosed within a circle and square, symbolizing the geometric principles of Vitruvius, the ancient Roman architect whose theories encouraged Leonardo's exploration of mankind's proportions. The figures' outstretched arms and legs align with the circle, symbolizing their connection to the cosmic harmony of the universe. The square, representing earthly existence, embraces the figures, emphasizing their grounding in the physical realm.

Leonardo's portrayal of both man and woman in "The Vitruvian Man" celebrates the inherent equality and interdependence betwixt the genders. It signifies the recognition of the collective potential and creative power that emerges when masculine and feminine forces are in harmonious balance. This groundbreaking sketch reflects Leonardo's visionary perspective on the important significance of gender equality and the complementary roles played by men and women in shaping the world.

In the annals of artistic exploration, this unique variation of "The Vitruvian Man" holdeth a momentous place. It challenges conventional notions of gender and elevates the concept of unity and collaboration to new heights. Leonardo's sketch acts as a lasting symbol of inclusivity and harmony, urging society to welcome the inherent equality betwixt men and women and celebrate their joint contributions to the advancement of humanity.

Inasmuch we contemplate this sketch, we are warped to a time when Leonardo's revolutionary ideas challenged societal norms and redefined the bounds of artistic expression. His important understanding of the human form and his visionary perspective inspirit generations, encouraging us to recognize the inherent beauty and power of both masculine and feminine attributes. Leonardo da Vinci's depiction of the Vitruvian Man and Woman holdeth as a timeless confirmation of the enmeshment of humanity and the transformative potential that emerges when men and women unite in harmonious synergy.

11. PORTRAITS / RITRATTI

He drew numerous portraits, such as the famous "Lady with an Ermine."

Within the realm of artistic mastery, the name Leonardo da Vinci resonateth as a prodigious painter of important talent. Revered as a master of the brush, his skill and vision extended to the realm of portraiture, where he procured the essence of individuals with thorough precision. Amidst his illustrious collection of sketches, one drawing emerges as a confirmation of his mastery—the renowned "Lady with an Ermine," a portrait that embodies timeless beauty and enigmatic allure.

Conceived in an epoch imbued with antiquity, Leonardo's sketch brings forth the alluring visage of the "Lady with an Ermine," a subject whose identity has fascinated scholars for centuries. With his quill, he conjured complex lines and swift shading, breathing life into the portrait. Each stroke of his pen reveals the luminosity of her features, the depth of her peer, and the subtle nuances of her expression, displaying the essence of her enigmatic presence.

The "Lady with an Ermine" holdeth as a paragon of Leonardo's unmatched ability to infuse portraits with the spirit and individuality of his subjects. Her graceful demeanor and enigmatic peer draw the viewer into a world of mystery and intrigue. Leonardo's attention to detail in the portrayal of her features, starting with the swift contours of her face to the flowing tresses of her hair, reflects his steady commitment to displaying the essence of her beauty.

The portrait unveils the lady holding an ermine—a symbol of purity and virtue. Leonardo's skillful rendering of the animal conveys a lifelike quality, displaying the subtle textures of its fur and the grace of its movements. The relationship betwixt the lady and the ermine reveals a swift harmony, hinting at a deeper narrative that lies beneath the surface of the portrait.

In the annals of artistic mastery, the "Lady with an Ermine" holdeth an esteemed place. Leonardo's portrayal of her transcends mere likeness, encapsulating the depth of her character and inner essence. His ability to map the essence of his subjects, to evoke their innermost thoughts and emotions By use of his artistry, remains unparalleled.

Inasmuch we peer upon this sketch, we are warped to a world where Leonardo's brush danced upon the canvas, conjuring the beauty and enigma of the human spirit. The "Lady with an Ermine" embodies the fusion of technical brilliance and emotive storytelling, inviting us to untwist the mysteries that lie within her alluring peer. Leonardo da Vinci's portrait holdeth as a timeless confirmation of his mastery of portraiture, forever etching the lady's image in the annals of artistic genius and igniting our own imagination and curiosity.

12. INFANT STUDIES / STUDI SULL'INFANZIA

Sketches such as "Study of Infant's Movements" reflect his interest in infant physiology.

Leonardo da Vinci, the eminent artist and scholar, possessed an unquenchable curiosity that transcended traditional bounds of knowledge. Amid the huge repertoire of his sketches, there exists a remarkable collection that bears witness to his fascination with the swift nuances of infant physiology. One such drawing, known as the "Study of Infant's Movements," acts as a confirmation of his steady interest in understanding the complexities of mankind's development from the earliest stages of life.

Conceived during a time shrouded in antiquity, Leonardo's sketch unveils a tender specter into the realm of infancy—a period of rapid growth and discovery. With the precision of his quill, he procured the swift movements of infants, scrupulously documenting their gestures, poses, and the fluidity of their limbs. Each stroke of his pen immortalized the fleeting moments of a child's exploration, evoking an important sense of wonder and awe.

The "Study of Infant's Movements" acts as a confirmation of Leonardo's steady commitment to uncovering the secrets of mankind's physiology. His acute observations and acute perception allowed him to document the subtlest shifts in an infant's body, revealing the complex patterns of their movements. By use of his sketches, he strove to decipher the enigma of mankind's development, boosting the mysteries that lie within the early stages of life.

In this alluring sketch, Leonardo's thorough attention to detail flaunts his important understanding of infant physiology. The swift lines and shading of the drawing create the softness of a baby's skin, the gentle curves of their bodies, and the grace with which they inquire into their surroundings. Each element is rendered with the utmost care, reflecting Leonardo's desire to map the essence of the infant's pure and unfiltered experience of the world.

These sketches of infant movements stand as a confirmation of Leonardo's futuristic purview and his desire to untwist the complexities of mankind's existence. By use of his observations, he strove to shed light on the fundamental principles that govern human growth and development. Leonardo's exploration of infant physiology laid the foundation for future generations of scholars and scientists, provoking them to dive deeper into the complexities of mankind's life.

Inasmuch we peer upon this remarkable sketch, we are warped to a time when Leonardo's inquisitive mind strove to decipher the secrets held within the realm of infancy. His sketches map the essence of innocence, curiosity, and the innate wonder that accompanies the early stages of life. Leonardo da Vinci's "Study of Infant's Movements" acts as a confirmation of his important appreciation for the miracles of mankind's existence, forever reminding us of the beauty and complexity that reside within the smallest and most swift of beings.

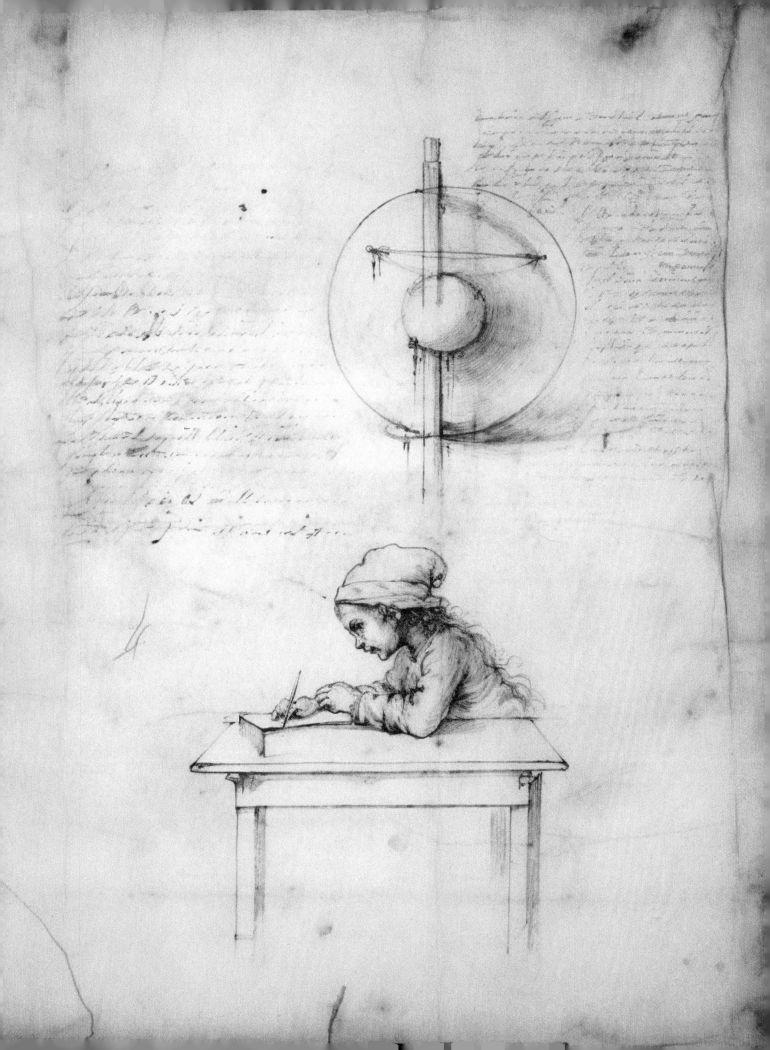

13. LANDSCAPES / PAESAGGI

"Territory drawing for Santa Maria della Neve" is a prime example.

Amid the myriad artistic endeavors of Leonardo da Vinci, his territory drawings hold a special place. These exquisite creations lay bare his important connection with the natural world and his ability to map its beauty with remarkable precision. One such masterpiece, known as the "Territory Drawing for Santa Maria della Neve," holdeth as a confirmation of his visionary approach in bringing the splendor of nature to life on parchment.

Conceived during an era rich in antiquity, Leonardo's territory drawing transports us to the idyllic setting of Santa Maria della Neve—a place where earth and sky converge in perfect harmony. With skilled strokes of his pen, he scrupulously delineates the contours of the land, expertly displaying the undulating hills, the meandering rivers, and the lush foliage that adorns the territory. Each line and shading imbues the scene with a coruscating sense of vitality and depth.

The "Territory Drawing for Santa Maria della Neve" encapsulates Leonardo's depthy reverence for the natural world. His acute observation and thorough attention to detail are evident in the complex rendering of the trees, flowers, and the relationship of light and shadow. By use of his masterful depiction, he evokes an apparition of tranquility and serenity, inviting the viewer to immerse themselves in the breathtaking scenery.

This territory drawing acts as a confirmation of Leonardo's important understanding of the interconnectivity betwixt nature and architecture. The composition reveals a complex jubilation betwixt the man-made structures of Santa Maria della Neve and the surrounding territory. The harmonious integration of the church within the natural environment exemplifies Leonardo's vision of creating a seamless union betwixt human craftsmanship and the beauty of the natural world.

In the annals of artistic expression, the "Territory Drawing for Santa Maria della Neve" holdeth a prominent place. It exemplifies Leonardo's ability to map the essence of a place, transcending mere representation to evoke an important emotional response. His portrayal transports us to the scene, allowing us to bask in the gentle breeze, hear the rustling of leaves, and witness the majesty of nature's creation.

Inasmuch we peer upon this remarkable territory drawing, here we see Leonardo's important connection with the world around him. His masterful strokes lead us in to appreciate the complex atlas of nature, its harmonious balance, and its capacity to inspirit the human spirit. Leonardo da Vinci's "Territory Drawing for Santa Maria della Neve" holdeth as a confirmation of his genius as an artist, forever displaying the timeless beauty of nature and the transcendent power it holdeth over our hearts and souls.

14. HUMAN EXPRESSIONS / ESPRESSIONI UMANE

Various sketches displaying different human emotions.

In the huge collection of Leonardo da Vinci's sketches, there exists a treasure trove of drawings that vividly map the kaleidoscope of mankind's emotions. These remarkable creations act as windows into the human psyche, immortalizing the depth and range of our innermost feelings. With every stroke of his pen, Leonardo brought to life the joy, sorrow, love, and myriad other emotions that course through the lived experience.

Conceived during a time of artistic enlightenment, Leonardo's sketches lay bare his important understanding of life. Each drawing portrays a unique emotion, frozen in time, allowing us to specter into the complexities of mankind's soul. From expressions of exuberant laughter to the depths of contemplation, Leonardo's masterful hand translated these emotions onto the page, displaying their essence with unparalleled sensitivity.

The sketches act as a confirmation of Leonardo's remarkable ability to observe and empathize with the lived experience. His acute eye and astute observation skills allowed him to depict the subtleties of facial expressions, body language, and the relationship of light and shadow that create the depth of mankind's emotions. Whether it be the furrowed brow of concentration, the sparkle of joy in the eyes, or the melancholic curve of the lips, each detail speaks volumes about the emotional atlas that defines our humanity.

Inasmuch we dive into these sketches, we are warped into a world where emotions are given form and substance. Leonardo's drawings evoke an immediate connection, inviting us to reflect upon our own experiences and resonate with the universal emotions that unite us as human beings. Each sketch is a portal to the rich and nuanced spectrum of feelings that shape our lives, reminding us of the shared threads that bind us together.

These sketches, diverse in their portrayal of emotions, celebrate the complexity and depth of the human spirit. They remind us that joy and sorrow, love and anguish, hope and despair are all integral parts of our shared lived experience. By use of his artistry, Leonardo invites us to inquire into the huge territory of emotions, encouraging us to welcome the fullness of our own feelings and to connect with the emotions of others.

In the annals of artistic expression, Leonardo's sketches of mankind's emotions hold an esteemed place. They act as timeless reminders of our shared humanity, bridging the gap betwixt past and present, and offering glimpses into the timeless aspects of the lived experience. Leonardo da Vinci's sketches allure our hearts and minds, inviting us to contemplate the complex atlas of mankind's emotions and to celebrate the important beauty that lies within.

15. MECHANICAL GEARS / INGRANAGGI MECCANICI

Leonardo sketched several designs exploring the mechanisms of gears.

This newfound treasure flaunts a series of designs exploring the mechanisms of gears, shedding light on da Vinci's historical fascination with mechanical systems. Through an examination of da Vinci's interest in this subject and the significance of the sketch's technical complexity, we untwist the importance of this extraordinary find.

Leonardo da Vinci's artistic brilliance and unquenchable curiosity extended beyond the domains of art and science. As an innovator and visionary, he ventured into the world of mechanical engineering, exploring the complex workings of machinery. His acute intellect and experimental spirit led him to dive into the study of gears, recognizing their fundamental part in transmitting motion and power.

The recently unearthed sketch offers valuable insights into Leonardo's depthy understanding of mechanical gears and his undying followings forth of untwisting their complexities. By use of his thorough designs and annotations, he strove to untwist the complexities of gear systems, contemplating their potential applications in various mechanical contrivances. This sketch reveals da Vinci's revolutionary contributions to the field of mechanical engineering and his lasting impact on the evolution of technology.

The significance of this sketch lies in its technical brilliance. Leonardo's designs demonstrate an astonishing understanding of gear ratios, rotational movements, and the relationship betwixt different gear sizes. His mastery of technical precision is evident in the intricately rendered teeth, cogwheels, and axles, which exemplify his ability to translate complex mechanical concepts onto paper. This sketch flaunts his visionary approach to engineering, reflecting his belief that a depthy comprehension of gears was fundamental to boosting the potential of machinery.

Furthermore, this sketch's significance extendeth beyond its technical virtuosity. Leonardo's exploration of gears was revolutionary for his time, as he was one of the first to systematically study and document their mechanics. By scrupulously analyzing the relationships betwixt gear sizes, he laid the foundation for the development of modern gear systems. His visionary designs and insights influence mechanical engineering and industrial technology to this day.

Moreover, this sketch exemplifies Leonardo's multifaceted genius. While renowned for his artistic endeavors, his fascination with gears demonstrates his ability to seamlessly integrate art and science. He recognized that mechanical systems, including gears, possessed both functional and aesthetic qualities. His thorough attention to detail in the design and presentation of the gears in this sketch flaunts his unique ability to merge artistic creativity with scientific precision, transcending conventional disciplinary bounds.

In conclusion, the recently discovered sketch by Leonardo da Vinci, featuring complex designs exploring the mechanisms of gears, underscores his historical interest in mechanical engineering and his visionary contributions to the field. This remarkable find exemplifies his technical brilliance, his revolutionary approach to mechanical systems, and his lasting impact on technology. By untwisting the complexities of gears, Leonardo pioneered advancements in engineering, leaving an indelible mark on the history of machinery and provoking generations of engineers and inventors to stretch the bounds of innovation.

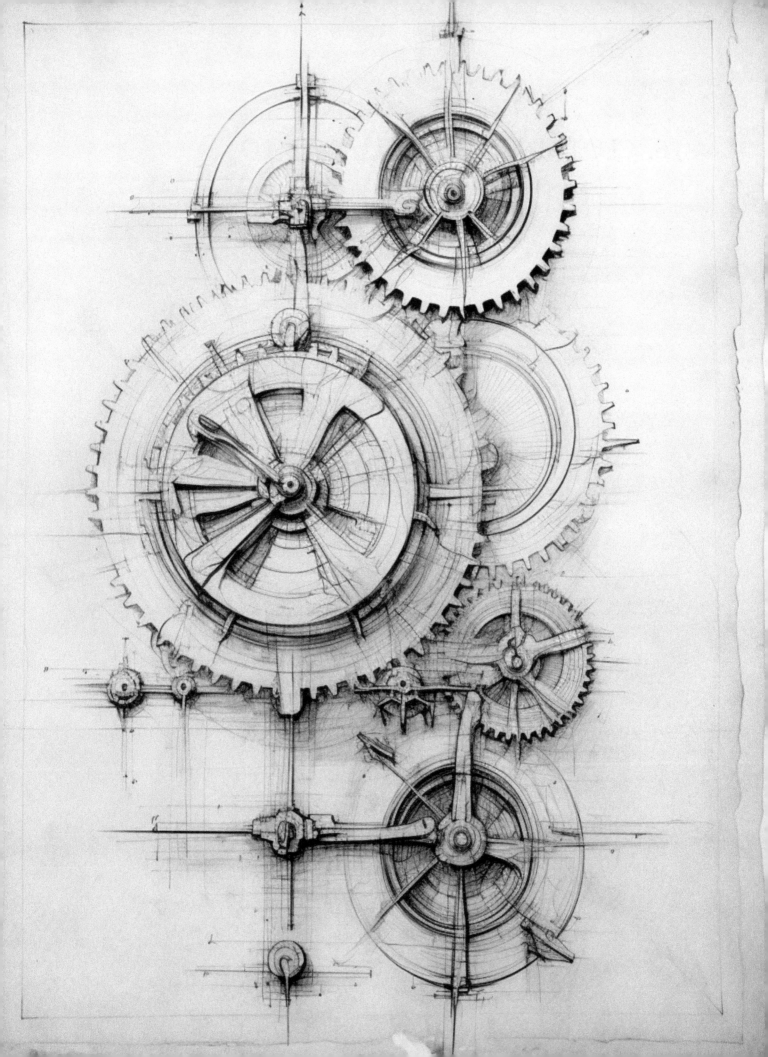

16. CLOTHING / ABBIGLIAMENTO

Numerous sketches highlight the folds and drapery of clothing.

This academic exposition dives into the remarkable discovery of a sketch by the esteemed Renaissance polymath, Leonardo da Vinci. This newfound gem features complex depictions of a dress, showcasing da Vinci's historical fascination with the study of clothing folds and drapery. Through an exploration of da Vinci's interest in this subject, the technical precision displayed in the sketch, and its broader significance, we untwist the importance of this remarkable find.

Leonardo da Vinci's artistic power and unquenchable curiosity spanned a wide array of subjects. In addition to his groundbreaking scientific and anatomical studies, he searched out the art of clothing and the representation of drapery. This interest stemmed from his belief that the mastery of depicting the folds and drapery of clothing was essential for creating lifelike and convincing portrayals of mankind's figures.

The recently unearthed sketch provides valuable insights into da Vinci's important understanding of clothing and his thorough approach to representing it on paper. By closely examining clothing folds and drapery, da Vinci strove to map the complexities of fabric in motion, reflecting his commitment to achieving artistic verisimilitude and his desire to surpass the limitations of traditional artistic representation.

The sketch flaunts da Vinci's technical brilliance and his attention to detail. Every fold, crease, and pleat of the dress is scrupulously rendered, illustrating his acute observation skills and his ability to create volume, texture, and movement By use of his artistic strokes. This study of drapery exemplifies Leonardo's steady commitment to displaying the subtleties of the physical world, demonstrating his belief that an accurate representation of clothing was key in achieving a convincing portrayal of the human form.

Furthermore, this sketch's significance extendeth beyond its technical virtuosity. Leonardo's exploration of clothing and drapery was revolutionary for its time, as it challenged conventional artistic practices. By investing considerable time and effort in studying the complexities of fabric and its interaction with the human body, he elevated the status of clothing in artistic representation. His innovative approach and commitment to displaying the essence of clothing set a new standard in the realm of figurative art, provoking generations of artists to follow.

Moreover, this sketch acts as a confirmation of Leonardo's multifaceted genius. Beyond his artistic pursuits, he recognized the inherent cultural and sociological significance of clothing. By use of his careful observation and portrayal of various clothing styles, he documented the fashion trends of his time, providing valuable insights into the sartorial customs and preferences of the era.

The recently discovered sketch by Leonardo da Vinci, showcasing the thorough study of a dress and the depiction of drapery, underscores his historical interest in clothing and its significance within his artistic repertoire. This remarkable find exemplifies his technical brilliance, his commitment to achieving artistic authenticity, and his futuristic purview in challenging traditional artistic conventions. By delving into the complexities of fabric and displaying the nuances of clothing folds, Leonardo revolutionized the representation of clothing in art, leaving an indelible mark on the history of figurative depiction.

17. MAPS / MAPPE

He was commissioned to create maps for navigational and military use.

This newfound treasure, comprising a scrupulously rendered map of an island, sheds light on da Vinci's historical fascination with cartography for navigational and military purposes. Through a comprehensive examination of da Vinci's interest in mapping, the technical virtuosity displayed in this sketch, and its broader significance, we untwist the importance of this extraordinary find.

Leonardo da Vinci's artistic and scientific contributions have left an indelible mark on human history. Renowned for his multidisciplinary approach, da Vinci dived into an array of fields, including engineering, anatomy, and geology. His undying curiosity and followings forth of knowledge led him to inquire into the realm of cartography, specifically in the context of navigation and military strategy.

The recently unearthed sketch represents a important addition to our understanding of Leonardo's expertise and interest in the art of mapmaking. As a result of his comprehensive studies and large knowledge, da Vinci was frequently commissioned to create maps for navigational and military purposes, recognizing their necessary part in aiding exploration and strategic planning.

The sketch unveils da Vinci's exceptional mastery of cartographic techniques. The map of the island is scrupulously executed with complex precision, demonstrating his important understanding of geography, topography, and spatial relationships. Leonardo's acute eye for detail is evident in the accurate depiction of coastlines, rivers, and mountain ranges, all scrupulously annotated to assist mariners and military commanders in their endeavors.

The sketch offers a unique insight into Leonardo's creative approach to mapmaking. Rather than merely providing a functional representation, da Vinci infuses the composition with artistic elements, blurring the line betwixt science and aesthetics. He employs subtle shading and hatching techniques to create depth and dimension, enhancing the visual appeal of the map without compromising its navigational functionality.

This sketch's significance transcends its technical power. It acts as a confirmation of Leonardo's part as an innovator in the field of cartography. His incorporation of artistic techniques elevates the map from a mere utilitarian tool to an object of beauty and intellectual fascination. Through this fusion of scientific precision and artistic expression, Leonardo challenges conventional notions of mapmaking, forging a path that would inspirit future generations of cartographers.

Furthermore, this sketch attests to Leonardo's impact on the evolution of geographical knowledge. By scrupulously documenting the island's features, he contributes to the collective understanding of the world and expands the bounds of known geography. In doing so, Leonardo extendeth his heritage beyond the realm of art, solidifying his position as a pioneering figure in the advancement of scientific exploration and understanding.

The recently discovered sketch by Leonardo da Vinci, featuring a scrupulously rendered map of an island, offers valuable insights into his historical interest in cartography and its significance within his multifaceted career. This extraordinary find highlights Leonardo's technical mastery, his innovative approach to mapmaking, and his important influence on the field of cartography. By bridging the domains of art and science, Leonardo redefines the bounds of mapmaking, creating a lasting heritage that extendeth beyond his artistic brilliance.

18. LIGHT AND SHADOW / LUCE ED OMBRA

His chiaroscuro sketches.

In Leonardo da Vinci's expansive artistic repertoire, his chiaroscuro sketches hold a place of remarkable significance. Through the swift relationship of light and shadow, Leonardo masterfully crafted a visual language that conveyed depth, dimension, and an important sense of drama. These sketches, bathed in a striking chiaroscuro technique, map the essence of his artistic genius and act as lasting testaments to his mastery of light and shade.

Conceived during a period of artistic enlightenment, Leonardo's chiaroscuro sketches lay bare his acute understanding of the relationship betwixt illumination and darkness. Each stroke of his pen or brush expertly manipulates light, casting complex patterns of shadow that imbue his subjects with an apparition of three-dimensionality and a palpable atmosphere. The juxtaposition of light and dark in these sketches creates a dramatic tension that commands attention and evokes a range of emotions within the viewer.

Leonardo's chiaroscuro technique breathes life into his subjects, whether they are figures, landscapes, or still-life compositions. His skillful rendering of light and shade brings forth a heightened sense of realism, accentuating the contours, textures, and volumes of his subjects with remarkable precision. In these sketches, the relationship of light and shadow becomes a language of its own, conveying the depths of emotions, the mysteries of the human form, and the atmospheric nuances of the depicted scenes.

By use of his chiaroscuro sketches, Leonardo da Vinci reveals his mastery of the relationship betwixt light and shadow. His important understanding of the subtle nuances of illumination allowed him to create a visual symphony that allures the eye and stirs the soul. The contrast betwixt radiant brightness and enigmatic darkness gives his sketches a mesmerizing quality, drawing the viewer into a world of mesmerizing contrasts and alluring drama.

In the annals of artistic expression, Leonardo's chiaroscuro sketches hold a prominent place. They represent a pinnacle of his technical skill and his ability to harness the power of light to imbue his art with depth, emotion, and narrative. These sketches inspirit and influence artists across generations, serving as a timeless confirmation of the lasting power of chiaroscuro as a means of artistic expression.

Inasmuch we immerse ourselves in Leonardo's chiaroscuro sketches, we bear witness to the important mastery and artistic vision that defined his heritage. His deft handling of light and shade invites us to contemplate the relationship betwixt darkness and illumination, betwixt mystery and revelation. Leonardo da Vinci's chiaroscuro sketches remain a confirmation of his steady commitment to the followings forth of artistic excellence and an invitation to dive into the alluring world of shadows and light.

19. CATS / GATTI

Studies and sketches of cats in various positions.

This sketch, comprising nine scrupulously rendered cats, unveils a hitherto unrecognized facet of da Vinci's artistic repertoire and provides valuable insights into his historical interest in the natural world. Through an examination of Leonardo's fascination with animal representation and the technical brilliance displayed in this sketch, we untwist the significance and lasting impact of this remarkable discovery.

Leonardo da Vinci's indelible mark on the world of art and science is widely recognized. His unquenchable curiosity and quest for knowledge transcended disciplinary bounds, as exemplified by his groundbreaking anatomical studies, botanical illustrations, and engineering designs. While his fascination with the human form is well-documented, his interest in the animal kingdom, particularly the enigmatic behavior of cats, has garnered less scholarly attention.

The recently unearthed sketch not merely enriches our understanding of Leonardo's multifaceted genius but also sheds light on his lesser-known engagement with the depiction of animals. As an artist whose work primarily revolved around religious and historical themes, this composition holdeth as a notable departure from his conventional subject matter, revealing his inclination to inquire into the diverse atlas of the natural world.

The sketch's central motif of nine cats unveils Leonardo's thorough observation and attentiveness to detail. Each cat is rendered with exceptional precision, showcasing a range of distinct poses, expressions, and coat patterns. This confirmation of Leonardo's unrivaled mastery of form and movement reveals his capacity to breathe life into his subjects, transcending mere representation to evoke an apparition of vitality.

Furthermore, the arrangement of the cats within the composition illustrates Leonardo's compositional finesse and spatial awareness. Through carefully orchestrated positioning, he creates a harmonious visual balance, accentuated by the relationship of their tails, paws, and alert ears. This display of artistic cleverness underscores Leonardo's steady commitment to achieving perfect harmony and proportion in his work.

Beyond its aesthetic allure, this sketch assumes a broader significance within the context of Leonardo's artistic heritage. It exemplifies his ability to bridge the domains of art and science, highlighting his belief that the study of the natural world was integral to the followings forth of artistic excellence. By focusing on feline subjects, Leonardo dived into the complexities of animal behavior, perceiving them as an integral part of the enmeshed nexus of life.

Moreover, this composition represents a groundbreaking departure from traditional animal portraiture of the time. Leonardo's important understanding of anatomy, acquired By use of his comprehensive study of mankind's physiology, is evident in the complex rendering of the cats' musculature and skeletal structure. This relationship betwixt scientific observation and artistic expression further exemplifies Leonardo's futuristic purview and his desire to stretch the bounds of artistic representation.

The discovery of Leonardo da Vinci's sketch featuring nine cats adds a new dimension to our understanding of his artistic power and his important appreciation for the natural world. This composition exemplifies his technical brilliance, thorough attention to detail, and unrelenting curiosity. By untwisting the historical context, technical virtuosity, and thematic significance of this sketch, we gain invaluable insights into Leonardo's artistic vision, his exploration of animal representation, and his lasting impact on the world of art.

20. ARTILLERY / ARTIGLIERIA

Including the design for a "33-barrelled organ."

Amidst Leonardo da Vinci's huge repertoire of artistic and scientific endeavors, his design for a "33-barrelled organ" holdeth as a confirmation of his cleverness and inventive spirit. This remarkable creation, conceived in an era of important curiosity, flaunts Leonardo's unlimited imagination and his remarkable skill in the realm of musical innovation.

The design for the "33-barrelled organ" unveils a mesmerizing instrument that fuses artistry, engineering, and musical craftsmanship. With thorough attention to detail, Leonardo envisioned a complex mechanism composed of numerous barrels, each containing a distinct melody or musical composition. This innovative design allowed for a symphony of harmonies to be played with the turn of a handle, creating a alluring auditory experience.

The complex structure of the organ, as procured in Leonardo's design, flaunts his depthy understanding of acoustics and his desire to stretch the bounds of musical expression. The 33 barrels, each scrupulously crafted to produce a unique set of notes, offered a huge repertoire of melodies that could be interchanged at will. Leonardo's design demonstrated his important appreciation for the art of music and his commitment to elevating the auditory experience to new heights.

In this visionary design, Leonardo da Vinci showcased his multidisciplinary approach, intertwining his artistic sensibility with his scientific and engineering power. The "33-barrelled organ" transcended the traditional confines of musical instruments, representing a fusion of artistry, technology, and musicality. Leonardo's undying followings forth of innovation is evident in every detail, as he strove to create an instrument that would allure and inspirit both musicians and audiences alike.

Although the "33-barrelled organ" design remained unrealized in Leonardo's lifetime, its significance in the chronicles of musical history cannot be overstated. It acts as a confirmation of Leonardo's far-reaching vision and his ability to imagine possibilities beyond the confines of his time. His design remains to inspirit contemporary musicians and instrument makers, encouraging them to inquire into new domains of musical expression and stretch the bounds of artistic innovation.

Inasmuch we dive into Leonardo's design for the "33-barrelled organ," we are warped to a world where music intertwines with engineering and imagination knows no bounds. His visionary approach invites us to consider the important impact of innovation and the transformative power of merging different disciplines. Leonardo da Vinci's design for the "33-barrelled organ" remains a lasting confirmation of his genius and a glimmer of the limitless potential that lies at the intersection of art, science, and human imagination.

21. BRIDGES / PONTI

Such as the design for a self-supporting bridge.

Amid Leonardo da Vinci's extraordinary array of designs, his concept for a self-supporting bridge holdeth as a confirmation of his brilliance as an engineer and visionary. Conceived during an era of unlimited curiosity and exploration, this remarkable design flaunts Leonardo's innovative approach to solving complex architectural challenges.

The design for the self-supporting bridge reveals Leonardo's depthy understanding of structural mechanics and his ability to harness the forces of nature to create a harmonious balance. With thorough precision, he envisioned a bridge that could span great distances without the need for external support. The design incorporated graceful arches and strategic distribution of weight, enabling the bridge to bear its own load and stand firm in the face of physical forces.

Leonardo's self-supporting bridge design demonstrates his important appreciation for the inherent strength and resilience of materials. His careful calculations and understanding of physics allowed him to create a structure that could withstand the test of time. By use of his innovative design, he strove to create a bridge that not merely acted as a practical solution for crossing obstacles but also showcased the beauty and elegance of engineering.

Although the self-supporting bridge design remained unrealized in Leonardo's lifetime, its significance in the realm of architectural innovation cannot be overstated. It holdeth as a confirmation of Leonardo's ability to think beyond convention and challenge existing notions of structural design. His design remains to inspirit contemporary engineers and architects, serving as a catalyst for exploring new possibilities in bridge construction and pushing the bounds of architectural imagination.

Inasmuch we examine Leonardo's design for the self-supporting bridge, here we see his steady commitment to blending artistic vision with scientific understanding. His ability to unite aesthetics with functionality is evident in every curve and contour of the bridge design. Leonardo da Vinci's self-supporting bridge remains an emblem of his genius and a symbol of humanity's ceaseless quest for progress and innovation in the realm of architecture.

In contemplating this extraordinary design, we are invited to inquire into the limitless possibilities of mankind's cleverness and the transformative power of merging art and science. Leonardo's vision of a self-supporting bridge challenges us to think beyond conventional limitations, to welcome the inherent strength within ourselves and the world around us. His design acts as a timeless glimmer of the indomitable human spirit and the power of imagination to shape our physical reality.

22. PARACHUTE / PARACADUTE

His drawing of a parachute is much revered.

Amid the revered works of Leonardo da Vinci, his drawing of a parachute holdeth a special place. This remarkable creation flaunts his visionary mind and futuristic purview, as he dived into the realm of aeronautics and searched out the possibilities of mankind's flight.

Conceived during an era characterized by intellectual curiosity and bold exploration, Leonardo's drawing of a parachute reveals his important understanding of physics and his undying followings forth of innovative ideas. With thorough detail, he sketched a device that would allow a person to descend safely from great heights, harnessing the forces of air resistance to slow their descent and ensure a gentle landing.

The drawing of the parachute reflects Leonardo's remarkable ability to merge artistry and scientific inquiry. Each line and stroke of his pen captures the complex design and functionality of this revolutionary apparatus. The concept of the parachute, with its canopy and suspension lines, is scrupulously rendered, showcasing Leonardo's acute understanding of aerodynamics and his drive to lay bare the secrets of mankind's flight.

Although Leonardo's parachute design was ahead of its time and remained unrealized during his era, its significance in the realm of aeronautics cannot be overstated. His vision and pioneering approach paved the way for future generations of inventors and aviators, provoking them to inquire into the possibilities of mankind's flight. Leonardo's drawing of the parachute holdeth as a confirmation of his indomitable spirit and his steady belief in the limitless potential of mankind's cleverness.

Inasmuch we contemplate this extraordinary drawing, here we see Leonardo's unquenchable curiosity and his undying followings forth of knowledge. His exploration of the parachute represents a culmination of his scientific and artistic talents, merging technical precision with aesthetic grace. Leonardo da Vinci's drawing of the parachute remains to inspirit and allure, igniting the imagination of those who dare to dream of reaching new heights and defying the limits of gravity.

In reflecting upon this revered work, we honor Leonardo's heritage as a firstman and visionary. His drawing of the parachute symbolizes humanity's unyielding quest for progress and our innate desire to bypass the confines of our earthly existence. Leonardo's steady belief in the power of mankind's cleverness acts as a guiding light, provoking us to stretch the bounds of what is possible and to soar to new heights in our own creative endeavors.

23. ANATOMICAL COMPARISONS / CONFRONTI ANATOMICI

He compared the physiology of humans and other animals.

Leonardo da Vinci, the renowned polymath, began on an important exploration of the natural world, comparing the physiology of humans with that of other animals. By use of his thorough observations and detailed sketches, he strove to untwist the complex similarities and differences that exist across the animal kingdom.

In his followings forth of knowledge, Leonardo recognized the enmeshment of all living beings. His comparative studies of mankind's and animal physiology aimed to shed light on the shared foundations of life, while also highlighting the unique adaptations that distinguish each species. With his acute eye and extraordinary attention to detail, he scrupulously documented the anatomical structures, skeletal systems, and muscular arrangements of diverse creatures, from birds and horses to fish and reptiles.

Leonardo's comparative studies of mankind's and animal physiology transcended mere anatomical exploration. They were a confirmation of his unquenchable curiosity and his steady belief in the unity of nature. By use of his sketches and writings, he strove to understand the underlying principles that governed life's complex workings, recognizing the potential for insights that could revolutionize fields ranging from medicine to engineering.

In examining Leonardo's comparative studies, we witness his depthy appreciation for the beauty and complexity of the natural world. His sketches and annotations provide glimpses into the shared features and evolutionary adaptations that have shaped life on Earth. By use of his thorough observations, he relayed the mysteries of nature, untwisting the fascinating connections that bind all living organisms.

Leonardo's comparative physiology studies inspirit scientists, artists, and thinkers of all disciplines. They remind us of the importance of embracing a holistic understanding of life and recognizing the relationship betwixt humans and the wider animal kingdom. Leonardo da Vinci's work acts as a timeless glimmer of our place within the grand atlas of nature, encouraging an apparition of awe and reverence for the incredible diversity and enmeshment of life.

Inasmuch we dive into Leonardo's comparative studies of mankind's and animal physiology, we are invited to contemplate the beauty and wonder of existence. His sketches and writings not merely deepen our understanding of the natural world but also ignite an apparition of curiosity and appreciation for the complex nexus of life. Leonardo da Vinci's lasting heritage lies in his ability to bridge the gap betwixt art and science, illuminating the mysteries of the universe and provoking generations to dive deeper into the domains of knowledge and discovery.

24. FOSSILS / FOSSILI

Da Vinci sketched and studied fossils to understand the concept of depthy time.

Leonardo da Vinci, the brilliant polymath, dived into the study of fossils as he strove to grasp the concept of depthy time. By use of his thorough sketches and acute observations, he began on a quest to untwist the mysteries of the Earth's history and gain insights into the huge expanses of time that preceded the present.

In his followings forth of knowledge, Leonardo recognized that fossils held the key to understanding the ancient past. He scrupulously documented the shapes, textures, and complex details of these preserved remnants of ancient life. His sketches revealed the imprints of long-extinct creatures, displaying their forms in astonishing detail and breathing life into their long-lost existence.

Leonardo's study of fossils was a confirmation of his unquenchable curiosity and his drive to uncover the secrets of the natural world. By use of his careful examination, he strove to decipher the stories embedded within these ancient relics, piecing together a narrative that spanned millions of years. His sketches and observations provided glimpses into the evolution of life on Earth, offering an important understanding of the concept of depthy time.

As Leonardo dived into the study of fossils, he embraced the notion that the Earth's history stretched far beyond the span of a human lifetime. His explorations nurtured an apparition of awe and wonder for the immense passage of time and the ever-changing nature of the world. By use of his sketches, he bridged the gap betwixt past and present, igniting an apparition of connection to the huge continuum of life that had inhabited the Earth before our time.

Leonardo's commitment to understanding depthy time through the study of fossils remains to inspirit scientists, paleontologists, and thinkers of all disciplines. His sketches act as a confirmation of the importance of embracing the vastness of geological time and recognizing our place within the grand atlas of life's evolution. Leonardo da Vinci's work urges us to contemplate the complex nexus of existence, humbling us in the face of the ancient past and propelling us to inquire across the nexus of our planet's history.

Inasmuch we dive into Leonardo's sketches and studies of fossils, here we see the important connections that bind us to the Earth and the incredible timeline of life. His thorough observations awaken an apparition of wonder, prompting us to ponder the mysteries of our planet's past and welcome the immense stretches of time that have shaped our world. Leonardo da Vinci's lasting heritage lies in his ability to lay bare the secrets of depthy time, encouraging a depthy appreciation for the ever-unfolding story of life on Earth.

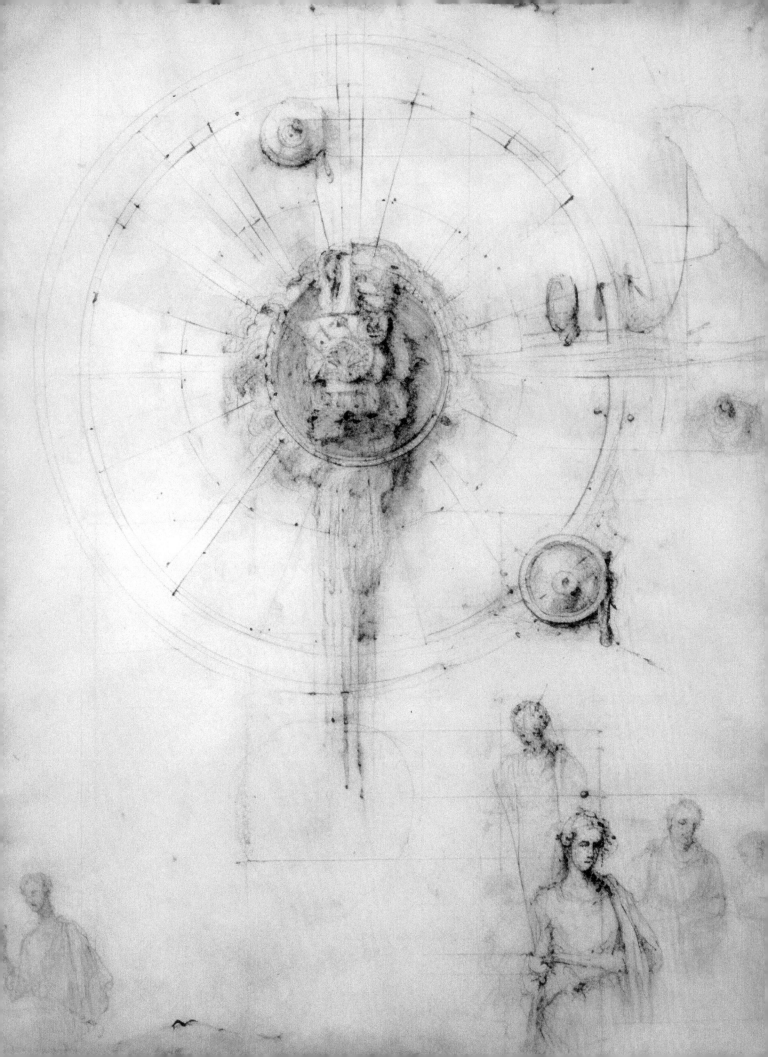

25. HUMAN AGING / INVECCHIAMENTO UMANO

Studies of the human face showcasing the process of aging.

Leonardo da Vinci, the esteemed artist and scholar, committed his acute eye and artistic power to the study of the human face, displaying its ever-evolving process of aging. By use of his thorough observations and sketches, he began on an important exploration of the passage of time and the transformative effects it has on the human visage.

Leonardo's studies of the human face went beyond mere artistic representation. With steady commitment, he strove to untwist the secrets of aging, documenting the subtle changes and nuanced details that mark the progression of time on the human countenance. His sketches revealed the lines etched by wisdom, the gentle sagging of skin, and the transformative power of life's experiences, all encapsulated within the complex territory of the face.

In his quest to understand the aging process, Leonardo's studies procured the essence of humanity's shared quest. His observations revealed the beauty and vulnerability inherent in the passage of time, highlighting the inevitability of change and the inherent grace that accompanies each stage of life. By use of his sketches, he embraced the imperfections and unique characteristics that make each face a confirmation of a life well-lived.

Leonardo's studies of the aging face were a confirmation of his important understanding of mankind's nature and his ability to map its essence on paper. With each stroke of his pen, he unraveled the complexities of the aging process, conveying the stories etched upon each face with empathy and insight. His sketches act as a mirror that reflects our shared humanity, reminding us of the transient nature of existence and the beauty that lies within the passage of time.

Inasmuch we dive into Leonardo's studies of the human face, we are confronted with the universality of aging. His sketches evoke an apparition of empathy and reverence for the journeys we all undertake, celebrating the wisdom that comes with the accumulation of years. Leonardo da Vinci's work inspires us to welcome the changes that time brings, to appreciate the unique stories written upon our faces, and to recognize the inherent beauty in the ebb and flow of life.

By use of his studies, Leonardo da Vinci offered an important exploration of the aging process, shedding light on the transformative power of time and the intrinsic beauty that emerges as faces mature. His sketches allure our imagination, prompting us to reflect on our own journeys and find solace in the complex lines and contours that bear witness to a life fully lived. Leonardo's lasting heritage lies in his ability to map the essence of the lived experience, immortalizing the beauty of aging in his timeless works of art.

26. THEATER DESIGN / PROGETTAZIONE TEATRALE

Leonardo was involved in designing pageants and theatrical productions.

Leonardo da Vinci, the celebrated artist and visionary, showcased his multifaceted talents not merely in the realm of fine art but also in the coruscating world of pageants and theatrical productions. His involvement in designing and conceptualizing these spectacles brought forth a harmonious blend of artistic creativity and theatrical grandeur.

With his acute eye for aesthetics and thorough attention to detail, Leonardo lent his artistic power to the creation of alluring pageants and theatrical performances. His designs and ideas encompassed a wide array of elements, including elaborate stage sets, exquisite costumes, and innovative stage mechanisms. By use of his contributions, he elevated the art of spectacle, alluring audiences with his imaginative visions.

Leonardo's involvement in pageants and theatrical productions showcased his ability to seamlessly merge artistic expression with the dynamic nature of live performances. His designs not merely strove to visually allure but also aimed to engage the audience on a deeper emotional level. From grand processions to elaborate stage illusions, he infused his creations with an apparition of wonder, inviting spectators into a realm of enchantment and awe.

In his quest to create unforgettable theatrical experiences, Leonardo combined his knowledge of perspective, light, and movement to craft immersive and visually stunning productions. His innovative stage designs and mechanical contraptions brought scenes to life, transforming the stage into a dynamic and alluring space. By use of his contributions, he pushed the bounds of what was possible, leaving an indelible mark on the world of theatrical arts.

Leonardo's involvement in designing pageants and theatrical productions reflects his innate ability to harness the power of storytelling and visual aesthetics. His creations were not merely ornamental, but rather acted as integral components that enhanced the narrative and heightened the emotional impact of the performances. Leonardo's designs breathed life into the theatrical realm, providing a rich atlas of sights and sounds that immersed audiences in an unforgettable experience.

Inasmuch we reflect on Leonardo's contributions to pageants and theatrical productions, here we see his undying followings forth of artistic excellence and his ability to inspirit wonder and imagination. His designs influence and shape the world of theater, propelling future generations to inquire into new frontiers of creativity and innovation. Leonardo da Vinci's heritage in this realm remains an illuminant of artistic brilliance, forever etching his name in the annals of theatrical history.

27. MUSICAL INSTRUMENTS / STRUMENTI MUSICALI

He designed a number of novel musical instruments.

Leonardo da Vinci, the extraordinary polymath, applied his unlimited creativity and cleverness to the design of novel musical instruments. In his undying followings forth of innovation, he strove to stretch the bounds of musical expression and create instruments that would allure the senses and evoke important emotions.

Leonardo's designs for musical instruments were a confirmation of his depthy understanding of acoustics, aesthetics, and the human connection to sound. With his visionary approach, he envisioned instruments that would produce unique timbres, expand the tonal range, and inspirit musicians to inquire into new domains of musicality.

From the whimsical to the sublime, Leonardo's designs encompassed a diverse array of instruments. His sketches relayed instruments with innovative mechanisms, unconventional shapes, and imaginative embellishments. Whether it was a groundbreaking keyboard instrument or a mesmerizing stringed instrument, each design showcased Leonardo's ability to harmonize form and function.

Leonardo's designs for novel musical instruments were not merely an exercise in artistic expression, but an important exploration of the human relationship with sound. He understood the power of music to stir emotions, uplift the spirit, and bypass language. His designs aimed to amplify this emotional connection, offering musicians and audiences alike a transformative musical experience.

Although many of Leonardo's musical instrument designs were never realized during his lifetime, their significance in the realm of music cannot be understated. His visionary approach and innovative concepts inspirit instrument makers, composers, and musicians to this day. Leonardo's designs act as a catalyst for pushing the bounds of musical invention, nurturing a spirit of exploration and experimentation.

Inasmuch we dive into Leonardo's designs for novel musical instruments, here we see his steady commitment to expanding the frontiers of mankind's creativity. His sketches transport us to a world where imagination meets craftsmanship, where the language of music transcends conventional bounds. Leonardo da Vinci's lasting heritage in the realm of musical instrument design remains an impetus, forever resonating with the harmonies and melodies that connect us all.

28. FOOTWEAR / CALZATURE

Studies of different types of footwear and their impact on gait.

Leonardo da Vinci, the inquisitive scholar and artist, dived into the study of different types of footwear and their influence on human gait. By use of his thorough observations and sketches, he strove to untwist the complex relationship betwixt footwear design and the way we move.

In his exploration of footwear, Leonardo recognized that the choice of shoes could profoundly impact an individual's gait and overall movement patterns. He scrupulously documented various types of shoes, from sturdy boots to swift slippers, analyzing their structures, materials, and the effects they had on the human body in motion.

Leonardo's studies went beyond mere fashion or aesthetics. He strove to understand how different footwear designs affected balance, stability, and the natural rhythm of walking. His sketches revealed the subtle nuances of foot placement, weight distribution, and the complex interactions betwixt the foot and the ground.

By use of his careful examination of footwear and its impact on gait, Leonardo shed light on the ways in which shoes can either enhance or hinder our natural movement. He recognized that the design of shoes could either promote ease and efficiency or impose limitations and discomfort. His studies highlighted the importance of finding a harmonious balance betwixt style, functionality, and the inherent needs of the human body.

Leonardo's insights into footwear and gait resonate in the domains of biomechanics and ergonomic design. His thorough observations and sketches act as a valuable resource for researchers, designers, and individuals seeking to optimize their movement and enhance their prosperity. Leonardo da Vinci's work drives home the important enmeshment betwixt our bodies and the objects we interact with, offering valuable lessons for creating footwear that supports natural movement.

Inasmuch we reflect on Leonardo's studies of footwear and their impact on gait, here we see the significance of mindful design and the potential to optimize human movement. His thorough observations and sketches encourage us to consider the relationship betwixt form and function, reminding us that the choices we make in footwear can have an important impact on our physical prosperity. Leonardo da Vinci's lasting heritage in the realm of footwear studies inspires us to seek a harmonious fusion of style, comfort, and human movement, Inasmuch we navigate the world on our own unique paths.

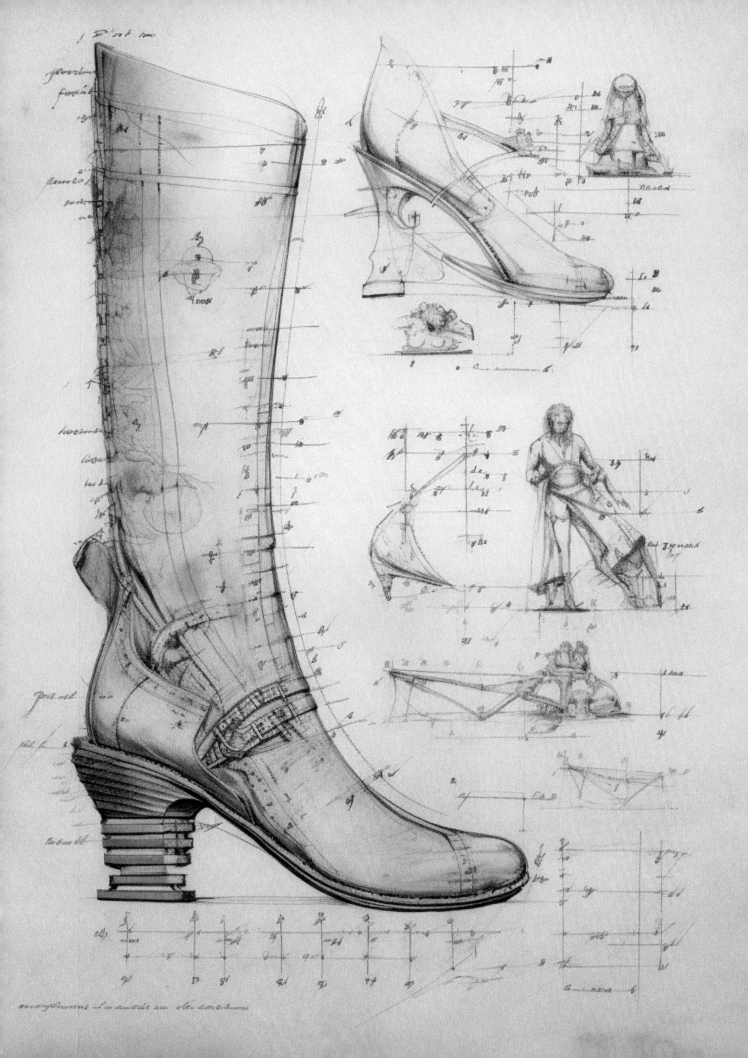

29. THE SUN AND MOON / IL SOLE E LA LUNA

Studies of their movement across the sky.

Leonardo da Vinci, the visionary artist and scholar, devoted himself to the study of celestial bodies and their graceful movement across the expanse of the sky. Through thorough observations and contemplative sketches, he strove to lay bare the mysteries of the heavens and comprehend the complex jubilation of celestial objects.

In his quest to understand the movement of celestial bodies, Leonardo turned his peer upward, immersing himself in the wonders of the night sky. With his acute observational skills, he scrupulously recorded the trajectories, positions, and interactions of the stars, planets, and other celestial phenomena.

Leonardo's studies of celestial movement went beyond mere astronomical observations. He strove to comprehend the underlying mechanics and forces that governed the majestic choreography of the heavens. His sketches procured the essence of the celestial ballet, showcasing the fluidity and grace with which celestial objects traversed the cosmic stage.

By use of his studies, Leonardo discovered patterns and rhythms within the celestial realm. He recognized the cyclical nature of celestial movements, the jubilation of the planets as they orbited the sun, and the mesmerizing procession of stars across the night sky. His sketches and notes mirrored his awe and reverence for the complex celestial symphony that unfolded above.

Leonardo's studies of celestial movement inspirit astronomers, scientists, and dreamers alike. His thorough observations act as a foundation for our understanding of the cosmos, fueling further discoveries and shaping our exploration of the universe. Leonardo's work drives home the unlimited wonders that await us in the vastness of space, beckoning us to peer skyward with an apparition of wonder and curiosity.

Inasmuch we contemplate Leonardo's studies of celestial movement, here we see the important enmeshment betwixt the Earth and the cosmos. His sketches and observations lead us in to ponder our place in the grand atlas of the universe, to swoon at the celestial objects that have guided humanity throughout history. Leonardo da Vinci's lasting heritage in the study of celestial movement encourages us to keep exploring, questioning, and seeking answers to the mysteries that unfold above us.

By use of his studies, Leonardo da Vinci began on a celestial quest, displaying the poetry of the heavens in his sketches. His observations of celestial movement act as a confirmation of his unquenchable curiosity, reminding us to look beyond our earthly bounds and welcome the infinite possibilities that await us in the cosmic expanse.

30. FLUID DYNAMICS / DINAMICA DEI FLUIDI

Studies and sketches of water and air movement.

Leonardo da Vinci, the brilliant mind of the Renaissance, immersed himself in the study of the dynamic forces of nature, focusing on the movement of water and air. By use of his acute observations and detailed sketches, he strove to untwist the mysteries of these elemental phenomena and map their essence on paper.

In his followings forth of knowledge, Leonardo recognized the fundamental part that water and air play in shaping the world around us. He scrupulously observed the fluid motion of water as it cascaded, swirled, and flowed, displaying its graceful movements in his sketches. Similarly, he studied the ethereal jubilation of air, observing its currents, turbulence, and gentle breezes.

Leonardo's studies and sketches of water and air movement were more than mere scientific observations. They revealed his important appreciation for the beauty and power of nature. His complex renderings mirrored the complex patterns and relationship of these elements, portraying their ever-changing forms and displaying the essence of their motion.

By use of his observations, Leonardo unraveled the complex dynamics of water and air, recognizing their impact on the natural world. His sketches showcased the complexities of fluid dynamics, starting with the gentle ripples on a calm lake to the crashing waves of the sea. In his depictions of air movement, he procured the invisible forces that shape our environment, starting with the gentle caress of a breeze to the tumultuous gusts of a storm.

Leonardo's studies and sketches of water and air movement inspirit scientists, engineers, and artists alike. His observations laid the Earthly foundation for our understanding of fluid dynamics and aerodynamics, shaping fields such as hydrology and aeronautics. His sketches act as a glimmer of the complex and enmeshed nature of the elements that surround us.

Inasmuch we contemplate Leonardo's studies and sketches of water and air movement, here we see the ceaseless jubilation of nature and our place within it. His thorough observations lead us in to appreciate the beauty and complexity of the natural world, encouraging us to seek harmony with these elemental forces. Leonardo da Vinci's lasting heritage in the study of water and air movement acts as a confirmation of his unquenchable curiosity and his ability to map the essence of nature's dynamic welcome.

By use of his studies and sketches, Leonardo da Vinci set free the secrets of water and air movement, painting a vivid picture of the ever-changing world around us. His observations and depictions allure our imagination, reminding us of the awe-provoking forces that shape our planet and provoking us to further inquire into the mysteries of nature.

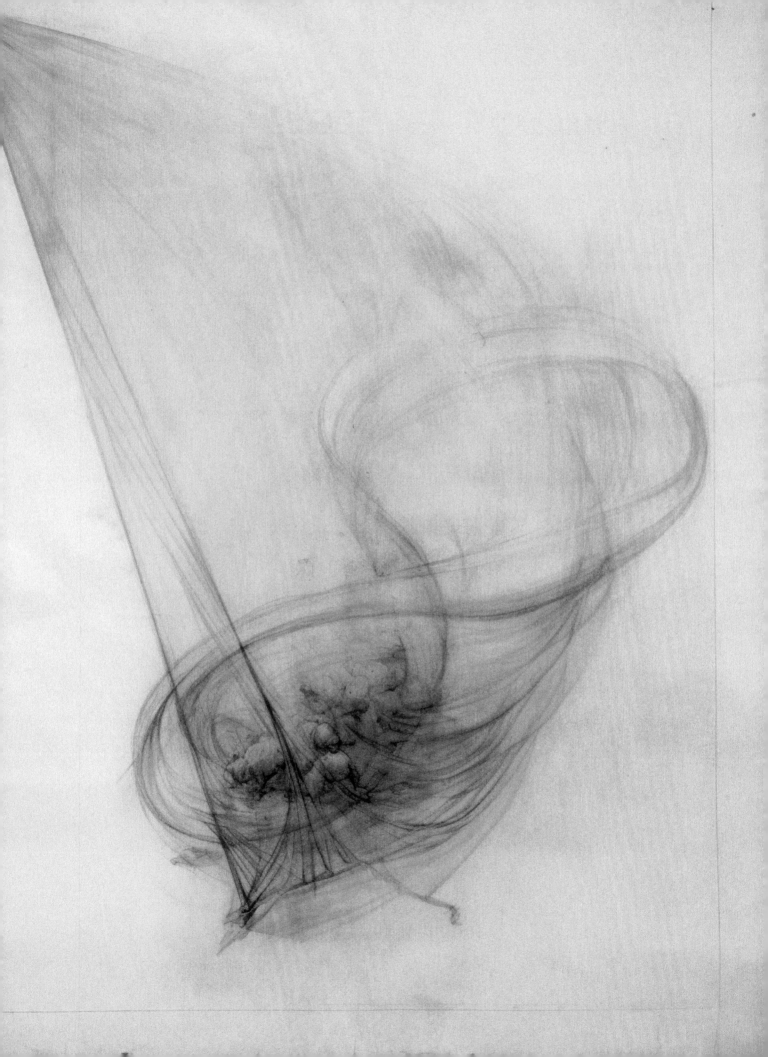

31. ASTRONOMY / ASTRONOMIA

Sketches of the night sky.

Leonardo da Vinci, the visionary artist and scholar, turned his peer to the heavens above, displaying the ethereal beauty of the night sky in his remarkable sketches. With his acute eye and important curiosity, he strove to unveil the mysteries of the celestial realm and translate its splendor onto paper.

By use of his thorough observations and swift strokes of the pen, Leonardo depicted the grandeur of the night sky in his sketches. He immortalized the twinkling stars, the gentle glow of the moon, and the celestial bodies that adorned the huge expanse of darkness. Each stroke of his hand procured the intangible magic that enveloped the nocturnal canopy.

Leonardo's sketches of the night sky transcended mere representation. They breathed life into the cosmic ballet, evoking an apparition of wonder and awe. His careful renderings conveyed the vastness of space, the infinite possibilities that lay beyond our reach, and the enmeshment of the celestial objects that adorned the atlas of the night.

By use of his studies, Leonardo strove to understand the patterns and movements of the celestial bodies. He documented the phases of the moon, the constellations that traced their paths across the sky, and the elusive beauty of shooting stars. His sketches became a visual language, displaying the fleeting moments and eternal majesty of the heavens.

Leonardo's sketches of the night sky inspirit astronomers, stargazers, and dreamers alike. They act as a glimmer of the limitless expanse of the universe and our place within it. His artistry and important understanding of the cosmos echo through the ages, inviting us to contemplate the mysteries that lie beyond our earthly confines.

Inasmuch we peer upon Leonardo's sketches of the night sky, we are warped to a realm where time holdeth still and imagination takes flight. His complex observations and masterful renderings awaken an apparition of wonder within us, encouraging us to ponder the infinite possibilities that lie in the depths of the universe. Leonardo da Vinci's lasting heritage in displaying the essence of the night sky acts as a glimmer of the beauty, mystery, and enmeshment of the cosmos.

By use of his sketches, Leonardo da Vinci revealed the sublime beauty of the night sky, forever preserving its enchantment on paper. His observations and artistic renderings ignite our imagination, beckoning us to look upward and swoon at the celestial wonders that surround us. Leonardo's heritage as a visionary artist and scholar remains to inspirit us to inquire into, discover, and connect with the celestial realm above.

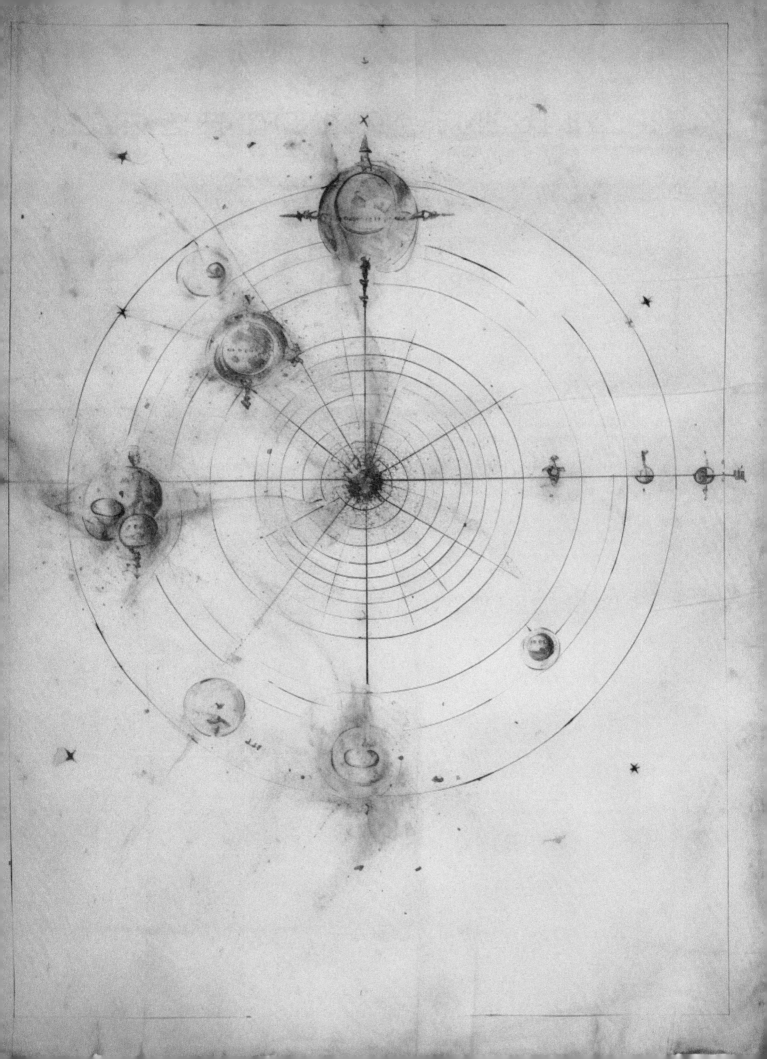

32. CIVIL ENGINEERING / INGEGNERIA CIVILE

Design of a city with a multi-tier layout.

Leonardo da Vinci, the visionary artist and architect, turned his creative genius towards the design of a city with a multi-tier layout. In his visionary sketches, he strove to reimagine urban spaces, introducing a dynamic and harmonious structure that embraced the vertical dimension.

Leonardo's design envisioned a cityscape that defied traditional flat landscapes. His sketches showcased a multi-tier layout, where buildings and infrastructure rose in a cascading fashion, creating a three-dimensional atlas of urban life. This innovative approach to city planning aimed to maximize space efficiency while providing a harmonious balance betwixt function and aesthetics.

With thorough attention to detail, Leonardo's sketches procured the complex relationship of streets, walkways, and public spaces across different tiers. His design incorporated architectural elements that harmonized with the natural topography, seamlessly blending human structures with the surrounding environment. The multi-tier layout allowed for the efficient flow of people, goods, and services, creating a coruscating and enmeshed urban ecosystem.

Leonardo's design of a multi-tier city embodied his visionary spirit and his understanding of the evolving needs of urban dwellers. The tiered structure offered unique opportunities for diverse urban experiences, with each level catering to specific functions, such as residential, commercial, cultural, and recreational spaces. This innovative approach aimed to enhance livability, promote social interaction, and optimize the utilization of available land.

Beyond its functional aspects, Leonardo's design of a multi-tier city celebrated the beauty of architectural form and spatial composition. His sketches showcased a harmonious balance of proportions, light, and shadow, creating a visually alluring cityscape that encouraged awe and wonder. The verticality of the design added depth and perspective to the urban fabric, elevating the lived experience within the city.

While Leonardo's design for a multi-tier city remained a vision on paper, its influence and forward-thinking concepts inspirit urban planners and architects today. His sketches challenge conventional notions of urban design and encourage a more holistic approach that considers the vertical dimension as an integral part of the urban territory.

Inasmuch we inquire into Leonardo's design of a city with a multi-tier layout, here we see the unlimited potential for innovation in urban planning. His visionary sketches prompt us to envision cities that bypass traditional bounds, embracing the vertical dimension and creating dynamic urban environments that enhance our lives.

Leonardo da Vinci's design of a multi-tier city reflects his unquenchable curiosity, his ability to merge aesthetics and functionality, and his lasting heritage as a visionary thinker. His sketches remind us that the city is not merely a collection of buildings and infrastructure but a living, breathing entity that shapes our daily experiences. Leonardo's design challenges us to reimagine our urban environments and strive for a harmonious balance betwixt human needs, natural surroundings, and architectural expression.

33. GEOMETRY / GEOMETRIA

His sketches on geometrical shapes.

Leonardo da Vinci, the renowned artist and scholar, dived into the realm of geometrical shapes, displaying their essence in his thorough sketches. By use of his acute observations and masterful strokes, he searched out the complexities and inherent beauty of these fundamental forms.

Leonardo's sketches on geometrical shapes were a confirmation of his fascination with the underlying principles of structure and proportion. With precision and artistic finesse, he depicted circles, squares, triangles, and other geometric figures, revealing their symmetries, relationships, and relationship.

In his followings forth of understanding, Leonardo recognized that geometric shapes formed the foundation of the physical world. His sketches went beyond mere representations, encapsulating the essence of these shapes and their inherent mathematical properties. By use of his artwork, he aimed to create the harmony, balance, and order that underlie the universe.

Leonardo's sketches on geometrical shapes showcased his important understanding of their significance in both art and science. He recognized their part in architectural design, spatial composition, and the depiction of form. His attention to detail and his exploration of the geometric principles allowed him to create visually alluring and mathematically precise compositions.

Beyond their aesthetic appeal, Leonardo's sketches on geometrical shapes acted as a tool for exploration and experimentation. They laid the Earthly foundation for his further studies on perspective, light and shadow, and the relationship of forms. These sketches became a visual language through which he communicated his understanding of the world around him.

Leonardo's sketches on geometrical shapes inspirit artists, mathematicians, and thinkers of all disciplines. They remind us of the important enmeshment betwixt art and science, the marriage of aesthetics and mathematical precision. His sketches act as a confirmation of the lasting power of geometric forms in shaping our perception and understanding of the world.

Inasmuch we contemplate Leonardo's sketches on geometrical shapes, here we see the universal language that these forms speak. They bypass cultural bounds and time, offering a visual vocabulary that communicates fundamental principles. Leonardo da Vinci's lasting heritage in the exploration of geometrical shapes invites us to appreciate the elegance, harmony, and inherent order that exist within the realm of mathematics and artistic expression.

By use of his sketches, Leonardo da Vinci unraveled the mysteries of geometrical shapes, displaying their essence on paper. His observations and artistic renderings inspirit us to perceive the world through a geometric lens, encouraging a deeper appreciation for the complex beauty and mathematical foundations that underlie our existence.

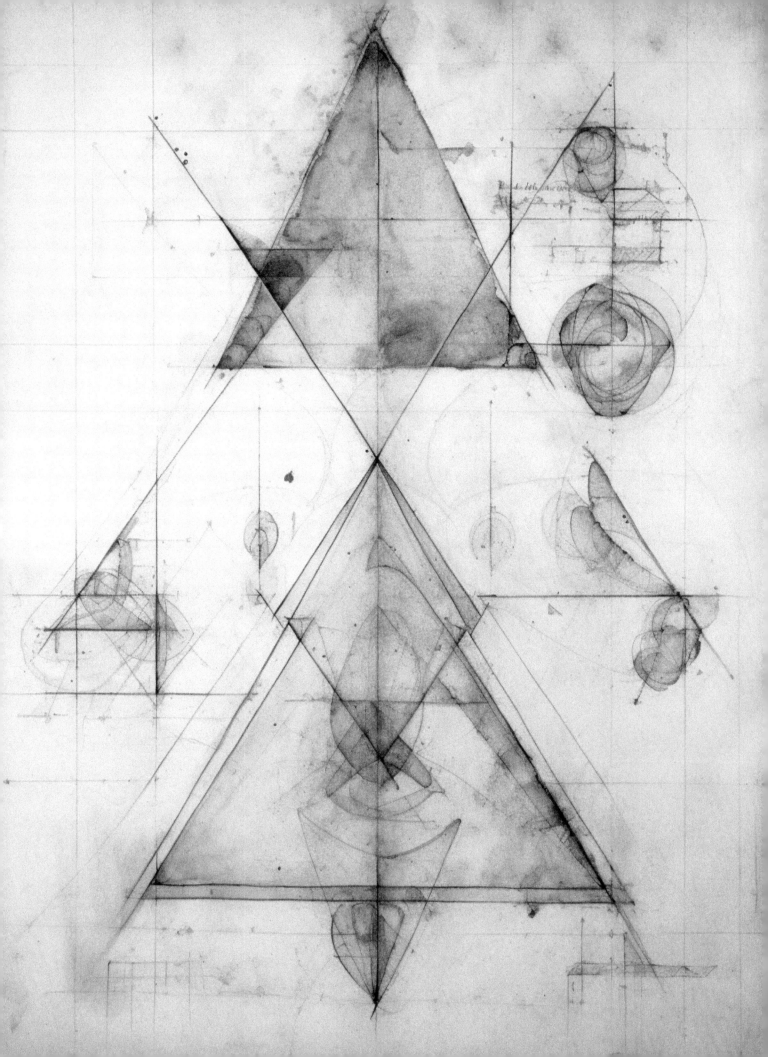

34. WAX CASTING / COLATA DI CERA

Leonardo described and sketched the process of making sculptures with wax.

Leonardo da Vinci, the visionary artist and scholar, immersed himself in the art of sculpture, documenting and sketching the complex process of sculpting with wax. By use of his detailed descriptions and thorough renderings, he strove to untwist the secrets of this ancient craft and map its essence on paper.

Leonardo's fascination with wax as a medium for sculpture stemmed from its unique properties and malleability. He carefully observed and recorded the techniques used by sculptors to manipulate and shape wax into three-dimensional forms. His sketches depicted the swift hands of artists, guiding their tools and scrupulously sculpting wax into exquisite masterpieces.

In his descriptions and sketches, Leonardo procured the various stages of the sculpting process. He detailed the preparatory steps, such as creating armatures or frameworks to provide structure and support to the wax. He documented the gradual addition and subtraction of wax to refine the form, displaying the relationship of light and shadow on the sculpted surface.

Leonardo's sketches and descriptions of sculpting with wax were not limited to the technical aspects alone. He dived into the artistic sensibilities required to breathe life into the wax, emphasizing the importance of displaying the essence and spirit of the subject. His observations mirrored his depthy understanding of mankind's anatomy and the nuances of expression, as he strove to infuse his sculptures with an apparition of vitality and emotion.

By use of his thorough renderings and thoughtful explanations, Leonardo shed light on the craftsmanship and artistry involved in sculpting with wax. His sketches became a visual documentation of the sculptor's quest, unveiling the transformative process from raw material to finished artwork. They acted as a source of impetus for aspiring sculptors, encouraging them to inquire into the possibilities of wax as a medium of expression.

While Leonardo's exploration of sculpting with wax extended beyond his own artistic output, his sketches and descriptions offered valuable insights into this ancient practice. His documentation acts as a confirmation of his unquenchable curiosity and his desire to understand and share the complexities of the artistic process.

Inasmuch we contemplate Leonardo's descriptions and sketches of sculpting with wax, here we see the craftsmanship, skill, and creativity required to shape formless material into works of art. His observations and renderings lead us in to appreciate the commitment and precision of sculptors, and the transformative power of art.

Leonardo da Vinci's exploration of sculpting with wax acts as a confirmation of his multidisciplinary approach and his commitment to understanding the world through art. His sketches and descriptions inspirit artists, scholars, and enthusiasts, encouraging a deeper appreciation for the art of sculpture and its timeless ability to create the beauty and complexity of the lived experience.

35. TEXTILES / TESSUTI

Studies of textile patterns and weaving techniques.

Leonardo da Vinci, the visionary artist and polymath, immersed himself in the study of textile patterns and weaving techniques, allured by the complex beauty and craftsmanship of fabric. By use of his thorough observations and detailed sketches, he strove to untwist the secrets of textile artistry and map the essence of these complex patterns on paper.

Leonardo's studies of textile patterns and weaving techniques were a confirmation of his acute eye for detail and his appreciation for the artistry involved in fabric production. He closely observed the complex weaves, the swift relationship of colors, and the mesmerizing repetition of motifs found in textiles of his time.

His sketches documented the various weaving techniques, showcasing the skill and precision required to create complex patterns and textures. Leonardo's renderings procured the artful manipulation of threads, the careful arrangement of warp and weft, and the rhythm of the loom as it brought the fabric to life.

By use of his studies, Leonardo searched out the harmonious fusion of art and craftsmanship in the world of textiles. He recognized the cultural significance of fabric patterns, the symbolism they carried, and the stories they told. His sketches mirrored his depthy appreciation for the diversity of textile traditions and the mastery of artisans who transformed raw materials into works of art.

Leonardo's studies of textile patterns and weaving techniques extended beyond mere documentation. He dived into the principles of symmetry, repetition, and proportion that underpinned these complex designs. His sketches revealed his understanding of the mathematical foundations that governed the creation of textile patterns, reflecting his unquenchable curiosity and his desire to uncover the underlying principles of beauty and harmony.

These studies and sketches of textile patterns and weaving techniques remain a confirmation of Leonardo's lasting curiosity and his ability to find impetus in every aspect of the world around him. They remind us of the rich cultural heritage woven into fabrics and the skilled craftsmanship that brings them to life.

Inasmuch we inquire into Leonardo's studies of textile patterns and weaving techniques, here we see the complex artistry and the labor-intensive processes involved in creating textiles. His sketches lead us in to appreciate the beauty of these complex patterns and to recognize the important cultural significance embedded within the fabric of our lives.

Leonardo da Vinci's studies of textile patterns and weaving techniques act as a timeless tribute to the artistry and craftsmanship of textile production. His observations and sketches inspirit us to cherish the heritage of textile traditions, to seek beauty in the woven atlas of our world, and to recognize the skill and creativity of those who transform threads into works of art.

36. LIGHT REFRACTION / RIFRAZIONE DELLA LUCE

Sketches and notes exploring how light passes through water.

Leonardo da Vinci, the brilliant mind of the Renaissance, began on an important exploration of the relationship betwixt light and water. By use of his sketches and thorough notes, he strove to untwist the mysteries of how light passes through this fluid medium, displaying its ethereal beauty on paper.

Leonardo's sketches and notes on the interaction of light and water were a confirmation of his acute observation and scientific inquiry. He carefully studied the way light refracts, reflects, and diffuses as it traverses through water, documenting the complex patterns and mesmerizing effects that unfold beneath the surface.

His sketches depicted the play of light and shadow on the undulating waves, displaying the mesmerizing jubilation of colors and the shimmering reflections. With each stroke of his pen, he attempted to grasp the ephemeral qualities of light as it interacts with the fluidity of water, creating alluring images that evoke an apparition of wonder and tranquility.

By use of his thorough notes, Leonardo recorded his observations on the behavior of light in water. He documented how the angle and intensity of light affect its interaction with the liquid medium, noting the subtle nuances and transformations that occur as light pierces the surface and permeates the depths.

Leonardo's sketches and notes on light passing through water went beyond the realm of artistry. They revealed his scientific curiosity and his depthy understanding of optics. His explorations paved the way for advancements in our understanding of how light behaves in different mediums, influencing fields such as physics, photography, and underwater exploration.

Inasmuch we contemplate Leonardo's sketches and notes on light and water, here we see the swift relationship betwixt these two elemental forces. His artistic renderings and scientific observations lead us in to appreciate the mesmerizing effects that occur beneath the surface, offering a specter into the hidden wonders of the aquatic realm.

Leonardo da Vinci's sketches and notes on how light passes through water remain a confirmation of his unquenchable curiosity and his ability to map the essence of natural phenomena. They inspirit us to perceive the world with a discerning eye, to seek beauty in the relationship of light and water, and to recognize the important connections betwixt art, science, and the wonders of the natural world.

By use of his sketches and notes, Leonardo da Vinci unraveled the enigmatic relationship betwixt light and water, immortalizing their ethereal jubilation on paper. His observations allure our imagination and deepen our understanding of the swift balance betwixt nature's elements.

37. ARMOR / ARMATURE

Designs for different types of protective armor.

Leonardo da Vinci, the visionary artist and inventor, turned his creative genius towards the design of various types of protective armor. By use of his detailed sketches and innovative ideas, he strove to reimagine the concept of defense, blending functionality with artistic elegance.

Leonardo's designs for protective armor showcased his important understanding of mankind's anatomy, mechanics, and the art of warfare. His sketches depicted a range of armor designs, from helmets and breastplates to gauntlets and greaves, each scrupulously crafted to provide maximum protection without compromising mobility.

With thorough attention to detail, Leonardo searched out the complex relationship of form and function in his armor designs. He integrated innovative features, such as articulated joints and layered plates, to ensure flexibility and adaptability in battle. His sketches showcased his visionary approach, where aesthetics merged seamlessly with defensive capabilities.

Beyond their practicality, Leonardo's armor designs were true works of art. He infused his sketches with complex embellishments, engravings, and decorative motifs that added a touch of elegance and individuality. Each design was a confirmation of his ability to fuse the practical with the aesthetic, elevating the concept of armor to a form of artistic expression.

Leonardo's designs for protective armor went beyond conventional materials and techniques. He searched out the use of new materials and innovative construction methods to enhance both protection and comfort. His sketches revealed his mastery of engineering principles, as he strove to stretch the bounds of what was possible in the realm of defensive gear.

These designs were not just idle sketches; Leonardo's armor concepts aimed to revolutionize the field of personal protection. He envisioned a future where warriors would be equipped with not just functional armor, but pieces that mirrored their individuality and encouraged awe on the battlefield.

Although many of Leonardo's armor designs remained unrealized, their influence on the field of defensive gear cannot be overstated. His sketches inspirit contemporary armorers and designers, encouraging them to stretch the bounds of innovation and craftsmanship. Leonardo da Vinci's visionary approach to armor design remains a confirmation of his lasting heritage as a firstman of both art and technology.

Inasmuch we contemplate Leonardo's designs for protective armor, here we see his multidisciplinary approach and his steady commitment to exploring the intersection of art, science, and warfare. His sketches lead us in to appreciate the cleverness and craftsmanship that goes into creating effective and aesthetically pleasing armor, highlighting the importance of both protection and individual expression.

Leonardo da Vinci's designs for protective armor act as a timeless confirmation of his visionary spirit and his quest for excellence. His sketches and ideas inspirit us to rethink traditional notions of defense, encouraging us to welcome innovation, creativity, and the followings forth of a harmonious balance betwixt form and function.

38. MASONRY / MURATURA

Sketches of masonry techniques.

Leonardo da Vinci, the visionary artist and engineer, immersed himself in the study of masonry techniques, displaying their essence in his thorough sketches. By use of his acute observations and masterful strokes, he strove to untwist the secrets of this ancient craft and preserve its knowledge for future generations.

Leonardo's sketches of masonry techniques were a confirmation of his depthy appreciation for the artistry and technical precision involved in working with stone. With each stroke of his pen, he scrupulously depicted the tools, methods, and complex details of masonry construction.

His sketches documented the various stages of the masonry process, starting with the quarrying and shaping of stones to the assembly and joining of the masonry units. He searched out different techniques such as ashlar masonry, brickwork, and arch construction, displaying the complexities of their execution.

By use of his drawings, Leonardo emphasized the importance of proper proportion, stability, and structural integrity in masonry. His attention to detail extended to the ornamental aspects of masonry, as he searched out decorative motifs, carvings, and the relationship of light and shadow on the finished structures.

Leonardo's sketches of masonry techniques were not limited to architectural applications alone. He also searched out the use of masonry in various engineering projects, such as bridges, fortifications, and canal systems. His sketches acted as a confirmation of his understanding of the practical and aesthetic aspects of masonry across different disciplines.

Beyond the technical aspects, Leonardo's sketches mirrored his depthy appreciation for the beauty and permanence of masonry. He recognized the lasting heritage of stone structures and strove to map their essence By use of his artistic renderings. His sketches breathed life into the stones, conveying the timelessness and craftsmanship embedded within each structure.

While many of Leonardo's masonry projects remained unrealized, his sketches and ideas laid the foundation for future advancements in the field. His thorough documentation and exploration of masonry techniques provided a valuable resource for architects, engineers, and craftsmen who followed in his footsteps.

Inasmuch we contemplate Leonardo's sketches of masonry techniques, here we see the ancient artistry and technical mastery that goes into building with stone. His drawings lead us in to appreciate the skill, patience, and attention to detail required to create lasting structures that stand the test of time.

Leonardo da Vinci's sketches of masonry techniques act as a timeless tribute to the art and science of working with stone. His observations and renderings inspirit architects, engineers, and artisans, encouraging a deeper understanding of the complexities and possibilities of masonry construction.

By use of his sketches, Leonardo da Vinci immortalized the knowledge and beauty of masonry, displaying the essence of this ancient craft for future generations to admire and learn from. His thorough renderings and insightful observations stand as a confirmation of his lasting heritage as a master of both art and engineering.

39. CANALS AND LOCKS / CANALI E CHIUSE

Design for a system of canals and locks for navigation and irrigation.

Leonardo da Vinci, the visionary artist and engineer, dived into the design of a comprehensive system of canals and locks, envisioning a transformative connections that would facilitate navigation and irrigation. By use of his complex sketches and thorough notes, he strove to revolutionize the way water resources were managed and harnessed.

Leonardo's design for the system of canals and locks was a confirmation of his depthy understanding of hydraulic principles and his commitment to improving the efficiency of water transportation and distribution. His sketches depicted a huge connections of enmeshed canals, strategically designed to navigate through different terrains and facilitate the movement of goods and people.

With thorough attention to detail, Leonardo searched out the engineering complexities involved in constructing canals and locks. His sketches showcased the innovative mechanisms and structures that would allow for the controlled flow of water, enabling ships to traverse varying elevations and providing essential irrigation to agricultural lands.

Leonardo's design aimed to optimize the utilization of water resources, promoting both navigation and irrigation for the betterment of society. His sketches revealed his understanding of the enmeshment of water systems, demonstrating his vision for a sustainable and efficient connections that would meet the needs of both commerce and agriculture.

Beyond their practicality, Leonardo's sketches of the canal and lock system also showcased his artistic sensibilities. He envisioned structures that harmonized with the natural environment, seamlessly integrating into the surrounding territory. His drawings procured the grandeur and elegance of the envisioned canals, reflecting his belief in the unification of aesthetics and functionality.

While many of Leonardo's ambitious engineering projects remained unrealized, his sketches and ideas paved the way for advancements in hydraulic engineering and water management. His design concepts acted as a source of impetus for future generations of engineers and urban planners, shaping the development of canal systems and irrigation networks across the world.

Inasmuch we contemplate Leonardo's design for a system of canals and locks, here we see his important vision and his commitment to harnessing the power of water for the betterment of society. His sketches lead us in to inquire into innovative solutions to water management challenges and to appreciate the complex relationship betwixt engineering, artistry, and environmental sustainability.

Leonardo da Vinci's design for a system of canals and locks holdeth as a confirmation of his multidisciplinary approach and his undying followings forth of knowledge. His sketches and ideas inspirit us to reimagine our relationship with water, encouraging us to find innovative solutions that harmonize with the natural world and meet the diverse needs of society.

By use of his sketches, Leonardo da Vinci envisioned a transformative connections of canals and locks, displaying the essence of his engineering power and artistic vision. His designs remain a lasting confirmation of his heritage as a masterful thinker and a firstman in the domains of both art and engineering.

40. TOWNSCAPE / PANORAMA URBANO

Sketches of different townscapes.

Leonardo da Vinci, the visionary artist and observer of the world, committed his artistic genius to displaying the essence of townscapes By use of his remarkable sketches. With a acute eye for detail and an important understanding of perspective, he strove to immortalize the diverse beauty and architectural splendor of towns and cities.

Leonardo's sketches of townscapes were a confirmation of his thorough observation and his ability to create the character and atmosphere of urban environments. With each stroke of his pen, he procured the complex details of buildings, streets, and bustling city life, creating visual narratives that warped viewers to the heart of these coruscating settings.

By use of his sketches, Leonardo celebrated the diversity of architectural styles and the unique character of each town. From towering cathedrals and grand palaces to humble houses and winding alleyways, his drawings mirrored the rich atlas of mankind's habitation. He masterfully depicted the relationship of light and shadow, the rhythm of streets, and the bustling activity that animated these urban landscapes.

Leonardo's sketches not merely conveyed the physical structures of towns but also strove to map the spirit and energy that permeated these urban spaces. He sketched marketplaces teeming with vendors and shoppers, squares alive with social gatherings, and streets abuzz with daily life. His drawings breathed life into the scenes, evoking an apparition of movement, human interaction, and the passage of time.

With an steady attention to detail, Leonardo's sketches revealed his depthy understanding of perspective and spatial relationships. He wisely portrayed the depth and dimensionality of buildings, displaying the convergence of lines and the play of light on surfaces. His mastery of architectural rendering techniques allowed him to create realistic and immersive portrayals of townscapes.

Leonardo's sketches of townscapes were not limited to mere documentation. They were infused with his artistic sensibilities, showcasing his ability to create mood, emotion, and the essence of a place. Whether displaying the grandeur of a city square or the intimacy of a quiet street, his drawings evoked an apparition of place, inviting viewers to immerse themselves in the beauty and complexity of urban life.

Inasmuch we contemplate Leonardo's sketches of townscapes, here we see the important connection betwixt human creativity and the built environment. His drawings lead us in to appreciate the architectural marvels that shape our cities, to observe the rhythms and interactions of urban life, and to find impetus in the diversity and vibrancy of the townscape.

Leonardo da Vinci's sketches of townscapes act as a timeless confirmation of his artistic vision and his ability to map the essence of the built environment. His observations and renderings inspirit artists, architects, and urban enthusiasts, encouraging a deeper understanding and appreciation for the complex atlas of mankind's habitation.

By use of his sketches, Leonardo da Vinci immortalized the beauty, diversity, and spirit of townscapes, providing us with glimpses into the urban world as he saw it. His drawings stand as a confirmation of his lasting heritage as a masterful observer of life and a firstman in the art of displaying the essence of place.

41. WEATHER PHENOMENA / FENOMENI METEOROLOGICI

Studies of clouds, storms, and atmospheric effects.

Leonardo da Vinci, the visionary artist and acute observer of nature, committed himself to studying the ethereal phenomena of clouds, storms, and atmospheric effects. By use of his thorough studies and detailed sketches, he strove to untwist the mysteries of the ever-changing sky and map its transient beauty on paper.

Leonardo's studies of clouds, storms, and atmospheric effects were a confirmation of his depthy fascination with the natural world. With steady curiosity, he observed the shifting formations of clouds, the dramatic play of light and shadow, and the tumultuous energy of storms. His sketches documented the complex patterns, textures, and movements that unfolded across the expansive canvas of the sky.

By use of his observations, Leonardo strove to understand the complex dynamics that shaped the atmospheric realm. He studied the relationship of air currents, the formation of clouds, and the subtle changes in color and light that accompanied different weather conditions. His sketches procured the essence of these atmospheric phenomena, inviting viewers to contemplate the beauty and power of nature's ever-changing moods.

Leonardo's studies of clouds, storms, and atmospheric effects went beyond artistic appreciation. They mirrored his scientific inquiry and his desire to comprehend the mechanisms that governed the behavior of the sky. He scrupulously recorded his observations, noting the subtle nuances and complexities that made each cloud formation or atmospheric phenomenon unique.

His sketches were not mere reproductions of what he saw; they were an attempt to map the ephemeral qualities of the sky. By use of his mastery of light and shade, Leonardo conveyed the dynamic relationship betwixt the elements, the dramatic contrasts that unfolded during storms, and the sublime tranquility that enveloped the sky during serene moments.

Inasmuch we contemplate Leonardo's studies of clouds, storms, and atmospheric effects, here we see the awe-provoking beauty and power of nature. His sketches lead us in to look upward, to immerse ourselves in the ever-changing drama of the sky, and to appreciate the complexities and enmeshment of our natural environment.

Leonardo da Vinci's studies of clouds, storms, and atmospheric effects act as a timeless tribute to his acute observation skills and his ability to map the essence of natural phenomena. His observations and sketches inspirit artists, scientists, and nature enthusiasts, encouraging a deeper understanding and appreciation for the wonders of the sky.

By use of his sketches, Leonardo da Vinci immortalized the fleeting beauty and dynamic energy of clouds, storms, and atmospheric effects, providing us with glimpses into the ever-changing theater of the sky. His drawings stand as a confirmation of his lasting heritage as a masterful observer of nature and a firstman in the art of displaying the essence of atmospheric phenomena.

42. ALLEGORICAL FIGURES / FIGURE ALLEGORICHE

Sketches such as "Angel in the Flesh."

Amid Leonardo da Vinci's exquisite sketches, there exists a masterpiece known as "Angel in the Flesh." This remarkable artwork captures the ethereal beauty and grace of a celestial being, rendered with thorough attention to detail and an unrivaled sense of artistic mastery.

In this sketch, Leonardo da Vinci unveils his important fascination with the human form, transcending the bounds of earthly existence to portray a heavenly figure. The angelic subject is depicted with swift lines, flowing contours, and an apparition of divine serenity that emanates from every stroke of the artist's pen.

Leonardo's "Angel in the Flesh" flaunts his remarkable ability to map the essence of the human figure in all its ethereal splendor. The complex details of the figure's wings, the gentle curves of the body, and the serene expression upon the face reflect the artist's steady commitment to the followings forth of artistic excellence.

The sketch reveals Leonardo's important understanding of anatomy and his mastery of proportion. Each line and curve is scrupulously crafted to create an apparition of grace, balance, and harmony. The wings, extending with an apparition of weightlessness and yet inherent strength, map the viewer's imagination and transport them to a realm beyond the earthly realm.

Through the "Angel in the Flesh," Leonardo da Vinci invites us to contemplate the ethereal and the divine. The sketch captures a snapshot frozen in time, where the celestial and the mortal intersect, evoking an apparition of wonder, awe, and spiritual contemplation.

Leonardo's sketch is not merely a representation of an angelic figure, but an important exploration of the human spirit and our connection to the divine. It acts as a confirmation of the artist's ability to bypass the physical and map the essence of the metaphysical By use of his extraordinary artistic vision.

Inasmuch we peer upon the "Angel in the Flesh," here we see the unlimited imagination and artistic genius of Leonardo da Vinci. The sketch inspires us to contemplate the beauty and mystery of the celestial realm, to reflect upon our own spiritual nature, and to recognize the infinite possibilities that exist within the realm of art.

Leonardo da Vinci's "Angel in the Flesh" holdeth as a confirmation of his lasting heritage as a masterful artist. The sketch allures the imagination, evoking an apparition of wonder and reverence for the divine. It remains to inspirit generations, reminding us of the important connection betwixt art, spirituality, and the unlimited depths of mankind's creativity.

Inasmuch we behold the "Angel in the Flesh," here we see Leonardo da Vinci's extraordinary ability to map the sublime in his sketches. His artistic vision transcends time, inviting us to inquire into the domains of the ethereal and the divine through the power of his artistry.

43. FURNITURE / MOBILI

He had sketched and designed furniture like chairs.

Leonardo da Vinci, the visionary artist and master of multiple disciplines, applied his creative genius to the world of furniture design. Amid his diverse sketches and designs, he searched out the artistry and functionality of chairs, leaving behind a remarkable heritage of innovation and craftsmanship.

Leonardo's sketches and designs of chairs exemplify his steady attention to detail and his quest for aesthetic harmony. With each stroke of his pen, he procured the elegant contours, structural integrity, and ergonomic considerations that went into creating these essential pieces of furniture.

In his exploration of chair design, Leonardo pushed the bounds of artistic expression while ensuring optimal comfort and usability. His sketches lay bare a depthy understanding of form and function, as he carefully considered the materials, proportions, and structural elements that would make each chair a harmonious blend of beauty and practicality.

Leonardo's chair designs encompassed a wide range of styles, from simple and utilitarian to intricately ornate. His sketches showcased the diverse possibilities in terms of shape, embellishments, and decorative elements, reflecting his versatile artistic sensibilities.

While some of Leonardo's chair designs remained conceptual, his sketches acted as a source of impetus for future furniture makers. His innovative ideas and attention to craftsmanship influenced the evolution of chair design, leaving an indelible mark on the furniture industry.

By use of his sketches, Leonardo da Vinci not merely revolutionized the aesthetics of chair design but also dived into the exploration of ergonomics and human comfort. His acute observations of mankind's anatomy and his understanding of mankind's movement informed his approach to creating chairs that provided optimal support and functionality.

Inasmuch we dive into Leonardo's sketches and designs of chairs, here we see his undying followings forth of excellence and his ability to fuse artistic vision with practicality. His contributions to furniture design inspirit us to seek beauty, innovation, and comfort in our everyday surroundings, reminding us that even the most utilitarian objects can be elevated to works of art.

Leonardo da Vinci's sketches and designs of chairs stand as a confirmation of his lasting heritage as a visionary artist and innovator. His exploration of form, function, and beauty remains to influence furniture design to this day, reminding us of the important impact that art can have on our lived experiences.

Inasmuch we admire Leonardo's chair sketches, here we see the power of creativity and the transformative nature of design. His ability to infuse artistry into every aspect of life, even in the simplest of objects like chairs, is a confirmation of his artistic brilliance and his steady commitment to excellence.

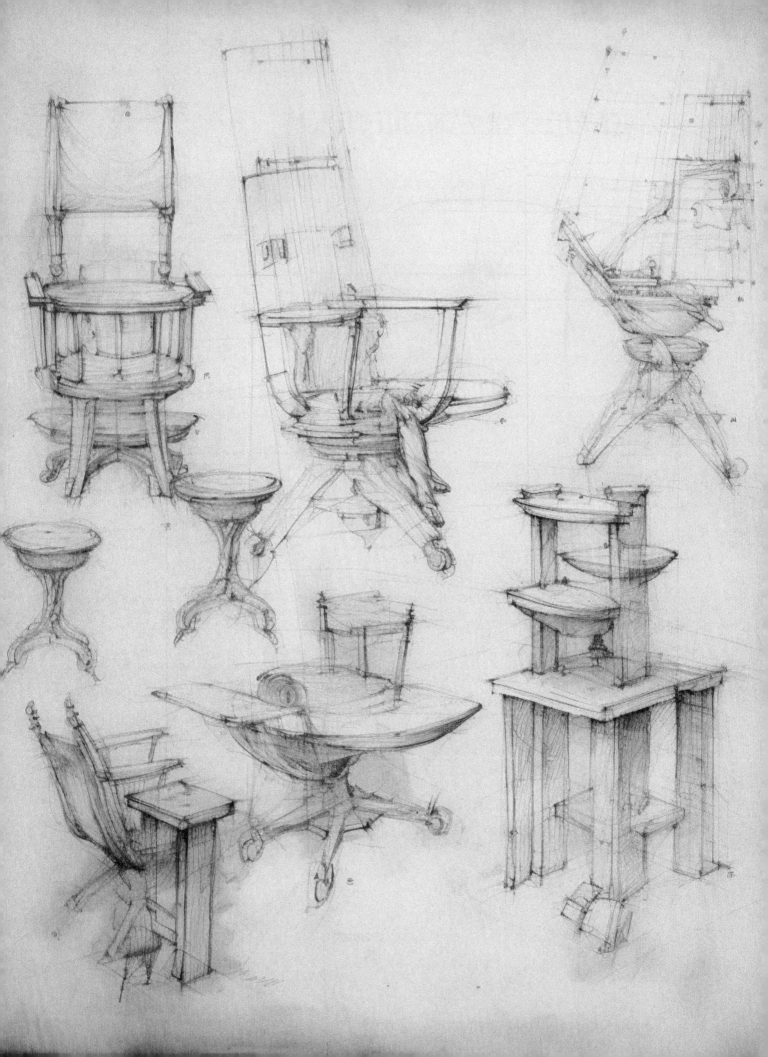

44. SCULPTURE / SCULTURA

Studies of existing sculptures and designs for new ones.

Leonardo da Vinci, the visionary artist and sculptor, committed his artistic pursuits to the study of existing sculptures and the creation of new ones. By use of his thorough studies and innovative designs, he strove to stretch the bounds of sculptural art and leave a lasting mark on the world of three-dimensional expression.

Leonardo's studies of existing sculptures were a confirmation of his admiration for the classical masters and his desire to understand the techniques and aesthetics that defined their works. With thorough attention to detail, he observed and sketched renowned sculptures of antiquity, untwisting the secrets of their composition, form, and proportions.

Through these studies, Leonardo strove to internalize the essence of the sculptures he encountered. He scrupulously examined the complex folds of drapery, the swift curves of the human form, and the subtleties of facial expressions, displaying them in his sketches and using them as a foundation for his own artistic creations.

In addition to studying existing sculptures, Leonardo da Vinci also ventured into the realm of designing new ones. His sketches and designs showcased his visionary approach to sculptural art, blending classical elements with his own innovative ideas. His designs encompassed a range of themes, from mythological figures to religious icons and allegorical representations.

Leonardo's designs for new sculptures were marked by an important understanding of anatomy, proportion, and movement. He searched out the relationship betwixt light and shadow, seeking to create sculptures that would come to life in their surroundings, evoking emotions and engaging viewers in a dialogue betwixt art and the lived experience.

While many of Leonardo's sculptural designs remained unrealized, his sketches and concepts acted as a wellspring of impetus for future sculptors. His visionary approach to form, his attention to detail, and his followings forth of artistic excellence influence sculptural art to this day.

Leonardo's studies of existing sculptures and designs for new ones were not limited to the realm of aesthetics. They also mirrored his desire to express important ideas, emotions, and narratives through the medium of sculpture. His sketches and designs were imbued with symbolism, inviting viewers to inquire across the nexus of mankind's existence and contemplate the complexities of life.

Inasmuch we dive into Leonardo's studies of existing sculptures and designs for new ones, here we see his important impact on the world of sculptural art. His observations and creative endeavors inspirit sculptors, artists, and art enthusiasts, fueling a perpetual followings forth of artistic innovation and exuberance.

By use of his sketches and designs, Leonardo da Vinci immortalized the beauty and power of sculpture, both as an homage to the classical tradition and as a manifestation of his own artistic vision. His heritage as a sculptor and innovator resonateth through the ages, reminding us of the transformative potential of three-dimensional art and its capacity to bypass time and space.

Leonardo da Vinci's studies of existing sculptures and designs for new ones stand as a confirmation of his lasting heritage as a master sculptor. His sketches and concepts lead us in to start on a visual quest, exploring the rich atlas of sculptural art and contemplating the important beauty that can be brought to life through the masterful hands of an artist.

45. LIONS / LEONI

Drawings and studies of lions.

Leonardo da Vinci, the visionary artist and acute observer of nature, committed himself to studying and displaying the majestic beauty of lions By use of his extraordinary drawings and studies. With thorough attention to detail and a depthy understanding of anatomy, he strove to untwist the essence of these regal creatures and bring their magnificence to life on paper.

Leonardo's drawings and studies of lions stand as a confirmation of his fascination with the natural world and his desire to inquire into the complexities of animal anatomy. By use of his sketches, he procured the grace, power, and unique characteristics that define lions as the kings of the animal kingdom.

In his quest to understand and depict lions, Leonardo began on detailed anatomical studies. He carefully observed their musculature, skeletal structure, and distinctive features, rendering them with precision and accuracy. His drawings lay bare the inner workings of these magnificent beasts, showcasing his depthy respect for the complexities of nature.

Beyond displaying their physical attributes, Leonardo's sketches also aimed to create the spirit and personality of lions. He strove to portray their majestic presence, their piercing peer, and their inherent strength. By use of his masterful use of shading and texture, he brought an apparition of life and vitality to his drawings, allowing viewers to specter the untamed spirit of these remarkable creatures.

Leonardo's studies of lions were not limited to static representations. He dived into their movements, displaying their agility, grace, and the fluidity of their forms. His sketches revealed the dynamic nature of these beasts in motion, showcasing their hunting power and the raw energy that radiates from their every stride.

Inasmuch we peer upon Leonardo's drawings and studies of lions, here we see the complex beauty and untamed power of nature. His thorough observations and artistic renderings lead us in to appreciate the sublime elegance of these awe-provoking creatures and to contemplate the swift balance betwixt humans and the animal kingdom.

Leonardo da Vinci's drawings and studies of lions act as a timeless tribute to his acute observation skills and his ability to map the essence of the natural world. His depictions of these majestic beasts inspirit artists, scientists, and nature enthusiasts, encouraging a deeper connection with the wonders of the animal kingdom.

By use of his sketches, Leonardo da Vinci immortalized the regal grace and untamed spirit of lions, providing us with glimpses into their world. His drawings stand as a confirmation of his lasting heritage as a masterful artist and observer of nature, reminding us of the important beauty that exists in the animal realm.

Inasmuch we swoon at Leonardo's drawings and studies of lions, here we see his artistic brilliance and his steady commitment to understanding and displaying the wonders of the natural world. His sketches act as a bridge betwixt human civilization and the untamed wilderness, inviting us to appreciate and protect the extraordinary creatures that share our planet.

46. DANCERS / BALLERINI

Sketches of dancers in motion.

Leonardo da Vinci, the visionary artist and master of mankind's anatomy, procured the alluring beauty and fluidity of dancers in motion By use of his extraordinary sketches. With his acute observation skills and thorough attention to detail, he strove to untwist the graceful movements and expressiveness of these talented performers on paper.

In his sketches of dancers, Leonardo aimed to map the essence of their artistry, the rhythm of their movements, and the harmony betwixt body and music. With swift strokes of his pen, he depicted the dynamic poses, the flowing lines, and the sense of weightlessness that defined their performances.

Leonardo's sketches of dancers lay bare his important understanding of mankind's anatomy and his ability to portray the subtleties of movement. He studied the muscles, the lines of tension, and the relationship of limbs, displaying the energy and grace that radiated from the dancers as they moved through space.

By use of his sketches, Leonardo strove to create not just the physicality of jubilation but also the emotions and narratives conveyed by the performers. He procured the expressions on their faces, the gestures of their hands, and the nuances of their body language, allowing viewers to specter into the stories being told through their movements.

Leonardo's sketches of dancers go beyond mere representations of mankind's figures in motion. They show off his ability to evoke the atmosphere, rhythm, and emotions of a jubilation performance. His mastery of light and shadow, combined with his understanding of anatomy and movement, brought an apparition of vitality and dynamism to his sketches, as if freezing a time of artistic expression in time.

Inasmuch we dive into Leonardo's sketches of dancers, we are warped to a world of grace, beauty, and artistic expression. His drawings lead us in to appreciate the commitment, skill, and creativity of these performers, as well as the universal language of movement that transcends cultural and linguistic barriers.

Leonardo da Vinci's sketches of dancers stand as a confirmation of his lasting heritage as a masterful observer of the human form and a firstman in displaying movement on paper. His studies inspirit artists, dancers, and art enthusiasts, encouraging a deeper appreciation for the art of jubilation and its ability to create important emotions and stories.

By use of his sketches, Leonardo immortalized the fleeting moments of jubilation, preserving the essence of movement and the spirit of artistic expression. His drawings act as a glimmer of the transformative power of the human body and the lasting beauty of the performing arts.

Inasmuch we swoon at Leonardo's sketches of dancers, here we see his artistic brilliance and his steady commitment to displaying the essence of mankind's expression. His sketches inspirit us to appreciate the beauty and grace of movement, encouraging us to welcome the artistry and creativity that jubilation brings to our lives.

47. GROTESQUE FIGURES / FIGURE GROTTESCHE

Various sketches of figures with exaggerated features.

Leonardo da Vinci, the visionary artist and master of mankind's form, searched out the realm of artistic expression By use of his sketches of figures with exaggerated features. With his acute eye and unlimited imagination, he dived into the realm of distortion, creating alluring drawings that challenged conventional notions of beauty and pushed the bounds of artistic representation.

In his sketches of figures with exaggerated features, Leonardo strove to inquire into the realm of the extraordinary and the fantastical. He played with proportions, elongating limbs, enlarging facial features, and distorting the human form to create an apparition of heightened drama and intrigue.

Through these sketches, Leonardo aimed to map the essence of emotions, to create narratives, or to express his own artistic vision. By exaggerating certain features, he brought attention to specific aspects of the human form, emphasizing their expressive potential and inviting viewers to contemplate the deeper meaning behind these exaggerated representations.

Leonardo's sketches of figures with exaggerated features also acted as a vehicle for his exploration of the human psyche and the complexities of mankind's nature. By distorting the external appearance, he strove to peel back the layers of superficiality and lay bare the underlying emotions, desires, and vulnerabilities that define our shared lived experience.

While these sketches may have been departures from the traditional ideals of beauty, they demonstrated Leonardo's artistic daring and his refusal to conform to established norms. By use of his exaggerations, he challenged viewers to question their preconceived notions of aesthetics, encouraging them to welcome the unconventional and to see beauty in its myriad forms.

Leonardo's sketches of figures with exaggerated features were not merely exercises in artistic experimentation; they were reflections of his important understanding of life. By distorting the familiar, he strove to provoke introspection, to elicit emotional responses, and to prompt viewers to question their own perceptions and assumptions.

Inasmuch we examine Leonardo's sketches of figures with exaggerated features, we are invited to welcome the unconventional, to challenge our preconceptions, and to celebrate the diversity of mankind's expression. These drawings remind us that beauty lies not merely in perfection but also in the nuances, imperfections, and idiosyncrasies that make each individual unique.

Leonardo da Vinci's sketches of figures with exaggerated features stand as a confirmation of his artistic genius and his undying exploration of the human form. They inspirit us to look beyond surface appearances, to dive deeper into the realm of emotions and expressions, and to appreciate the extraordinary potential that lies within every individual.

By use of his sketches, Leonardo immortalized the power of artistic interpretation and the unlimited nature of mankind's creativity. His drawings challenge us to welcome the unconventional, to celebrate individuality, and to recognize the inherent beauty that resides in the diversity of mankind's experiences.

Inasmuch we immerse ourselves in Leonardo's sketches of figures with exaggerated features, here we see his artistic brilliance and his steady commitment to pushing the bounds of artistic expression. His sketches inspirit artists, ignite conversations, and provoke us to question and reimagine the world around us.

48. OXEN / BOVINI

Studies of oxen in motion and at rest.

Leonardo da Vinci, the visionary artist and acute observer of nature, devoted his artistic endeavors to studying and displaying the essence of oxen in motion and at rest. By use of his thorough studies and detailed sketches, he strove to untwist the grace, strength, and unique characteristics of these magnificent creatures.

In his studies of oxen in motion, Leonardo scrupulously observed their movements, carefully displaying the subtle shifts in their weight, the powerful strides of their legs, and the rhythmic swaying of their bodies. With each stroke of his pen, he immortalized the dynamic energy and vitality of these animals as they navigated their surroundings.

Leonardo's sketches of oxen at rest showcased his ability to depict their majestic presence and their serene tranquility. By use of his acute observation of their postures, he procured the relaxed poses, the powerful physiques, and the innate dignity that define these noble creatures in repose.

Beyond displaying their physical appearance, Leonardo's studies of oxen dived into the essence of their nature. He strove to understand the relationship betwixt their physical attributes and their behavioral patterns, delving into the subtleties of their expressions and their relationship with their environment.

Leonardo's sketches of oxen revealed his depthy appreciation for the harmony betwixt form and function. He paid thorough attention to the anatomical structure of oxen, studying their muscles, bone structure, and proportions. His acute eye for detail allowed him to map the essence of their physique and movement with remarkable accuracy.

By use of his studies of oxen, Leonardo strove not merely to depict their external appearance but also to create their significance in the lived experience. Oxen were necessary contributors to human civilization, serving as beasts of burden, sources of sustenance, and symbols of agricultural prosperity. Leonardo's sketches mirrored his understanding of their indispensable part in shaping the course of mankind's history.

Inasmuch we immerse ourselves in Leonardo's studies of oxen in motion and at rest, here we see the important connection betwixt humans and the natural world. His sketches lead us in to appreciate the beauty and significance of these powerful animals and to contemplate our interdependence with the animal kingdom.

Leonardo da Vinci's studies of oxen stand as a confirmation of his extraordinary ability to map the essence of nature through art. His sketches act as a bridge betwixt scientific observation and artistic interpretation, inviting us to inquire into the complexities of the natural world and to deepen our understanding of the creatures that share our planet.

By use of his sketches, Leonardo immortalized the timeless beauty and alluring presence of oxen, reminding us of the swift balance betwixt humanity and the animal kingdom. His heritage as an artist and naturalist remains to inspirit us to swoon at the wonders of the natural world and to nurture a depthy respect for all living beings.

Inasmuch we contemplate Leonardo's studies of oxen in motion and at rest, here we see his artistic brilliance and his steady commitment to displaying the essence of life in all its forms. His sketches act as a confirmation of the power of observation, the followings forth of knowledge, and the transformative potential of art to illuminate our understanding of the world around us.

49. PERSPECTIVE STUDIES / STUDI DI PROSPETTIVA

He searched out linear perspective in his sketches.

Leonardo da Vinci, the visionary artist and master of artistic techniques, dived into the realm of linear perspective in his sketches. With his acute eye for detail and steady commitment to artistic exploration, he strove to untwist the mysteries of spatial representation and create an apparition of depth and realism in his artworks.

In his sketches, Leonardo scrupulously studied the principles of linear perspective, which allowed him to accurately depict three-dimensional space on a two-dimensional surface. He observed how objects appear smaller and converge towards a vanishing point as they recede into the distance, and he applied this knowledge to his drawings, imbuing them with an apparition of depth and realism.

Leonardo's exploration of linear perspective in his sketches went beyond mere technical accuracy. He used this technique as a tool to enhance the visual impact of his artworks and to create an apparition of immersion for the viewers. By manipulating the lines and angles in his drawings, he was able to guide the eye and create a dynamic visual experience.

By use of his mastery of linear perspective, Leonardo brought a new level of realism and spatial depth to his sketches. He scrupulously calculated the proportions and positioning of objects, buildings, and landscapes, ensuring that they were harmoniously integrated within the composition. This attention to detail allowed viewers to immerse themselves in the depicted scenes and feel an apparition of presence within the artwork.

Leonardo's exploration of linear perspective was not limited to architectural drawings or landscapes; he applied this technique to various subjects, including figures, still life, and even narrative compositions. By employing linear perspective, he added an apparition of realism and spatial coherence to his artworks, enhancing the overall visual impact and engaging the viewer on a deeper level.

Inasmuch we examine Leonardo's sketches that show off his exploration of linear perspective, we are invited to appreciate the thorough calculations and artistic choices that he made to bring his drawings to life. His understanding and application of this technique transformed his sketches into immersive visual experiences, alluring viewers and transporting them into the depicted worlds.

Leonardo da Vinci's exploration of linear perspective in his sketches holdeth as a confirmation of his undying followings forth of artistic excellence and his steady commitment to mastering the technical aspects of his craft. His sketches inspirit artists and art enthusiasts, serving as a glimmer of the transformative power of perspective in creating compelling and realistic artworks.

By use of his exploration of linear perspective, Leonardo da Vinci immortalized the beauty and complexity of the visual world. His sketches act as a confirmation of his artistic brilliance, his commitment to understanding the principles of perception, and his ability to translate that knowledge into visually stunning artworks that allure and inspirit audiences to this day.

Inasmuch we contemplate Leonardo's sketches and their mastery of linear perspective, here we see his important impact on the world of art and his lasting heritage as a visionary artist. His exploration of this technique expanded the possibilities of visual representation and set a standard for artistic realism that remains to influence artists and art movements throughout history.

50. MORTARS / MORTAI

Designs for different types of mortars.

Leonardo da Vinci, the visionary artist and ingenious inventor, devoted his creative energy to designing various types of mortars. With his remarkable technical expertise and innovative spirit, he strove to revolutionize the field of warfare and develop more efficient and effective weapons for battle.

In his designs for mortars, Leonardo focused on optimizing their functionality, range, and destructive power. He scrupulously studied the mechanics of these weapons, analyzing their structure and experimenting with different configurations to enhance their performance on the battlefield.

Leonardo's designs for mortars incorporated his depthy understanding of physics and engineering principles. He considered factors such as projectile trajectory, propellant power, and structural integrity to create mortars that were not merely formidable in their destructive capabilities but also reliable and easy to operate.

By use of his sketches and technical drawings, Leonardo procured the complex details of his mortar designs. He searched out different shapes, sizes, and materials, aiming to create weapons that would maximize accuracy and efficiency while minimizing the risk to the operators.

In addition to their destructive potential, Leonardo's mortar designs also mirrored his cleverness in addressing practical challenges. He strove to develop mortars that could be easily warped and assembled, allowing for greater mobility on the battlefield. His designs considered factors such as portability, stability, and ease of maintenance, ensuring that the mortars would be effective and practical tools of warfare.

Leonardo's designs for mortars went beyond the mere function of weaponry; they mirrored his depthy understanding of the strategic aspects of warfare. He considered the tactical advantages that mortars could offer on the battlefield, envisioning how they could be integrated into larger military operations to gain an upper hand in conflicts.

Inasmuch we inquire into Leonardo's designs for mortars, here we see his multidisciplinary approach to invention and his undying followings forth of technological advancement. His sketches and technical drawings show off his ability to bridge the domains of art and science, fusing creativity with practicality to shape the course of military technology.

Leonardo da Vinci's designs for mortars embody his important fascination with the mechanics of warfare and his undying followings forth of innovation. His sketches act as a confirmation of his visionary spirit, forever etching his name in the annals of military history and provoking future generations of inventors, engineers, and strategists.

Inasmuch we examine Leonardo's designs for mortars, here we see his lasting heritage as a mastermind of invention and his ability to translate his ideas into tangible designs. His sketches allure our imagination, reflecting his important impact on the fields of engineering, military technology, and the art of war.

By use of his designs for mortars, Leonardo da Vinci embraced the challenge of harnessing destructive power while pushing the bounds of scientific understanding. His sketches remind us of the swift balance betwixt innovation and responsibility in the realm of weaponry, prompting us to consider the ethical implications of technological advancements in the context of mankind's conflicts.

Inasmuch we reflect on Leonardo's designs for mortars, we are encouraged by his undying curiosity, his commitment to pushing the bounds of knowledge, and his steady commitment to shaping the course of mankind's history By use of his inventive genius. His designs stand as a confirmation of his lasting impact on the fields of art, science, and military innovation.

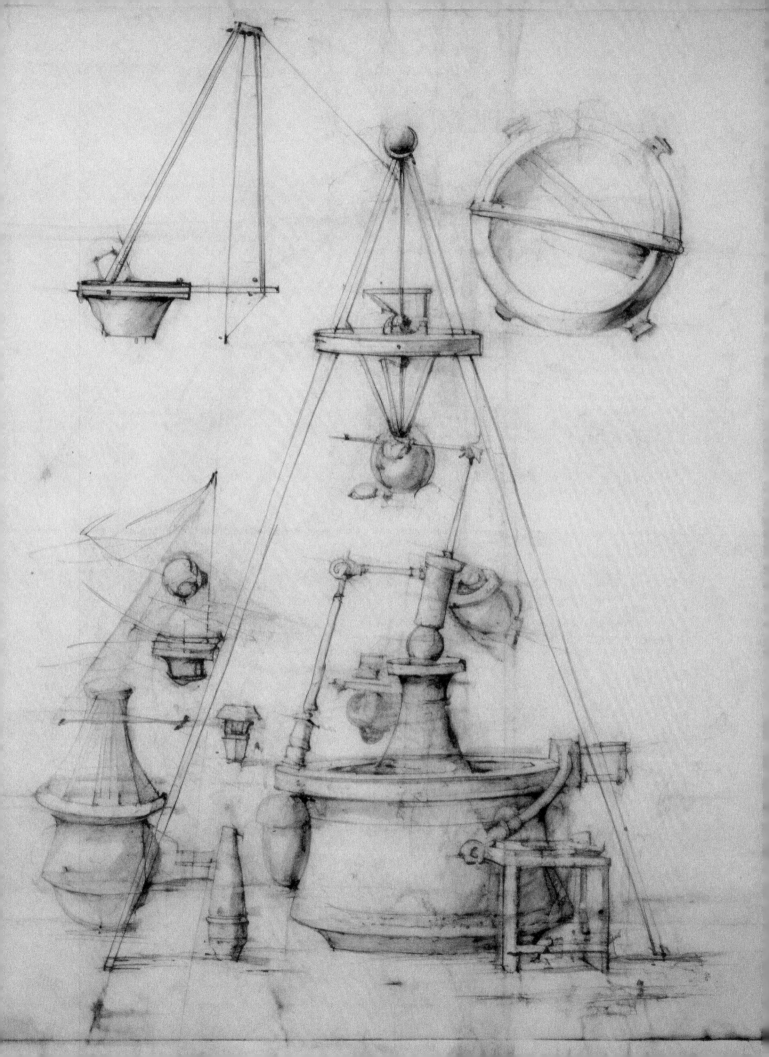

51. RIVERS / FIUMI

Sketches and studies of river landscapes.

Leonardo da Vinci, the visionary artist and acute observer of nature, committed his artistic talent to displaying the beauty and serenity of river landscapes By use of his sketches and studies. With his thorough attention to detail and important appreciation for the natural world, he strove to immortalize the alluring essence of rivers and their surrounding landscapes.

In his sketches of river landscapes, Leonardo scrupulously observed the flow of water, the meandering curves of the riverbanks, and the relationship of light and shadow upon the surface. With each stroke of his pen, he endeavored to map the dynamic energy and the ever-changing nature of these majestic waterways.

By use of his studies, Leonardo searched out the complex details of river landscapes, paying close attention to the unique features of each scene. He observed the vegetation that lined the riverbanks, the geological formations that shaped the land, and the diverse array of wildlife that thrived in these environments. His sketches mirrored his depthy understanding of the enmeshment of the elements within a river ecosystem.

Leonardo's studies of river landscapes went beyond mere representation; they conveyed an apparition of tranquility, harmony, and the passage of time. He procured the essence of the ever-flowing water, the subtle reflections, and the serene ambiance of these natural settings, inviting viewers to immerse themselves in the contemplation of nature's beauty.

By use of his sketches, Leonardo not merely celebrated the aesthetic qualities of river landscapes but also recognized their significance in human life. Rivers have been integral to the development of civilizations, providing sustenance, transportation, and impetus throughout history. Leonardo's studies procured the symbiotic relationship betwixt humans and rivers, showcasing the important impact that these waterways have on our lives and our connection to the natural world.

Inasmuch we dive into Leonardo's sketches of river landscapes, we are warped to a world of serene beauty and tranquility. His drawings lead us in to appreciate the majesty of nature, to swoon at the complex balance of its elements, and to contemplate the importance of preserving and cherishing our precious natural resources.

Leonardo da Vinci's sketches of river landscapes stand as a confirmation of his artistic brilliance and his depthy reverence for the natural world. His studies inspirit artists, environmentalists, and nature enthusiasts, encouraging a deeper connection to the rivers that sustain life and reminding us of our responsibility to protect and preserve these invaluable ecosystems.

By use of his sketches, Leonardo immortalized the timeless beauty and serenity of river landscapes, reminding us of the swift balance betwixt human existence and the natural world. His heritage as an artist and naturalist remains to inspirit us to appreciate the wonders of the natural environment, to seek solace in its welcome, and to recognize the important impact of rivers on our collective prosperity.

Inasmuch we contemplate Leonardo's sketches of river landscapes, here we see his artistic brilliance and his steady commitment to displaying the essence of nature. His studies act as a confirmation of the power of art to bypass time and space, transporting us to the peaceful welcome of river landscapes and reminding us of our intrinsic connection to the flow of life.

52. FISH / PESCI

Studies of various fish and their movements.

Leonardo da Vinci, the visionary artist and curious observer of the natural world, committed his artistic talent to studying and displaying the grace and beauty of various fish species and their movements. By use of his thorough studies and detailed sketches, he strove to untwist the mysteries of aquatic life and the fascinating dynamics of fish in their underwater realm.

In his studies of fish, Leonardo carefully observed their anatomical structure, their scales, fins, and tails, and their unique adaptations for swimming. He scrupulously procured their distinct features, bringing their forms to life on the parchment with remarkable accuracy and attention to detail.

Leonardo's sketches not merely depicted the external appearance of fish but also aimed to create their movements through water. He observed how they propelled themselves with elegant strokes, their bodies gracefully bending and undulating, and their fins and tails propelling them forward. His studies procured the fluidity and agility of fish as they navigated their aquatic environment.

By use of his acute observation and scientific curiosity, Leonardo strove to understand the mechanics behind the movements of fish. He studied the principles of hydrodynamics, analyzing how fish created thrust and maneuvered in water. His sketches were not mere representations of fish, but rather visual records of his in-depth exploration of their behavior and the physical forces at play.

Leonardo's studies of fish encompassed a wide range of species, starting with the majestic movements of larger fish to the swift fluttering of smaller ones. He documented their unique characteristics, their patterns of behavior, and their interactions within their aquatic ecosystems. His sketches acted as a window into the rich and diverse world beneath the water's surface.

Inasmuch we dive into Leonardo's studies of fish and their movements, we are warped to the enchanting realm of underwater life. His sketches lead us in to appreciate the incredible diversity and intricacy of aquatic ecosystems, as well as the harmony and balance that exist within them. They inspirit us to recognize the swift relationship betwixt living organisms and their natural environments.

Leonardo da Vinci's studies of fish stand as a confirmation of his undying followings forth of knowledge and his important appreciation for the wonders of the natural world. His sketches allure and inspirit scientists, artists, and nature enthusiasts alike, offering a specter into the fascinating realm of underwater life and encouraging us to deepen our understanding and respect for the ecosystems that sustain it.

By use of his studies, Leonardo immortalized the beauty and elegance of fish, forever displaying their mesmerizing movements upon the parchment. His sketches act as a glimmer of the enmeshment of all living beings and the marvels of the natural world, urging us to protect and preserve the fragile ecosystems that support the abundance of life on Earth.

Inasmuch we contemplate Leonardo's studies of fish and their movements, here we see his unquenchable curiosity, his commitment to scientific exploration, and his ability to map the essence of life through art. His heritage as an artist, scientist, and naturalist remains to inspirit us to swoon at the wonders of the natural world and to strive for a deeper understanding of the complex and diverse atlas of life that surrounds us.

53. WINDS / VENTI

Diagrams illustrating the flow and effects of wind.

Leonardo da Vinci, the visionary artist and acute observer of nature, committed his artistic talent to displaying and understanding the flow and effects of wind By use of his complex diagrams. With his undying curiosity and thorough attention to detail, he strove to untwist the mysteries of this invisible force and its impact on the world around us.

In his diagrams, Leonardo scrupulously depicted the patterns and directions of wind currents. He studied how the wind flowed over different landscapes, such as hills, valleys, and bodies of water, and how it interacted with various objects and structures in its path. His diagrams procured the complex jubilation of air molecules, conveying the dynamic nature of wind.

By use of his observations and sketches, Leonardo strove to understand the effects of wind on the natural environment and human activities. He examined how wind influenced the growth and dispersal of seeds, the formation of clouds, and the behavior of birds in flight. His diagrams revealed the complex relationship betwixt wind and the elements of the natural world.

Leonardo's diagrams of wind also mirrored his fascination with the practical applications of this natural phenomenon. He searched out how wind could be harnessed for various purposes, such as powering mills, driving ships, and enhancing the efficiency of architectural structures. His diagrams showcased his innovative ideas and his ability to apply scientific principles to real-world challenges.

By use of his thorough studies, Leonardo not merely procured the visual aspects of wind but also strove to understand its underlying principles. He examined the factors that influenced wind speed and direction, such as temperature differentials, atmospheric pressure, and topographical features. His diagrams mirrored his depthy understanding of the scientific principles that governed the behavior of wind.

Inasmuch we examine Leonardo's diagrams illustrating the flow and effects of wind, we are invited to appreciate the complexities of this natural phenomenon. His thorough observations and sketches allow us to gain a deeper understanding of the forces that shape our environment and influence our daily lives.

Leonardo da Vinci's diagrams of wind stand as a confirmation of his unquenchable curiosity and his undying followings forth of knowledge. His sketches inspirit scientists, engineers, and environmentalists, serving as a glimmer of the important impact that natural forces have on our world.

By use of his diagrams, Leonardo strove to untwist the secrets of the wind and its effects, forever immortalizing its invisible power upon the parchment. His heritage as an artist, scientist, and inventor drives home the beauty and complexity of the natural world and encourages us to cultivate a deeper appreciation for the swift balance of forces that shape our planet.

Inasmuch we contemplate Leonardo's diagrams illustrating the flow and effects of wind, here we see his genius and his ability to combine artistic expression with scientific inquiry. His sketches act as a timeless glimmer of the enmeshment of art and science, inviting us to swoon at the wonders of the natural world and to keep our exploration and understanding of its complex mechanisms.

54. BEAR / ORSI

Studies of bears.

Leonardo da Vinci, the visionary artist and curious observer of the natural world, committed his artistic talent to studying and displaying the majestic presence of bears By use of his studies and sketches. With his acute eye for detail and depthy appreciation for the diversity of life, he strove to untwist the mysteries of these powerful creatures and map their essence on paper.

In his studies of bears, Leonardo scrupulously observed their physical characteristics, their muscular build, their distinct facial features, and their unique adaptations for survival. He carefully documented their anatomy, their movement patterns, and their behavior, aiming to portray their true nature and spirit in his sketches.

Leonardo's sketches of bears were not mere representations but rather windows into their world. By use of his artistry, he procured their strength and grace, their playfulness and ferocity, and their ability to adapt to different environments. His studies revealed the complex balance of power and vulnerability that defines these remarkable creatures.

In his quest to understand bears, Leonardo ventured beyond their external appearance. He dived into their habitat, studying the ecosystems they inhabit, the vegetation they rely on, and the prey they pursue. His sketches procured the symbiotic relationship betwixt bears and their surroundings, highlighting their integral part in the natural balance of ecosystems.

By use of his studies, Leonardo aimed to create the importance of bears in the complex atlas of life. His sketches celebrated their unique place in the animal kingdom and underscored the need for their conservation and protection. They acted as a glimmer of our responsibility to coexist with and preserve these magnificent creatures and the habitats they depend upon.

Inasmuch we dive into Leonardo's studies of bears, we are warped to a world of awe-provoking wildlife and untamed beauty. His sketches lead us in to appreciate the grandeur of these creatures, to admire their resilience and adaptability, and to recognize the necessary part they play in maintaining the swift equilibrium of our natural world.

Leonardo da Vinci's studies of bears stand as a confirmation of his unquenchable curiosity and his important reverence for the wonders of the natural world. His sketches allure and inspirit nature enthusiasts, artists, and conservationists, encouraging a deeper connection to the magnificent creatures that share our planet.

By use of his sketches, Leonardo immortalized the majesty and enigma of bears, forever displaying their essence upon the parchment. His heritage as an artist and naturalist drives home the complex beauty of wildlife and urges us to protect and preserve the habitats that sustain these remarkable creatures.

Inasmuch we contemplate Leonardo's studies of bears, here we see his undying followings forth of knowledge and his ability to translate his observations into timeless works of art. His sketches act as a glimmer of the enmeshment of all living beings and the importance of encouraging harmony betwixt humanity and the natural world.

Leonardo da Vinci's studies of bears inspirit us to appreciate the magnificence of wildlife, to deepen our understanding of their significance in the nexus of life, and to nurture an apparition of responsibility in safeguarding their future. By use of his artistry, Leonardo invites us to join him in celebrating the extraordinary creatures that grace our planet and to welcome our part as stewards of their prosperity.

55. DENTISTRY / ODONTOIATRIA

He made detailed studies of teeth.

Leonardo da Vinci, the visionary artist and inquisitive scholar, devoted his acute observational skills and artistic talent to studying and documenting the complex details of teeth. By use of his thorough studies, he strove to untwist the secrets concealed within these small but essential components of the human anatomy.

In his followings forth of understanding teeth, Leonardo scrupulously observed their structure, shape, and arrangement. He dived into the complexities of their composition, examining the enamel, dentin, and pulp that make up these remarkable dental structures. His studies procured the relationship betwixt form and function, revealing the remarkable efficiency and resilience of teeth.

Leonardo's sketches of teeth were not simply representations; they were a confirmation of his unquenchable thirst for knowledge. He scrupulously documented the various types of teeth, from incisors to molars, exploring their different shapes and sizes. His studies dived into the complexities of tooth morphology, highlighting the distinct characteristics that enable teeth to perform their essential roles in biting, chewing, and grinding.

Beyond their physical attributes, Leonardo's studies of teeth also searched out their connections to overall health and prosperity. He recognized the key part that teeth play in the digestion process and their impact on speech and facial aesthetics. His sketches procured the enmeshment of teeth with other anatomical structures, shedding light on their importance in the broader context of mankind's physiology.

Leonardo's studies of teeth extended beyond the individual tooth. He observed their arrangement within the jaw, studying the alignment and occlusion of teeth to understand the complexities of bite mechanics. His sketches revealed the harmonious relationship betwixt the upper and lower dental arches, emphasizing the complex relationship of forces during mastication.

By use of his studies, Leonardo's fascination with teeth went beyond the surface level. He searched out the effects of aging, dental diseases, and tooth loss, recognizing the important impact that these factors have on overall oral health. His sketches acted as a visual record of his depthy understanding of the complexities and vulnerabilities of the human dentition.

Leonardo's studies of teeth were not confined to the realm of anatomy; they were a confirmation of his holistic approach to understanding the human body. His sketches highlighted the enmeshment of various anatomical systems and the impact that teeth have on overall prosperity. They showcased his undying followings forth of knowledge and his desire to comprehend the complexities of mankind's physiology.

Inasmuch we dive into Leonardo's studies of teeth, here we see his extraordinary ability to combine scientific inquiry with artistic expression. His sketches inspirit and inform the field of dentistry, providing a foundation for further research and understanding. They remind us of the significance of oral health in the broader context of mankind's health and prosperity.

Leonardo da Vinci's studies of teeth stand as a confirmation of his steady commitment to exploring the wonders of the human body. His sketches allure and educate, inviting us to appreciate the remarkable complexities of our dental anatomy and the essential part that teeth play in our daily lives.

By use of his thorough observations and detailed sketches, Leonardo immortalized the beauty and complexity of teeth, forever displaying their essence upon the parchment. His heritage as an artist and scholar acts as a glimmer of the huge potential for discovery and understanding that lies within the realm of mankind's anatomy.

Inasmuch we contemplate Leonardo's studies of teeth, we are encouraged to welcome the significance of oral health and to recognize the important impact that a healthy dentition has on our overall prosperity. His sketches act as a timeless glimmer of the importance of caring for our teeth and nurturing a lifelong commitment to dental health.

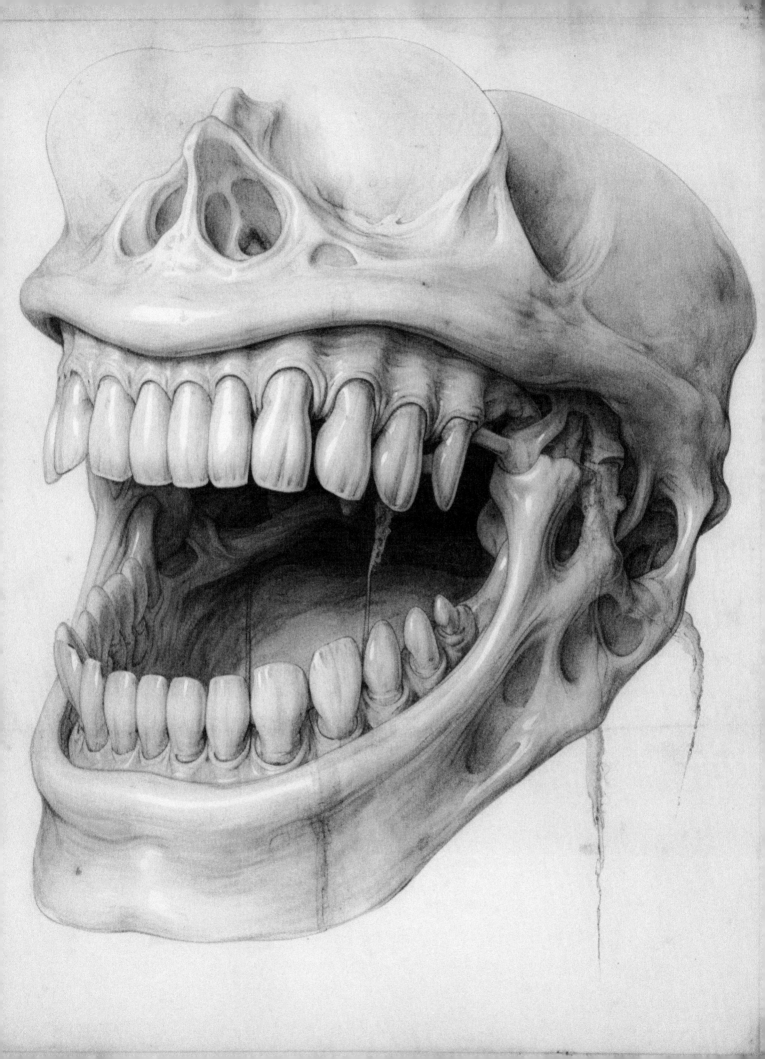

56. RELIGIOUS FIGURES / FIGURE RELIGIOSE

Sketches of saints and other religious figures.

Leonardo da Vinci, the visionary artist and important observer of humanity, devoted his artistic talent to sketching and displaying the essence of saints and other religious figures. By use of his exquisite sketches, he strove to dive into the spiritual realm and evoke an apparition of divine presence.

In his sketches of saints and religious figures, Leonardo scrupulously depicted their serene expressions, displaying the depth of their devotion and the inner peace that radiated from within. His sketches strove to create the spiritual grace and wisdom that these figures embodied, inviting viewers to contemplate the important messages they conveyed.

Leonardo's sketches went beyond mere representations; they aimed to encapsulate the essence of spirituality and the human connection with the divine. He studied the subtle nuances of facial features, the swift play of light and shadow, and the harmonious positioning of hands and gestures. Each stroke of his pen or brush conveyed an apparition of reverence and awe, bringing the spiritual figures to life on the canvas or parchment.

By use of his sketches, Leonardo searched out the diversity of religious figures, displaying the distinct attributes and symbolism associated with each saint. He strove to create their individual stories, their struggles, and their ultimate transcendence. His sketches acted as visual narratives, inviting viewers to contemplate the virtues and lessons embodied by these revered figures.

Leonardo's sketches of saints were not confined to a specific religious tradition; rather, they mirrored his depthy respect and appreciation for the universal aspects of spirituality. His drawings encompassed saints from different cultures and faiths, emphasizing the shared human longing for connection with the divine.

In his followings forth of displaying the essence of religious figures, Leonardo strove to illuminate the human capacity for spiritual elevation and transcendence. His sketches invoked an apparition of introspection and contemplation, encouraging viewers to connect with their own inner spirituality and the universal quest for meaning and purpose.

Leonardo's sketches of saints and religious figures inspirit and allure audiences today. They act as a glimmer of the important impact that spirituality has on the lived experience and the lasting quest for a connection with the divine. His sketches bypass time and cultural bounds, touching the hearts and souls of individuals across generations.

Inasmuch we peer upon Leonardo's sketches of saints and religious figures, here we see the depth and richness of mankind's spirituality. His artistry invites us to inquire into our own beliefs and convictions, to seek solace and guidance in the divine, and to welcome the universal values of love, compassion, and selflessness.

Leonardo da Vinci's sketches of saints and religious figures stand as a confirmation of his important appreciation for the spiritual aspects of humanity. His sketches ignite our imagination, inviting us to reflect on the timeless themes of faith, devotion, and the search for transcendent meaning.

By use of his sketches, Leonardo immortalized the ethereal beauty and serenity of saints and religious figures, forever displaying their divine essence upon the parchment. His heritage as an artist and spiritual observer drives home the important impact that the quest for spiritual enlightenment has on mankind's soul.

Inasmuch we contemplate Leonardo's sketches of saints and religious figures, we are encouraged to welcome the universal aspects of spirituality and to cultivate a deeper understanding of our shared lived experience. His sketches act as a timeless glimmer of the power of art to uplift the spirit and provide glimpses into the transcendent domains of faith and devotion.

57. METALLURGY / METALLURGIA

Notes and sketches on smelting and metal working techniques.

Leonardo da Vinci, the visionary artist and acute observer of the world, committed his artistic talent to exploring the complex processes of smelting and metalworking By use of his thorough notes and sketches. With his unquenchable curiosity and attention to detail, he strove to untwist the secrets of transforming raw materials into refined metal objects.

In his notes and sketches on smelting and metalworking, Leonardo scrupulously documented the various techniques and tools used in the process. He studied the properties of different metals, their melting points, and the methods for extracting them from their ores. His sketches procured the complex furnaces, crucibles, and molds employed in the smelting process.

Leonardo's fascination with metalworking extended beyond the technical aspects. He dived into the artistic possibilities that metal offered, exploring the ways in which it could be shaped, molded, and adorned. His sketches showcased the complex designs, engravings, and ornamental elements that could be incorporated into metal objects, elevating them to works of art.

By use of his notes and sketches, Leonardo strove to understand the chemical reactions and physical transformations that occurred during the smelting and metalworking processes. He searched out the part of heat, the use of fluxes and additives, and the importance of precise temperature control in achieving desired results. His sketches acted as a visual record of his discoveries and experiments.

Leonardo's studies on smelting and metalworking were not limited to a single metal or technique. He investigated a wide range of metals, including iron, copper, bronze, and gold, and searched out various methods such as casting, forging, and soldering. His sketches demonstrated his versatility and his ability to adapt his knowledge to different materials and processes.

Beyond the practical aspects, Leonardo recognized the artistic and aesthetic potential of metalworking. He searched out the ways in which metal could be used to create functional and decorative objects, from tools and weapons to jewelry and ornamental pieces. His sketches revealed his innovative ideas and his ability to combine form and function in his designs.

Leonardo's notes and sketches on smelting and metalworking inspirit and inform the field of metallurgy. They act as a confirmation of his undying followings forth of knowledge and his desire to untwist the mysteries of the natural world. His sketches provide a foundation for further exploration and experimentation, encouraging advancements in the techniques and understanding of metalworking.

Inasmuch we dive into Leonardo's notes and sketches on smelting and metalworking, here we see his genius and his ability to merge artistry with scientific inquiry. His studies act as a glimmer of the lasting human fascination with transforming raw materials into objects of beauty and utility. They lead us in to appreciate the artistry and craftsmanship inherent in the ancient and noble craft of metalworking.

Leonardo da Vinci's notes and sketches on smelting and metalworking stand as a confirmation of his steady commitment to untwisting the secrets of the natural world. His sketches allure and educate, providing a specter into the complexities of the metallurgical arts and provoking future generations of artists, artisans, and scientists.

By use of his thorough observations and detailed sketches, Leonardo immortalized the beauty and complexity of smelting and metalworking, forever displaying their essence upon the parchment. His heritage as an artist and scholar drives home the limitless possibilities of mankind's creativity and the transformative power of artistic expression.

58. CRUCIFIXES / CROCIFISSI

Designs and sketches of crucifixes.

Leonardo da Vinci, the visionary artist and important observer of religious symbolism, committed his artistic talent to designing and sketching crucifixes. By use of his complex designs and thorough sketches, he strove to map the essence of this powerful symbol of faith and redemption.

In his designs and sketches of crucifixes, Leonardo searched out the symbolism and significance of the crucifixion in Christian theology. He studied the proportions, positions, and expressions of the figure of Christ, seeking to portray the depth of his suffering and the magnitude of his sacrifice. His sketches conveyed an apparition of important reverence and empathy for the subject matter.

Leonardo's designs went beyond the traditional representations of the crucifixion. He strove to infuse his sketches with an apparition of artistic innovation and emotional depth. By use of his attention to detail, he procured the swift balance betwixt agony and serenity, portraying the human and divine aspects of the crucified Christ.

In his followings forth of creating meaningful crucifix designs, Leonardo searched out various artistic techniques and materials. He experimented with different poses, angles, and compositions to create the timeless message of salvation. His sketches demonstrated his acute understanding of mankind's anatomy, allowing him to depict the crucified figure with both accuracy and empathy.

Beyond the figure of Christ, Leonardo also searched out the artistic possibilities of the cross itself. He experimented with different shapes, materials, and ornamental details, seeking to create crucifixes that would inspirit awe and contemplation. His designs showcased his innovative approach to incorporating symbolism and artistic elements into the form of the cross.

By use of his designs and sketches of crucifixes, Leonardo aimed to evoke an important emotional response in viewers. He wanted his artwork to act as a source of solace, impetus, and spiritual reflection. His sketches were not just technical drawings but expressions of his depthy faith and his desire to create the transformative power of the crucifixion.

Leonardo's designs and sketches of crucifixes resonate with audiences today. They act as a glimmer of the lasting significance of the crucifixion in Christian belief and the power of visual representation to create spiritual and emotional truths. His artwork inspires contemplation, introspection, and a deeper understanding of the important mysteries of faith.

Inasmuch we contemplate Leonardo's designs and sketches of crucifixes, here we see the lasting power of religious symbolism and the capacity of art to create important truths. His artwork invites us to reflect on the meaning of the crucifixion, to connect with the divine, and to find solace and hope in times of struggle.

Leonardo da Vinci's designs and sketches of crucifixes stand as a confirmation of his steady devotion to exploring the mysteries of faith and displaying its essence through art. His sketches allure and inspirit, inviting us to contemplate the timeless message of love, sacrifice, and redemption embodied in the crucifixion.

By use of his thorough observations and artistic brilliance, Leonardo immortalized the beauty and significance of the crucifix, forever displaying its essence upon the parchment. His heritage as an artist and spiritual observer drives home the lasting power of visual representation to illuminate the depths of our souls and connect us to the divine.

Inasmuch we contemplate Leonardo's designs and sketches of crucifixes, we are encouraged to welcome the transformative power of faith and to seek solace and impetus in the lasting message of the crucifixion. His artwork acts as a timeless glimmer of the important impact that religious symbolism has on the human spirit and the ability of art to bypass time and touch the deepest recesses of our hearts.

59. MILITARY FORTIFICATIONS / FORTIFICAZIONI MILITARI

Designs for fortified structures and cities.

Leonardo da Vinci, the visionary artist and architectural genius, devoted his artistic talent to designing fortified structures and cities. By use of his thorough designs and visionary sketches, he strove to create fortified spaces that combined functionality, innovation, and strategic defense.

In his designs for fortified structures and cities, Leonardo approached architecture with a depthy understanding of military tactics and the art of defense. He studied the principles of fortification, analyzing the strengths and weaknesses of existing structures to inform his own designs. His sketches showcased his innovative ideas, blending form and function to create fortified spaces that were both aesthetically pleasing and strategically sound.

Leonardo's designs incorporated a variety of architectural elements aimed at enhancing defensive capabilities. He searched out the use of moats, drawbridges, and thick walls to create formidable barriers against potential invaders. His sketches demonstrated his understanding of the importance of strategic positioning, utilizing towers and bastions to provide optimal vantage points for surveillance and defense.

Beyond their defensive aspects, Leonardo's designs for fortified structures and cities also considered the needs of the inhabitants. He incorporated elements of urban planning, envisioning cities that were not merely secure but also practical and aesthetically pleasing. His sketches depicted well-designed streets, squares, and public spaces, showcasing his appreciation for the harmony betwixt architectural beauty and functionality.

By use of his designs, Leonardo strove to revolutionize the concept of fortification, incorporating innovative ideas that pushed the bounds of traditional defensive architecture. His sketches showcased his visionary approach, where creativity merged with strategic thinking to create fortified structures that surpassed conventional norms.

Leonardo's designs for fortified structures and cities were not limited to a specific geographic location or time period. He searched out various architectural styles, drawing impetus from historical structures and blending them with his own imaginative concepts. His sketches procured the diversity and adaptability of his designs, catering to different terrains, climates, and cultural contexts.

While some of Leonardo's designs for fortified structures and cities remained unrealized, they acted as a confirmation of his undying followings forth of knowledge and his desire to improve upon existing architectural practices. His sketches inspirit and influence architects and urban planners, providing a foundation for the development of fortified spaces that balance security, aesthetics, and functionality.

Inasmuch we inquire into Leonardo's designs for fortified structures and cities, here we see his innovative spirit and his commitment to pushing the bounds of architectural design. His sketches lead us in to reimagine the possibilities of fortified spaces, emphasizing the importance of creativity, adaptability, and strategic thinking in the field of architecture.

Leonardo da Vinci's designs for fortified structures and cities stand as a confirmation of his lasting heritage as an architect and visionary. His sketches allure and inspirit, serving as a glimmer of the transformative power of architectural innovation. They lead us in to welcome the harmonious integration of form and function, to envision fortified spaces that not merely provide security but also enhance the quality of life for their inhabitants.

By use of his thorough observations and visionary sketches, Leonardo immortalized the beauty and practicality of fortified structures and cities, forever displaying their essence upon the parchment. His heritage as an architect and artist drives home the important impact that architecture has on our lives and the potential for design to shape our physical surroundings in ways that are both functional and provoking.

Inasmuch we contemplate Leonardo's designs for fortified structures and cities, we are encouraged to welcome the principles of innovation, sustainability, and human-centric design. His sketches act as a timeless glimmer of the transformative power of architecture to create spaces that promote security, prosperity, and harmonious coexistence within our built environment.

60. AGRICULTURAL TOOLS / ATTREZZI AGRICOLI

Sketches of farming equipment.

Leonardo da Vinci, the visionary artist and inventor, committed his artistic talent to sketching and designing various farming equipment. By use of his detailed sketches, he strove to improve the efficiency and productivity of agricultural practices, showcasing his innovative approach to farming technology.

In his sketches of farming equipment, Leonardo scrupulously procured the complex mechanisms and components that would revolutionize the way farming was conducted. He studied the needs of farmers, analyzed the challenges they faced, and strove to create solutions that would streamline their work and enhance agricultural output.

Leonardo's sketches encompassed a wide range of farming equipment, from plows and harrows to irrigation systems and seed planters. Each sketch demonstrated his depthy understanding of farming techniques and his desire to create tools that would alleviate the physical labor involved in agriculture.

By use of his sketches, Leonardo searched out the principles of mechanics and hydraulics, incorporating innovative features into his designs. He envisioned machines that would increase efficiency, reduce manual labor, and optimize resource utilization. His sketches showcased his cleverness and his commitment to improving the agricultural practices of his time.

Leonardo's designs for farming equipment were not limited to a single crop or region. He recognized the diverse needs of farmers and aimed to create adaptable solutions that could be employed across various agricultural contexts. His sketches procured the versatility and flexibility of his designs, catering to different soil types, terrains, and farming methods.

Beyond the practical aspects, Leonardo also considered the ecological impact of farming equipment. He strove to design machines that would minimize soil erosion, promote sustainable farming practices, and conserve natural resources. His sketches mirrored his holistic approach to agriculture, highlighting the importance of preserving the environment while enhancing agricultural productivity.

While some of Leonardo's sketches for farming equipment remained conceptual, they acted as a confirmation of his futuristic purview and his desire to improve the lives of farmers. His sketches inspirit and influence agricultural innovation, providing a foundation for the development of modern farming machinery.

Inasmuch we inquire into Leonardo's sketches of farming equipment, here we see his steady commitment to the betterment of society through technology and invention. His sketches lead us in to reflect on the key part of agriculture in sustaining human civilization and to seek innovative solutions that balance productivity with environmental sustainability.

Leonardo da Vinci's sketches of farming equipment stand as a confirmation of his lasting heritage as an inventor and advocate for human progress. His sketches allure and inspirit, serving as a glimmer of the transformative power of technological advancements in agriculture. They lead us in to welcome innovation, efficiency, and sustainability in our ongoing quest for global food security.

By use of his thorough observations and visionary sketches, Leonardo immortalized the potential of farming equipment, forever displaying their essence upon the parchment. His heritage as an artist and inventor drives home the important impact that agricultural innovation has on society and the importance of harnessing technology to address the challenges of feeding a growing population.

Inasmuch we contemplate Leonardo's sketches of farming equipment, we are encouraged to welcome a future where technology and agriculture harmoniously coexist, enabling us to cultivate the land more efficiently and sustainably. His sketches act as a timeless glimmer of the necessary part that innovation plays in shaping the future of farming and ensuring a prosperous and food-secure world.

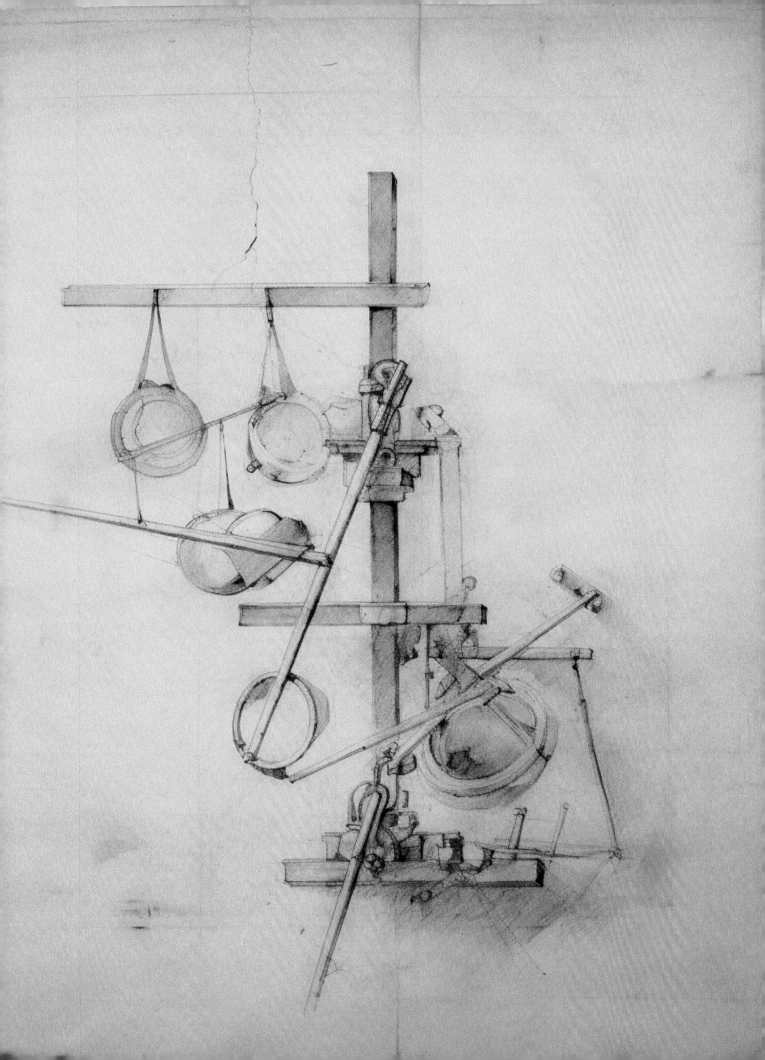

61. AQUEDUCTS / ACQUEDOTTI

Designs for improved water transportation.

Leonardo da Vinci, the visionary artist and inventor, committed his artistic talent to designing and sketching various improvements for water transportation. By use of his thorough designs and visionary sketches, he strove to enhance the efficiency and effectiveness of waterborne travel and commerce.

In his designs for improved water transportation, Leonardo recognized the necessary part that waterways played in connecting communities and facilitating trade. He studied the challenges faced by boats and ships, analyzing their designs and mechanisms to identify areas for improvement. His sketches showcased his innovative ideas, blending practicality and cleverness to create vessels that could navigate waterways with greater ease and efficiency.

Leonardo's designs encompassed a wide range of improvements for water transportation. He searched out advancements in hull designs, propulsion systems, and navigation instruments. His sketches depicted streamlined shapes and innovative features aimed at reducing drag, increasing maneuverability, and improving speed on the water.

By use of his sketches, Leonardo also dived into the concept of canals and water locks. He envisioned systems that could overcome elevation differences, allowing vessels to navigate through enmeshed waterways with minimal disruption. His designs incorporated innovative ideas to improve the efficiency of water transportation networks and facilitate the movement of goods and people.

Beyond the practical aspects, Leonardo's designs for improved water transportation also considered the comfort and safety of passengers. He searched out ideas for improved seating arrangements, onboard amenities, and even mechanisms for stability and stability control in rough waters. His sketches demonstrated his holistic approach to enhancing the overall water travel experience.

While some of Leonardo's designs for improved water transportation were not realized in his time, they acted as a confirmation of his forward-thinking mindset and his desire to stretch the bounds of existing technologies. His sketches inspirit and influence naval architecture and maritime engineering, providing a foundation for advancements in water transportation.

Inasmuch we inquire into Leonardo's designs for improved water transportation, here we see his innovative spirit and his commitment to improving the lived experience. His sketches lead us in to reimagine the possibilities of water travel, emphasizing the importance of efficiency, sustainability, and safety in the field of maritime technology.

Leonardo da Vinci's designs for improved water transportation stand as a confirmation of his lasting heritage as an inventor and visionary. His sketches allure and inspirit, serving as a glimmer of the transformative power of technological advancements in the field of transportation. They lead us in to welcome innovation and strive for more efficient and sustainable modes of water travel.

By use of his thorough observations and visionary sketches, Leonardo immortalized the beauty and potential of improved water transportation, forever displaying their essence upon the parchment. His heritage as an artist and inventor drives home the important impact that transportation innovation has on society and the importance of harnessing technology to improve the ways we connect and inquire into our world.

Inasmuch we contemplate Leonardo's sketches for improved water transportation, we are encouraged to welcome the possibilities of a future where water travel is more efficient, sustainable, and accessible. His sketches act as a timeless glimmer of the key part that innovation plays in shaping the future of transportation and encouraging global connectivity and prosperity.

62. PORTRAITURE TECHNIQUES / TECNICHE DI RITRATTO

Studies on different techniques to portray the human face.

Leonardo da Vinci, the masterful artist and acute observer of mankind's nature, committed his artistic talent to studying and exploring various techniques to portray the human face. By use of his detailed studies, he strove to map the complexities and nuances of facial expressions, revealing the depths of mankind's emotion and character.

In his studies on techniques to portray the human face, Leonardo dived into the domains of anatomy, psychology, and artistic expression. He scrupulously observed the features, proportions, and movements of the face, aiming to create lifelike representations that conveyed the essence of the individual.

Leonardo's studies encompassed a wide range of techniques, starting with the swift play of light and shadow, known as chiaroscuro, to the precise rendering of facial muscles and bone structure. His sketches searched out different angles, expressions, and gestures, as he strove to map the ever-changing nature of the human visage.

By use of his studies, Leonardo developed a depthy understanding of the relationship betwixt form and emotion. He recognized that the human face is a canvas of feelings, where each wrinkle, furrow, and curve tells a story. His sketches portrayed joy, sorrow, anger, and everything in betwixt, revealing the rich atlas of mankind's experiences.

Leonardo's techniques to portray the human face went beyond mere technical proficiency. He strove to create a connection betwixt the viewer and the subject, invoking empathy and understanding By use of his art. His sketches conveyed the complexities of mankind's nature, displaying the essence of individuals and inviting the viewer to contemplate their inner worlds.

Beyond the physical aspects, Leonardo also searched out the psychological dimensions of the human face. He saw the importance of microexpressions and subtle gestures, studying the ways in which emotions manifest themselves in fleeting moments. His sketches depicted the nuances of mankind's expression, revealing the depths of the human psyche.

While Leonardo's studies on techniques to portray the human face were large, they were also an ongoing followings forth of perfection. He understood that displaying the essence of a person required constant observation and refinement. His sketches acted as a visual diary of his quest to untwist the mysteries of the human countenance.

Inasmuch we inquire into Leonardo's studies on techniques to portray the human face, here we see his steady commitment to displaying the essence of humanity. His sketches lead us in to reflect on the complexities of mankind's emotion, to welcome the diversity of our experiences, and to celebrate the beauty of individuality.

Leonardo da Vinci's studies on techniques to portray the human face stand as a confirmation of his lasting heritage as an artist and observer of mankind's nature. His sketches allure and inspirit, serving as a glimmer of the transformative power of art to create the depth and complexity of the lived experience.

By use of his thorough observations and visionary sketches, Leonardo immortalized the beauty and complexities of the human face, forever displaying their essence upon the parchment. His heritage as an artist and scholar drives home the important impact that art has on our understanding of ourselves and others.

Inasmuch we contemplate Leonardo's studies on techniques to portray the human face, we are encouraged to welcome the power of art to connect, to communicate, and to lay bare the depths of our shared humanity. His sketches act as a timeless glimmer of the universal language of the human face and the transformative potential of artistic expression.

63. VESSELS / VASI

Sketches of various vessels, jars, and vases.

Leonardo da Vinci, the brilliant artist and observer of the world around him, committed his artistic talent to sketching and studying various vessels, jars, and vases. By use of his thorough sketches, he strove to map the beauty and complexities of these objects, showcasing his acute eye for detail and his appreciation for the artistry of craftsmanship.

In his sketches of vessels, jars, and vases, Leonardo dived into the study of form, proportion, and design. He observed the graceful curves, the complex patterns, and the swift craftsmanship of these objects, aiming to map their essence on paper. His sketches mirrored his fascination with the relationship betwixt function and aesthetics.

Leonardo's sketches encompassed a wide range of vessels, jars, and vases, from everyday objects to exquisite works of art. He studied their various shapes, sizes, and decorative elements, seeking to understand the principles of their construction and the artistry involved in their creation. His sketches celebrated the diversity and beauty of these vessels, displaying their unique characteristics and nuances.

By use of his sketches, Leonardo searched out the relationship betwixt form and function in these objects. He examined how their shapes and proportions influenced their practical use, as well as their visual appeal. His sketches showcased his understanding of the harmonious balance betwixt utility and artistic expression, highlighting the craftsmanship that went into their creation.

Beyond the technical aspects, Leonardo's sketches also revealed his appreciation for the cultural and historical significance of these vessels. He studied the influences of different civilizations and art movements, incorporating elements of their designs into his own sketches. His drawings acted as a visual documentation of the rich atlas of mankind's creativity and cultural heritage.

While some of Leonardo's sketches of vessels, jars, and vases remained conceptual, they acted as a confirmation of his acute observation skills and his desire to understand and appreciate the beauty in everyday objects. His sketches inspirit and influence artists and artisans, providing a foundation for the exploration of form, texture, and design.

Inasmuch we inquire into Leonardo's sketches of vessels, jars, and vases, here we see his ability to find impetus and beauty in the simplest of objects. His sketches lead us in to appreciate the craftsmanship, artistry, and cultural significance of these vessels, and to recognize the power of art to elevate the everyday into something extraordinary.

Leonardo da Vinci's sketches of vessels, jars, and vases stand as a confirmation of his lasting heritage as an artist and observer of the world. His sketches allure and inspirit, serving as a glimmer of the transformative power of art to evoke emotion, spark imagination, and celebrate the beauty found in the objects that surround us.

By use of his thorough observations and visionary sketches, Leonardo immortalized the beauty and artistry of vessels, jars, and vases, forever displaying their essence upon the parchment. His heritage as an artist and scholar drives home the important impact that art and craftsmanship have on our lives and our appreciation of the world around us.

Inasmuch we contemplate Leonardo's sketches of vessels, jars, and vases, we are encouraged to welcome the artistry and beauty that can be found in the simplest of objects. His sketches act as a timeless glimmer of the lasting allure of craftsmanship and the power of art to enrich our lives and deepen our connection to the world.

64. PROPELLERS / ELICHE

Design of screw-like propellers.

Leonardo da Vinci, the ingenious artist and inventor, committed his inventive spirit to designing and sketching screw-like propellers. By use of his thorough designs, he strove to harness the power of water and air to propel boats and aircraft with greater efficiency and speed.

In his designs of screw-like propellers, Leonardo searched out the principles of fluid dynamics and the mechanics of propulsion. He observed the swirling motion of water and air, seeking to replicate and enhance their natural forces By use of his inventive designs. His sketches procured the complex details and mechanisms that would revolutionize the field of propulsion.

Leonardo's designs encompassed a variety of screw-like propellers, each tailored to specific applications and intended to optimize performance. He examined different blade shapes, angles, and configurations, aiming to maximize thrust while minimizing resistance. His sketches mirrored his depthy understanding of the relationship betwixt form, function, and the movement of fluid mediums.

By use of his sketches, Leonardo also considered the practical aspects of propeller design, such as manufacturing techniques and material selection. He strove to create propellers that were not merely efficient and effective but also feasible to construct and operate. His designs showcased his engineering power and his commitment to practical innovation.

While some of Leonardo's designs for screw-like propellers were ahead of his time and remained conceptual, they acted as a confirmation of his visionary approach and his desire to stretch the bounds of existing technologies. His sketches inspirit and influence the field of propulsion, shaping the development of modern propeller systems.

Inasmuch we inquire into Leonardo's designs of screw-like propellers, here we see his undying followings forth of knowledge and his steady commitment to technological advancement. His sketches lead us in to reimagine the possibilities of fluid propulsion, emphasizing the importance of efficiency, sustainability, and innovation in the field of transportation.

Leonardo da Vinci's designs of screw-like propellers stand as a confirmation of his lasting heritage as an inventor and visionary. His sketches allure and inspirit, serving as a glimmer of the transformative power of technological advancements in the realm of propulsion. They lead us in to welcome innovation, efficiency, and environmental consciousness in our ongoing quest for more sustainable modes of transportation.

By use of his thorough observations and visionary sketches, Leonardo immortalized the beauty and potential of screw-like propellers, forever displaying their essence upon the parchment. His heritage as an artist and inventor drives home the important impact that propulsion innovation has on society and the importance of harnessing technology to propel us towards a more sustainable future.

Inasmuch we contemplate Leonardo's sketches of screw-like propellers, we are encouraged to welcome a future where transportation is not merely efficient and powerful but also environmentally conscious. His sketches act as a timeless glimmer of the transformative potential of propeller systems and the need to stretch the bounds of propulsion technology to create a better world for generations to come.

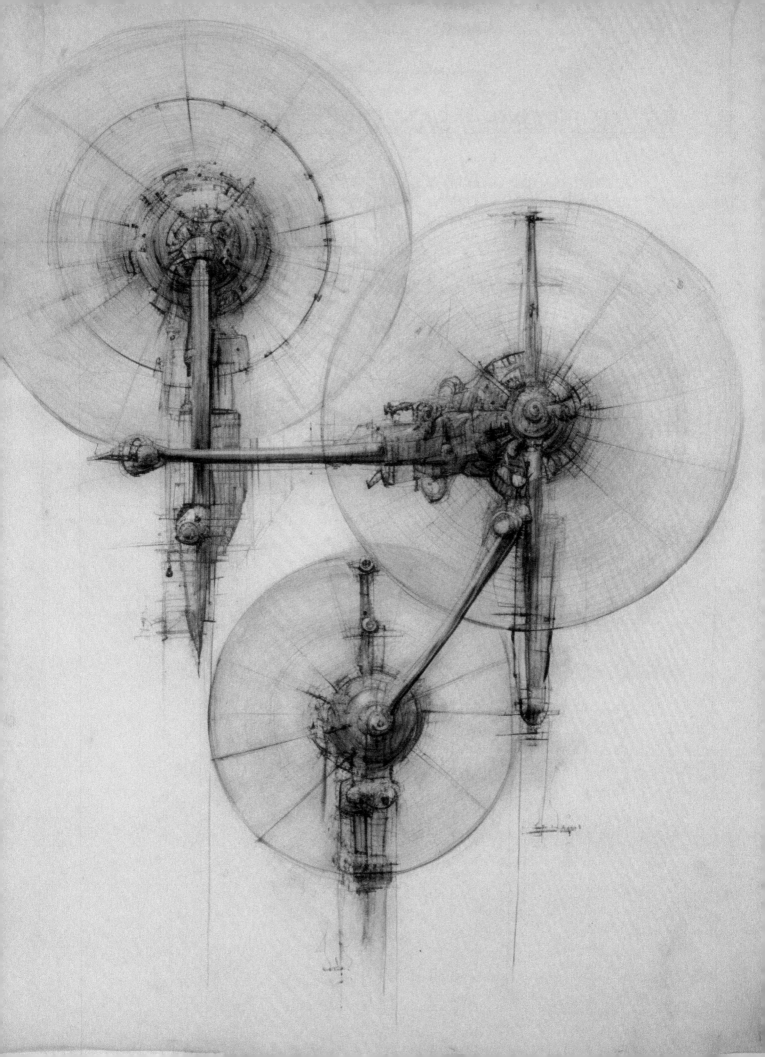

65. ST. JEROME / SAN GIROLAMO

A well-known unfinished painting of St. Jerome in the Wilderness.

A renowned and unfinished masterpiece attributed to Leonardo da Vinci is the painting of St. Jerome in the Wilderness. This alluring artwork portrays St. Jerome, a prominent Christian scholar and theologian, in a contemplative state amidst the serene and rugged wilderness.

Although the painting remains incomplete, it still exudes an apparition of important spirituality and depth. The image illustrates St. Jerome seated in a humble and introspective posture, engrossed in his studies and prayer. His weathered face and flowing beard reflect the passage of time and the wisdom that comes with a life committed to spiritual contemplation.

Leonardo's attention to detail is evident in the complex rendering of the surrounding territory. The untamed wilderness with its rocky cliffs, dense foliage, and distant mountains creates a harmonious backdrop, symbolizing the solitude and inner struggles faced by St. Jerome during his spiritual quest.

The composition of the painting is carefully constructed, with a balanced relationship of light and shadow. Soft rays of sunlight filter through the trees, illuminating St. Jerome's figure and casting a gentle glow on the scene. This contrast of light and dark adds depth and drama to the painting, inviting the viewer to immerse themselves in its contemplative atmosphere.

Although unfinished, the painting flaunts Leonardo's mastery of technique and his ability to map the essence of his subject. His skillful brushwork and swift use of color create an apparition of realism and emotional depth. Even in its incomplete state, the painting resonateth with a timeless quality that speaks to life and the followings forth of spiritual enlightenment.

St. Jerome in the Wilderness holdeth as a confirmation of Leonardo's artistic genius and his exploration of mankind's soul. Through this unfinished work, he invites us to contemplate the themes of introspection, solitude, and the eternal quest for meaning and enlightenment. The painting's enigmatic nature leaves room for interpretation, allowing each viewer to find their own connection and resonance with the subject matter.

Inasmuch we peer upon St. Jerome in the Wilderness, here we see the power of art to bypass time and touch the depths of our being. Leonardo's unfinished masterpiece acts as a glimmer of the imperfections and complexities of life, while also igniting our curiosity and imagination.

Although incomplete, St. Jerome in the Wilderness remains to allure and inspirit art lovers and scholars alike. Its enigmatic beauty and evocative atmosphere lead us in to dive across the nexus of our own spiritual quest and contemplate the timeless questions that have echoed through the ages.

Leonardo da Vinci's unfinished painting of St. Jerome in the Wilderness remains a confirmation of his artistic brilliance and his important understanding of life. It holdeth as a glimmer of the unfinished nature of life itself and the eternal quest for meaning and enlightenment. Through its enigmatic beauty, it invites us to start on our own introspective quest and find solace and impetus in the wilderness of our own souls.

66. DRAPERY STUDIES / STUDI DI DRAPPEGGI

Detailed studies of drapes and folds.

Leonardo da Vinci, the masterful artist and thorough observer of the world, committed his artistic talent to the detailed study of drapes and folds. By use of his large studies, he strove to map the complex relationship of fabric, light, and form, bringing a heightened sense of realism and texture to his artworks.

In his studies of drapes and folds, Leonardo dived into the realm of textile manipulation, exploring the way fabrics drape, fold, and interact with the human form. His thorough observations and sketches revealed his acute eye for the subtle nuances of fabric movement, allowing him to breathe life into his compositions.

Leonardo's studies encompassed a wide range of fabrics, from soft and flowing materials to stiffer and more structured textiles. He scrupulously observed and documented the way fabrics behaved in different conditions, displaying the graceful folds, the swift creases, and the complex patterns created by the relationship of cloth and gravity.

By use of his studies, Leonardo not merely focused on the visual aspects of drapes and folds but also on the tactile sensations they evoke. He aimed to create an apparition of touch and texture By use of his art, making viewers feel as though they could reach out and feel the weight and softness of the fabric depicted in his paintings.

Leonardo's attention to detail went beyond the surface level. He searched out the underlying mechanics of drapes and folds, understanding the principles of tension, gravity, and volume that govern their behavior. His sketches revealed his understanding of how these elements shape the visual appearance of fabric and contribute to the overall composition of his artworks.

By incorporating his studies of drapes and folds into his paintings, Leonardo brought a heightened sense of realism and depth to his artwork. The careful rendering of fabric textures and the thorough attention to the relationship of light and shadow created an apparition of presence and tangibility, making his subjects come to life on the canvas.

Beyond the technical aspects, Leonardo's studies of drapes and folds also acted as a confirmation of his appreciation for the beauty and artistry found in everyday objects. He saw the importance of textiles in human culture, both as functional items and as a means of exuberance. His sketches celebrated the diversity and richness of fabric patterns, colors, and textures.

Inasmuch we inquire into Leonardo's studies of drapes and folds, here we see his steady commitment to displaying the complex details and subtleties of the world around him. His sketches lead us in to appreciate the beauty and complexity of fabrics, and to recognize the artistic potential that lies within even the most mundane of objects.

Leonardo da Vinci's studies of drapes and folds stand as a confirmation of his lasting heritage as an artist and observer of the lived experience. His thorough observations and sketches allure and inspirit, serving as a glimmer of the transformative power of art to evoke emotion, create depth, and bring the world to life.

By use of his thorough observations and visionary sketches, Leonardo immortalized the beauty and complexities of drapes and folds, forever displaying their essence upon the parchment. His heritage as an artist and scholar drives home the important impact that the relationship of light, form, and texture has on our perception of the world and the power of art to elevate the everyday into something extraordinary.

Inasmuch we contemplate Leonardo's studies of drapes and folds, we are encouraged to welcome the beauty and artistry that can be found in the simplest of objects. His sketches act as a timeless glimmer of the lasting allure of fabric textures and the transformative potential of artistic expression.

67. BATHING / BAGNI

Sketches of people bathing and designs for baths.

Leonardo da Vinci, the brilliant artist and visionary, searched out the theme of bathing By use of his sketches, displaying the beauty and intimacy of this daily ritual. By use of his thorough observations and imaginative designs, he strove to create spaces that harmonized functionality, aesthetics, and tranquility, elevating the act of bathing to an art form.

In his sketches of people bathing, Leonardo aimed to map the human form in its natural state, celebrating the grace and vulnerability of the human body. His drawings depicted figures immersed in water, displaying the play of light and shadow on their skin, and the swift relationship of water droplets on their bodies. These sketches revealed his acute eye for anatomy and his ability to create an apparition of realism and sensuality.

Beyond the depiction of individuals bathing, Leonardo also searched out the design of baths themselves. He envisioned spaces that would provide comfort, relaxation, and a sensory experience for the bather. His designs incorporated elements such as natural light, harmonious proportions, and complex details to create an atmosphere conducive to rejuvenation and contemplation.

Leonardo's sketches of people bathing and his designs for baths mirrored his depthy understanding of the physical and emotional benefits of this ritual. He recognized the therapeutic and cleansing properties of water, and strove to create environments that would enhance these experiences. His sketches celebrated the human body, the element of water, and the holistic nature of the bathing experience.

By use of his sketches, Leonardo also considered the practical aspects of bath design, such as the circulation of water, drainage systems, and heating mechanisms. His designs showcased his engineering acumen and his commitment to creating functional spaces that would enhance the overall bathing experience.

Inasmuch we inquire into Leonardo's sketches of people bathing and his designs for baths, here we see the importance of self-care and the power of water as a source of rejuvenation and relaxation. His sketches lead us in to contemplate the beauty and vulnerability of the human form, and to appreciate the transformative potential of a well-designed bathing environment.

Leonardo da Vinci's sketches of people bathing and his designs for baths stand as a confirmation of his holistic approach to art and his understanding of the enmeshment of the lived experience. His sketches allure and inspirit, serving as a glimmer of the transformative power of water, the beauty of the human body, and the importance of creating spaces that promote prosperity and tranquility.

By use of his thorough observations and visionary sketches, Leonardo immortalized the beauty and intimacy of bathing, forever displaying its essence upon the parchment. His heritage as an artist and scholar drives home the important impact that the act of bathing has on our physical and emotional prosperity, and the power of art to elevate everyday rituals into something extraordinary.

Inasmuch we contemplate Leonardo's sketches of people bathing and his designs for baths, we are encouraged to welcome the restorative and transformative qualities of water, and to create environments that promote relaxation, rejuvenation, and self-care. His sketches act as a timeless glimmer of the lasting allure of bathing and the potential for art and design to enhance our everyday lives.

68. DIVING EQUIPMENT / ATTREZZATURE PER IMMERSIONI

He designed a diving suit and sketched it.

Leonardo da Vinci, the brilliant artist and visionary, ventured into the realm of underwater exploration and protection By use of his innovative designs and sketches of a diving suit. With his characteristic curiosity and inventive spirit, he strove to create a garment that would enable humans to inquire across the nexus of the sea with safety and ease.

In his detailed sketches, Leonardo procured the complexities of the diving suit, envisioning a protective ensemble that would allow individuals to breathe and move freely underwater. His designs incorporated elements such as airtight compartments, breathing apparatus, and reinforced materials to ensure the safety and comfort of the diver.

Leonardo's diving suit designs were a confirmation of his understanding of the principles of buoyancy, pressure, and human physiology. He aimed to create a suit that would provide both protection and mobility, enabling divers to navigate the underwater world with confidence and grace.

By use of his sketches, Leonardo not merely focused on the functional aspects of the diving suit but also considered its aesthetic appeal. He strove to create a suit that was not merely practical but also visually striking, reflecting his belief that artistry and functionality could coexist harmoniously.

Although Leonardo's diving suit designs remained conceptual and were not realized during his lifetime, they foreshadowed the advancements in underwater exploration and the development of modern diving apparatus. His visionary sketches laid the foundation for future inventors and engineers to refine and bring to life the concept of a functional diving suit.

Inasmuch we inquire into Leonardo's sketches of the diving suit, here we see his unquenchable curiosity and his undying followings forth of knowledge. His designs lead us in to welcome the wonders of the underwater world and to stretch the bounds of mankind's exploration and innovation.

Leonardo da Vinci's sketches of the diving suit stand as a confirmation of his lasting heritage as an inventor and visionary. While his designs may not have materialized in his time, they inspirit and influence the field of underwater exploration and the development of protective garments for divers.

By use of his thorough observations and visionary sketches, Leonardo immortalized the concept of the diving suit, forever displaying its essence upon the parchment. His heritage as an artist and scholar drives home the transformative power of mankind's cleverness and the potential for invention to shape the course of history.

Inasmuch we contemplate Leonardo's sketches of the diving suit, we are encouraged to welcome the spirit of exploration and innovation. His sketches act as a timeless glimmer of the unlimited possibilities that lie beneath the surface of the sea and the unyielding human desire to venture into uncharted territories.

69. MEDIEVAL WEAPONS / ARMI MEDIEVALI

Studies of various weapons.

Leonardo da Vinci, the renowned artist and visionary, committed his artistic talent and analytical mind to the study of various weapons. By use of his thorough observations and detailed sketches, he strove to understand the mechanics, functionality, and destructive power of these instruments of warfare.

In his studies of weapons, Leonardo searched out a wide range of armaments, including swords, spears, bows, and cannons. He carefully examined their designs, materials, and construction, seeking to untwist the complexities of their mechanisms and the principles behind their effectiveness in combat.

Leonardo's sketches of weapons showcased his acute eye for detail and his ability to map the essence of these formidable tools. His drawings depicted the complex engravings, the balance and weight distribution, and the subtle curves and angles that made each weapon unique. By use of his thorough renderings, he aimed to preserve a record of these martial implements for posterity.

Beyond the technical aspects, Leonardo also dived into the psychological and strategic dimensions of weapons. He searched out their impact on the psychology of warfare, the strategies of combat, and the dynamics of power on the battlefield. His sketches procured not merely the physical form of the weapons but also the aura of intimidation and the sense of authority they conferred upon those who wielded them.

By use of his studies, Leonardo strove to advance the understanding of weapons and warfare. His sketches provided a valuable resource for military strategists, engineers, and artisans of his time, while also leaving a lasting impact on the development of weaponry and military technology in the centuries that followed.

Inasmuch we inquire into Leonardo's studies of weapons, here we see the dual nature of mankind's innovation—the ability to create tools for both destruction and defense. His sketches lead us in to contemplate the ethical and philosophical implications of the advancements in weaponry and the part they play in shaping the course of history.

Leonardo da Vinci's studies of weapons stand as a confirmation of his unquenchable curiosity and his commitment to untwisting the mysteries of the world. His thorough observations and detailed sketches allure and inspirit, reminding us of the complexities of mankind's cleverness and the impact of technological advancements on society.

By use of his sketches, Leonardo immortalized the forms and functions of various weapons, forever displaying their essence upon the parchment. His heritage as an artist, scientist, and scholar drives home the important influence that weaponry has had on human civilization and the importance of responsible and ethical use of technology.

Inasmuch we contemplate Leonardo's studies of weapons, we are encouraged to reflect on the swift balance betwixt innovation and responsibility, and to strive for a world where the followings forth of knowledge and progress is guided by wisdom and compassion. His sketches act as a timeless glimmer of the power of mankind's creativity and the need to wield it with conscientiousness and discernment.

70. TURBULENCE / TURBOLENZA

Leonardo made sketches studying turbulent water flow.

Leonardo da Vinci, the brilliant artist and scientific mind, committed his artistic talent and analytical skills to studying the fascinating phenomena of turbulent water flow. By use of his thorough observations and detailed sketches, he strove to untwist the complex patterns and dynamics of water in motion, displaying its energy and fluidity on paper.

In his studies of turbulent water flow, Leonardo searched out the complex relationship of currents, eddies, and vortices. He observed the way water behaved when faced with obstacles, such as rocks or riverbanks, and how it transformed as it moved through different environments. His sketches depicted the ever-changing shapes and patterns created by the turbulent flow, showcasing his acute eye for displaying the essence of this dynamic natural phenomenon.

By use of his sketches, Leonardo not merely documented the visual aspects of turbulent water flow but also strove to understand the underlying principles that governed its behavior. He dived into the domains of fluid dynamics, investigating the forces and factors that influenced the movement and transformation of water. His studies showcased his interdisciplinary approach, bridging the gap betwixt art and science.

Leonardo's sketches of turbulent water flow were a confirmation of his unquenchable curiosity and his desire to uncover the secrets of nature. He recognized the beauty and complexity of water in motion, appreciating its ever-changing forms and its power to shape the world around us. His drawings procured the essence of this dynamic force, inviting viewers to swoon at the complex jubilation of water molecules.

Beyond the scientific exploration, Leonardo's sketches of turbulent water flow also acted as a source of impetus for his artistic endeavors. He incorporated the fluidity and energy of water into his paintings, bringing an apparition of life and movement to his depictions of rivers, oceans, and waterfalls. His understanding of the dynamics of water flow enriched his artistic compositions, creating an apparition of realism and vitality.

Inasmuch we contemplate Leonardo's sketches of turbulent water flow, here we see his remarkable ability to observe and interpret the natural world. His studies lead us in to appreciate the beauty and complexity of water in motion and to recognize the enmeshment of art, science, and nature.

Leonardo da Vinci's sketches of turbulent water flow stand as a confirmation of his lasting heritage as a polymath and visionary. His thorough observations and detailed drawings allure and inspirit, reminding us of the wonders that await us in the natural world and the limitless potential of mankind's curiosity.

By use of his sketches, Leonardo immortalized the fleeting and ever-changing nature of turbulent water flow, forever displaying its essence upon the parchment. His heritage as an artist, scientist, and scholar drives home the important beauty and complexity of the natural world and the importance of observing and appreciating its wonders.

Inasmuch we contemplate Leonardo's studies of turbulent water flow, we are encouraged to cultivate an apparition of wonder and curiosity, and to welcome the transformative power of nature in our own lives. His sketches act as a timeless glimmer of the enmeshment of art, science, and the natural world, and the endless possibilities that arise when we dive across the nexus of knowledge and exploration.

71. GIANTS / GIGANTI

Sketches of mythical giants.

Leonardo da Vinci, the visionary artist and creative mind, dived into the realm of mythology By use of his alluring sketches of mythical giants. Inspired by ancient tales and legends, he strove to bring these larger-than-life creatures to life on paper, displaying their grandeur and awe-provoking presence.

In his sketches of mythical giants, Leonardo demonstrated his imaginative power and attention to detail. His drawings depicted these towering beings with remarkable realism, showcasing their massive proportions, muscular forms, and powerful features. With each stroke of his pen or brush, he breathed life into these mythical beings, allowing us to specter into a world of legends and imagination.

Leonardo's sketches of mythical giants were not merely a confirmation of his artistic skill but also mirrored his fascination with the human form and anatomy. He studied the proportions and musculature of these extraordinary beings, blending his understanding of mankind's anatomy with the fantastical elements of myth and folklore. His sketches procured the essence of these giants, portraying them as both formidable and alluring.

Beyond their artistic value, Leonardo's sketches of mythical giants also acted as a window into the human psyche and the universal fascination with the extraordinary. These larger-than-life creatures embodied our collective desires for power, strength, and transcendence, representing both the wonders and the dangers that lie beyond the realm of ordinary existence.

Inasmuch we inquire into Leonardo's sketches of mythical giants, we are warped to a realm where imagination knows no bounds. His drawings lead us in to suspend disbelief and start on a quest into the realm of mythology, where gods and heroes mingle with awe-provoking beings of immense size and power.

Leonardo da Vinci's sketches of mythical giants stand as a confirmation of his lasting heritage as a master of imagination and artistic expression. His ability to breathe life into these mythical beings remains to allure and inspirit, reminding us of the unlimited potential of the human mind and the power of art to transport us to extraordinary domains.

By use of his sketches, Leonardo immortalized the grandeur and majesty of mythical giants, forever displaying their essence upon the parchment. His heritage as an artist and storyteller drives home the lasting allure of myth and the important impact that tales of giants have had on human culture throughout history.

Inasmuch we contemplate Leonardo's sketches of mythical giants, we are encouraged to welcome our own creativity and imagination, and to inquire across the nexus of myth and folklore. His sketches act as a timeless glimmer of the lasting power of stories and the universal human longing for the extraordinary.

72. LIFTING DEVICES / DISPOSITIVI DI SOLLEVAMENTO

Various designs for cranes and other lifting devices.

Leonardo da Vinci, the masterful artist and ingenious inventor, committed his remarkable talent and inventive mind to the study and design of lifting devices. By use of his acute observations and thorough sketches, he strove to understand the principles of mechanical advantage and develop innovative solutions for lifting heavy loads.

In his diverse designs for cranes and other lifting devices, Leonardo searched out a range of mechanisms and configurations. His sketches showcased his depthy understanding of leverage, pulleys, and gears, as well as his ability to conceptualize and refine complex machinery.

Leonardo's designs for cranes were characterized by their efficiency, strength, and adaptability. He envisioned machines capable of hoisting heavy objects with precision and ease, whether it be for construction purposes or the transportation of goods. His sketches depicted the complex details of these devices, displaying the complex relationship of gears, pulleys, and counterweights.

Beyond their functional aspects, Leonardo's designs for cranes also exhibited his aesthetic sensibilities. He strove to harmonize form and function, creating machines that were not merely efficient but also visually appealing. His sketches demonstrated his ability to integrate elegance and practicality, reflecting his belief that beauty could be found in the marriage of art and engineering.

By use of his studies and sketches of lifting devices, Leonardo not merely advanced the understanding of mechanical principles but also influenced the development of construction and engineering practices. His ideas and designs acted as a source of impetus for future inventors and engineers, laying the Earthly foundation for the evolution of lifting technology.

Inasmuch we dive into Leonardo's designs for cranes and lifting devices, here we see his extraordinary ability to merge artistry with practicality. His sketches lead us in to appreciate the beauty and cleverness of machinery, and to recognize the transformative power of invention in shaping the world around us.

Leonardo da Vinci's sketches of cranes and lifting devices stand as a confirmation of his lasting heritage as an innovator and a visionary. His thorough observations and detailed drawings allure and inspirit, reminding us of the unlimited potential of mankind's imagination and the impact of technological advancements on society.

By use of his sketches, Leonardo immortalized the concepts and designs of various lifting devices, forever displaying their essence upon the parchment. His heritage as an artist, inventor, and scholar drives home the remarkable synergy betwixt art and engineering, and the remarkable feats that can be achieved through human creativity and cleverness.

Inasmuch we contemplate Leonardo's designs for cranes and lifting devices, we are encouraged to stretch the bounds of innovation and to seek solutions that combine functionality, efficiency, and aesthetic appeal. His sketches act as a timeless glimmer of the transformative power of mankind's cleverness and the limitless possibilities that arise when art, science, and engineering converge.

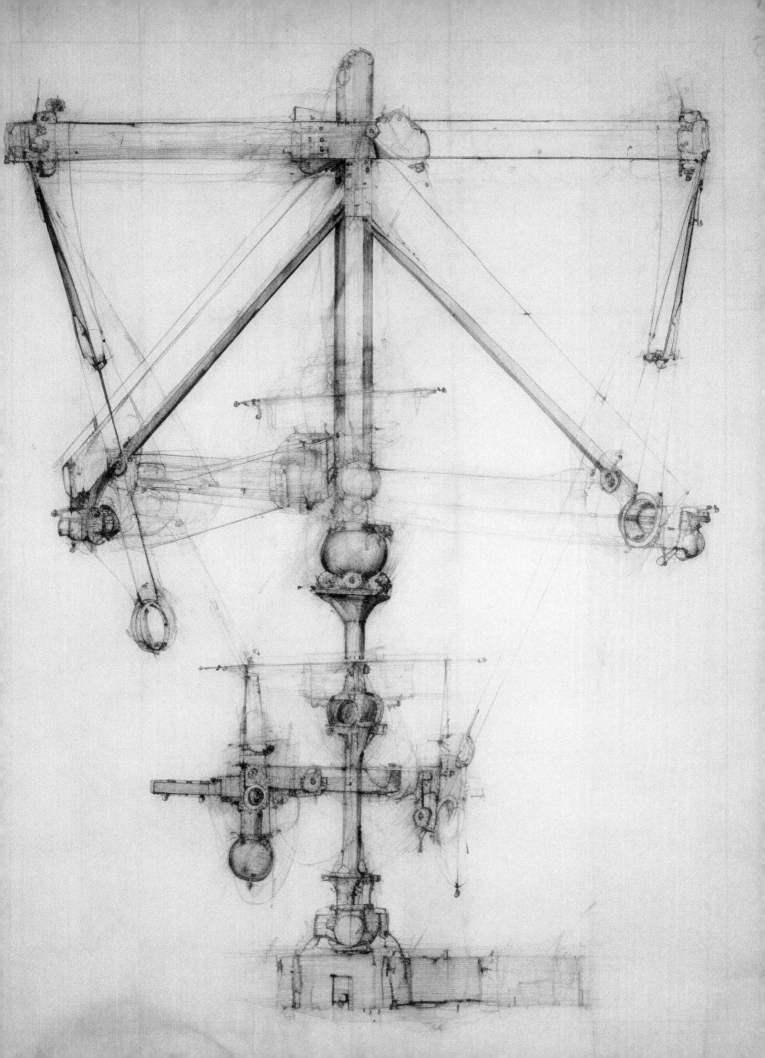

73. WHEELS / RUOTE

Studies of various types of wheel designs.

Leonardo da Vinci, the brilliant mind and visionary artist, committed his acute intellect and artistic talent to studying and sketching various types of wheel designs. By use of his thorough observations and detailed drawings, he strove to understand the mechanics and dynamics of these essential inventions that have shaped human civilization.

In his studies of wheel designs, Leonardo searched out a wide range of variations and configurations. He examined the complex relationship of spokes, rims, and axles, scrupulously displaying the details of each design. His sketches showcased his ability to analyze and interpret the functional aspects of wheels, including their efficiency, stability, and load-bearing capabilities.

Leonardo's drawings of wheel designs demonstrated his appreciation for both form and function. He recognized that the shape and structure of a wheel were not merely essential for its mechanical performance but also contributed to its aesthetic appeal. His sketches depicted the elegance and grace of various wheel designs, reflecting his belief that beauty could be found in the harmonious fusion of art and engineering.

By use of his studies, Leonardo strove to advance the understanding of wheel technology and inspirit new innovations. His sketches provided a foundation for future engineers and inventors, offering insights into the principles of rotational motion and the mechanics of wheel-based systems.

Inasmuch we inquire into Leonardo's studies of wheel designs, here we see the important impact that this simple yet revolutionary invention has had on human civilization. Wheels have enabled transportation, revolutionized industry, and shaped the development of countless technologies. Leonardo's sketches lead us in to appreciate the cleverness and versatility of wheels, and to recognize their significance in the progress of mankind's society.

Leonardo da Vinci's sketches of wheel designs stand as a confirmation of his lasting heritage as a master of both art and science. His thorough observations and detailed drawings allure and inspirit, reminding us of the remarkable intersection betwixt creativity and engineering.

By use of his sketches, Leonardo immortalized the essence of various wheel designs, forever displaying their significance upon the parchment. His heritage as an artist, scientist, and scholar drives home the remarkable cleverness of mankind's inventiveness and the power of curiosity to drive progress.

Inasmuch we contemplate Leonardo's studies of wheel designs, we are encouraged to appreciate the marvels of mankind's cleverness and to seek innovation that combines functionality, efficiency, and aesthetic appeal. His sketches act as a timeless glimmer of the transformative power of invention and the endless possibilities that arise when artistry and engineering converge.

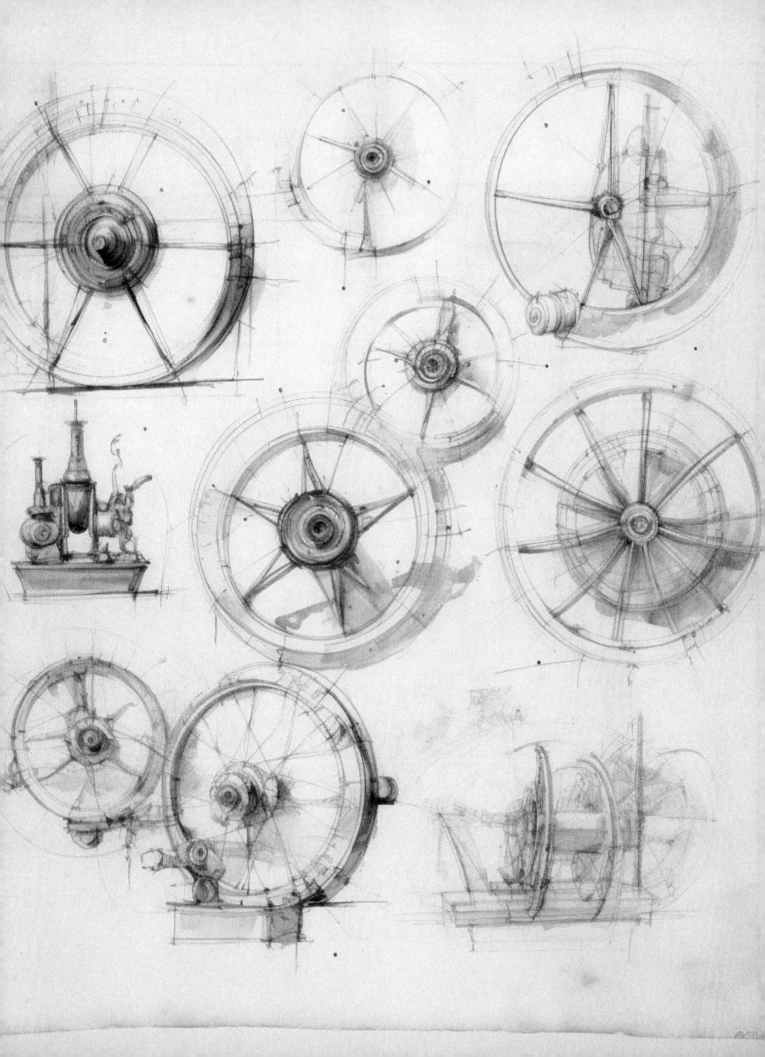

74. CAMOUFLAGE / MIMETIZZAZIONE

Designs for camouflaging military structures.

Leonardo da Vinci, the ingenious mind and artistic genius, applied his exceptional talent and strategic thinking to the design of camouflage techniques for military structures. By use of his visionary sketches and innovative ideas, he strove to develop methods to conceal and blend military installations seamlessly into their surroundings, rendering them difficult to detect by the enemy.

In his designs for camouflaging military structures, Leonardo searched out various strategies and concepts. His sketches depicted the clever use of natural elements, such as foliage, netting, and patterns, to disrupt the visual appearance and disguise the presence of military installations. He understood the importance of adapting to the environment and utilizing the surrounding elements to create an illusion of invisibility.

Leonardo's designs showcased his acute observation skills and understanding of optical illusions. He saw the importance of colors, shapes, and patterns in tricking the human eye and altering perception. His sketches demonstrated his ability to manipulate visual cues and distort depth perception, effectively concealing military structures from prying eyes.

Beyond their strategic value, Leonardo's designs for camouflaging military structures also mirrored his artistic sensibilities. He strove to harmonize the functional requirements of camouflage with aesthetics, considering the visual impact and integration of the structures within the natural territory. His sketches showcased his ability to blend artistry and practicality, creating designs that were both effective and visually appealing.

By use of his studies and sketches of camouflage techniques, Leonardo contributed to the evolution of military strategy and tactics. His ideas and concepts acted as a foundation for future developments in the field of military camouflage, influencing the design of military installations and the tactics employed in warfare.

Inasmuch we dive into Leonardo's designs for camouflaging military structures, here we see his extraordinary ability to merge artistry with innovation. His sketches lead us in to appreciate the power of perception and the strategic value of blending into the environment, highlighting the ever-evolving relationship betwixt warfare and the natural world.

Leonardo da Vinci's sketches of camouflage techniques stand as a confirmation of his lasting heritage as a master of both art and science. His thorough observations and innovative designs allure and inspirit, reminding us of the remarkable synergy betwixt creativity, strategy, and military innovation.

By use of his sketches, Leonardo immortalized the concepts and designs for camouflaging military structures, forever displaying their essence upon the parchment. His heritage as an artist, inventor, and scholar drives home the important impact of strategic thinking and the power of deception in the realm of warfare.

Inasmuch we contemplate Leonardo's designs for camouflaging military structures, we are encouraged to welcome the transformative power of creativity and innovation. His sketches act as a timeless glimmer of the importance of adaptability, cleverness, and the strategic use of art to influence the course of history.

75. CANNONS / CANNONI

Design for a multi-barrelled cannon.

Leonardo da Vinci, the ingenious artist and visionary inventor, turned his attention to the design of a remarkable multi-barrelled cannon. By use of his acute intellect and technical power, he strove to revolutionize the art of warfare with this innovative weapon of destructive power.

In his design for the multi-barrelled cannon, Leonardo envisioned a formidable weapon capable of delivering a undying barrage of firepower upon the enemy. His sketches showcased a scrupulously crafted apparatus, with multiple barrels arranged in a strategic configuration. Each barrel, carefully designed and positioned, represented a channel through which devastation could be unleashed.

Leonardo's design demonstrated his understanding of the principles of artillery and his ability to create a weapon that could significantly impact the course of battle. The multi-barrelled cannon symbolized his visionary approach to warfare, where innovation and cleverness merged with the destructive potential of technology.

The complexities of Leonardo's design for the multi-barrelled cannon went beyond mere functionality. His sketches revealed his attention to detail, displaying the precise mechanisms and complex inner workings of the weapon. Each component, scrupulously rendered, showcased his mastery of both form and function.

Beyond its practical applications, Leonardo's design for the multi-barrelled cannon mirrored his important fascination with the art of warfare. It represented his commitment to exploring new possibilities and pushing the bounds of conventional weaponry. His sketches stood as a confirmation of his steady commitment to boosting the potential of military technology.

Inasmuch we dive into Leonardo's design for the multi-barrelled cannon, here we see his visionary spirit and his important impact on the advancement of military innovation. His sketches lead us in to ponder the evolving nature of warfare and the part of technological advancements in shaping its outcomes.

Leonardo da Vinci's design for the multi-barrelled cannon holdeth as a confirmation of his lasting heritage as a master of invention and creativity. His thorough attention to detail, coupled with his visionary thinking, remains to inspirit generations of engineers and inventors, propelling the advancement of military technology and strategic thinking.

By use of his sketches, Leonardo immortalized the concept and design of the multi-barrelled cannon, forever displaying its essence upon the parchment. His heritage as an artist, inventor, and scholar drives home the remarkable synergy betwixt artistry and warfare, and the important impact that visionary ideas can have on the course of history.

Inasmuch we contemplate Leonardo's design for the multi-barrelled cannon, we are encouraged to stretch the bounds of innovation, to welcome the transformative power of technology, and to consider the complex relationship betwixt invention, warfare, and life.

76. DOMES / CUPOLE

Studies of architectural domes.

Leonardo da Vinci, the brilliant mind and visionary artist, devoted his acute intellect and artistic power to the study and sketching of architectural domes. By use of his thorough observations and detailed drawings, he strove to understand the structural complexities and aesthetic beauty of these magnificent architectural features.

In his studies of architectural domes, Leonardo searched out various designs, styles, and construction techniques. His sketches procured the graceful curves, proportions, and complex details that define these magnificent structures. With each stroke of his pen, he dived into the complexities of dome construction, seeking to untwist the secrets behind their stability and grandeur.

Leonardo's drawings of architectural domes revealed his depthy appreciation for the harmony betwixt form and function. He understood that a dome's structural integrity must be carefully balanced with its visual impact. His sketches showcased his ability to map the relationship of light and shadow, the elegant lines, and the alluring geometry that define these architectural marvels.

By use of his studies, Leonardo aimed to elevate the art of architecture and inspirit future generations of designers and builders. His sketches provided insights into the principles of dome construction, including the innovative use of materials, the distribution of weight, and the creation of complex ornamentation.

Inasmuch we dive into Leonardo's studies of architectural domes, here we see the important impact that these structures have had on human civilization. Domes have adorned sacred and monumental buildings throughout history, serving as symbols of grandeur, spirituality, and architectural achievement. Leonardo's sketches lead us in to appreciate the beauty and cleverness of these structures and to recognize their lasting heritage in shaping our built environment.

Leonardo da Vinci's sketches of architectural domes stand as a confirmation of his lasting heritage as a master of both art and science. His thorough observations and detailed drawings allure and inspirit, reminding us of the remarkable fusion of creativity, engineering, and artistic expression.

By use of his sketches, Leonardo immortalized the essence of architectural domes, forever displaying their significance upon the parchment. His heritage as an artist, inventor, and scholar drives home the remarkable achievements that can be accomplished through human cleverness and the limitless possibilities that arise when artistry and engineering converge.

Inasmuch we contemplate Leonardo's studies of architectural domes, we are encouraged to welcome the transformative power of architecture, to celebrate the beauty of our built environment, and to strive for excellence in both design and construction. His sketches act as a timeless glimmer of the lasting impact of architectural innovation and the important influence that architectural masterpieces have on our lives and collective identity.

77. PYRAMIDS / PIRAMIDI

Geometric studies of pyramids.

Leonardo da Vinci, the extraordinary mind and visionary artist, committed his unlimited curiosity and artistic talent to the exploration and sketching of geometric studies of pyramids. By use of his thorough observations and complex drawings, he strove to untwist the mathematical principles and inherent beauty of these famous structures.

In his geometric studies of pyramids, Leonardo dived into the fundamental properties and complex relationships that define these geometric wonders. His sketches procured the precise angles, symmetries, and proportions that characterize pyramids in their various forms and sizes. With each stroke of his pen, he began on a quest to understand the secrets of their construction and the harmony of their geometric configurations.

Leonardo's drawings of pyramids revealed his depthy appreciation for the relationship of shapes, lines, and volumes. He recognized that pyramids encapsulated the essence of geometric elegance and mathematical precision. His sketches showcased his ability to map the essence of these structures, conveying their grandeur and timeless appeal.

By use of his studies, Leonardo strove to uncover the underlying principles that govern the geometry of pyramids. His sketches provided insights into the symmetry, proportionality, and spatial relationships that define these remarkable structures. They acted as a confirmation of his analytical mind and his ability to translate complex mathematical concepts into visual representations.

Inasmuch we dive into Leonardo's geometric studies of pyramids, here we see the lasting fascination and allure of these geometric marvels. Pyramids have fascinated civilizations throughout history, serving as symbols of power, spirituality, and architectural achievement. Leonardo's sketches lead us in to contemplate the inherent beauty and mathematical harmony embedded within their geometric forms.

Leonardo da Vinci's sketches of geometric studies of pyramids stand as a confirmation of his lasting heritage as a master of both art and science. His thorough observations and complex drawings allure and inspirit, reminding us of the remarkable fusion of creativity and mathematical precision.

By use of his sketches, Leonardo immortalized the essence of geometric studies of pyramids, forever displaying their significance upon the parchment. His heritage as an artist, inventor, and scholar drives home the extraordinary achievements that arise from the synergy of artistry, mathematics, and intellectual curiosity.

Inasmuch we contemplate Leonardo's geometric studies of pyramids, we are encouraged to welcome the beauty of geometry, to appreciate the inherent order and harmony in the world around us, and to strive for excellence in both artistic expression and scientific inquiry. His sketches act as a timeless glimmer of the unlimited possibilities that arise when art, mathematics, and intellectual exploration converge.

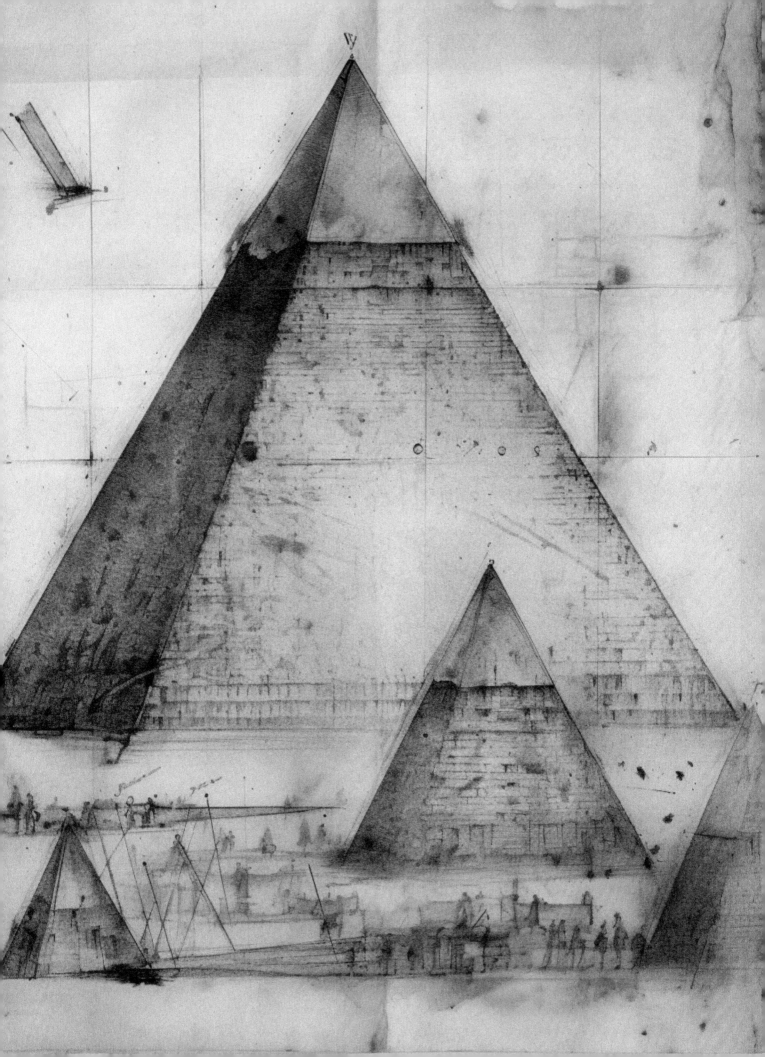

78. CAVERNS / CAVERNE

Sketches and studies of cavernous landscapes.

Leonardo da Vinci, the visionary artist and inquisitive mind, committed his talents to the exploration and sketching of cavernous landscapes. By use of his thorough observations and detailed studies, he strove to untwist the mysteries and map the awe-provoking beauty of these subterranean domains.

In his sketches and studies of cavernous landscapes, Leonardo dived across the nexus of these hidden worlds. His drawings portrayed the vastness, complex formations, and play of light and shadow within the caverns. With each stroke of his pen, he aimed to create the grandeur and enigmatic nature of these underground domains.

Leonardo's sketches revealed his depthy appreciation for the geological wonders that lie beneath the Earth's surface. He procured the majestic stalactites, stalagmites, and other unique formations that adorned the cavernous walls. By use of his thorough attention to detail, he brought to life the complex textures and patterns that define these alluring landscapes.

By use of his studies, Leonardo strove to understand the geological processes that shaped these cavernous landscapes. His sketches depicted the erosion, water flow, and geological forces that sculpted the complex features within the caves. He embraced the challenge of displaying the ethereal beauty and sense of wonder that emanates from these natural wonders.

Inasmuch we dive into Leonardo's sketches and studies of cavernous landscapes, here we see the hidden domains that exist beneath our feet. Caves have allured human imagination since ancient times, serving as mysterious and awe-provoking environments. Leonardo's sketches lead us in to contemplate the important connection betwixt the Earth's surface and the subterranean depths.

Leonardo da Vinci's sketches of cavernous landscapes stand as a confirmation of his lasting heritage as a master of both art and science. His thorough observations and detailed drawings allure and inspirit, reminding us of the remarkable fusion of artistic expression and scientific inquiry.

By use of his sketches, Leonardo immortalized the essence of cavernous landscapes, forever displaying their significance upon the parchment. His heritage as an artist, inventor, and scholar drives home the important beauty and complexity that exist in the natural world.

Inasmuch we contemplate Leonardo's sketches and studies of cavernous landscapes, we are encouraged to appreciate the wonders of our planet, to inquire into the hidden depths, and to recognize the enmeshment of the Earth's diverse landscapes. His sketches act as a timeless glimmer of the beauty that lies beneath the surface, inviting us to start on a quest of discovery and awe.

79. FOUNTAIN DESIGNS / DESIGN DI FONTANE

He had drafted several designs for fountains.

Leonardo da Vinci, the visionary artist and ingenious inventor, committed his creative mind to the drafting of several designs for fountains. By use of his thorough observations and imaginative sketches, he strove to map the beauty, functionality, and artistic essence of these water features.

In his designs for fountains, Leonardo searched out various concepts and techniques to create enchanting displays of water. His sketches portrayed the graceful shapes, complex details, and harmonious proportions that would define these architectural marvels. With each stroke of his pen, he aimed to bring to life the mesmerizing relationship of water and sculpture.

Leonardo's drawings revealed his depthy understanding of hydraulics, aesthetics, and the transformative power of water. He envisioned fountains that would not merely act as sources of refreshment and irrigation but also as awe-provoking works of art. His sketches procured the ingenious mechanisms, complex piping systems, and imaginative sculptural elements that would adorn these fountains.

By use of his designs, Leonardo strove to celebrate the ephemeral nature of water, harnessing its alluring movement and rhythmic flow. His sketches portrayed the enchanting jubilation of water droplets, cascades, and jets, evoking an apparition of tranquility and wonder. Each design mirrored his acute eye for beauty and his steady commitment to pushing the bounds of artistic expression.

Inasmuch we inquire into Leonardo's designs for fountains, here we see the important allure and symbolic significance of these water features. Fountains have allured human imagination throughout history, symbolizing life, purity, and the harmonious union of nature and artifice. Leonardo's sketches lead us in to contemplate the poetic beauty and the transformative power of water in our built environment.

Leonardo da Vinci's sketches of fountain designs stand as a confirmation of his lasting heritage as a master of both art and engineering. His thorough observations, technical expertise, and artistic sensibility inspirit and influence fountain design to this day.

By use of his sketches, Leonardo immortalized the essence of fountain design, forever displaying their significance upon the parchment. His heritage as an artist, inventor, and scholar drives home the remarkable fusion of creativity, engineering, and the elemental forces of nature.

Inasmuch we contemplate Leonardo's designs for fountains, we are encouraged to welcome the beauty and symbolism of these water features, to appreciate the harmony betwixt human creativity and the natural world, and to strive for excellence in both form and function. His sketches act as a timeless glimmer of the transformative power of water and its ability to enhance our surroundings with its mesmerizing presence.

80. HUMAN FIGURES IN MOTION / FIGURE UMANE IN MOVIMENTO

Numerous sketches of mankind's figures in various activities.

Leonardo da Vinci, the masterful artist and acute observer of mankind's nature, filled his sketchbooks with numerous drawings of mankind's figures engaged in various activities. By use of his thorough studies and detailed sketches, he strove to map the essence of mankind's movement, expression, and the complexities of the human form.

In his sketches of mankind's figures, Leonardo searched out the huge range of mankind's activities and emotions. His drawings depicted individuals engaged in everyday tasks, dynamic actions, and contemplative poses. With each stroke of his pen, he endeavored to create the vitality, grace, and diversity of mankind's existence.

Leonardo's sketches revealed his depthy understanding of mankind's anatomy, proportion, and the relationship of light and shadow on the human form. He scrupulously observed the nuances of posture, gesture, and facial expressions, displaying the essence of mankind's emotion and the subtleties of physical movement. His drawings celebrated the beauty and complexity of the human figure, showcasing his remarkable ability to portray the lived experience through art.

By use of his sketches, Leonardo strove to depict the human figure as a conduit for storytelling and expression. His drawings celebrated the human form in all its diversity, showcasing individuals from different walks of life, engaged in various activities, and expressing a wide range of emotions. Each sketch mirrored his acute eye for detail, his curiosity about human behavior, and his important appreciation for life.

Inasmuch we inquire into Leonardo's sketches of mankind's figures, here we see the timeless fascination and endless possibilities of the human form. Human figures have been a central subject of artistic expression throughout history, displaying the essence of humanity, its triumphs, struggles, and aspirations. Leonardo's sketches lead us in to contemplate the depth and richness of the lived experience and to connect with the universal aspects of our shared humanity.

Leonardo da Vinci's sketches of mankind's figures stand as a confirmation of his lasting heritage as a master of both art and observation. His thorough studies and detailed drawings inspirit and influence artists, displaying the essence of the human spirit and the beauty of mankind's form.

By use of his sketches, Leonardo immortalized the diversity and vitality of the human figure, forever displaying their significance upon the parchment. His heritage as an artist, inventor, and scholar drives home the important depth and complexity of the lived experience.

Inasmuch we contemplate Leonardo's sketches of mankind's figures, we are encouraged to welcome the beauty and diversity of the human form, to appreciate the richness of mankind's expression, and to celebrate the universal aspects of our shared humanity. His sketches act as a timeless glimmer of the power of art to map the essence of mankind's existence and to bypass the bounds of time and space.

81. ST. JOHN THE BAPTIST / SAN GIOVANNI BATTISTA

He painted a portrait of St. John the Baptist.

Leonardo da Vinci, the revered artist and master of portraiture, graced the canvas with his exquisite brushwork to create a remarkable portrait of St. John the Baptist. In this alluring painting, Leonardo's skillful hand and acute artistic vision brought to life the enigmatic figure of the revered saint.

The portrait of St. John the Baptist flaunts Leonardo's ability to map the essence of his subject with unparalleled depth and realism. By use of his thorough brushstrokes, he portrayed the saint's radiant countenance, his penetrating peer, and the air of contemplation that emanates from his serene expression. Each stroke of the brush conveyed an apparition of spiritual reverence and an important understanding of the human form.

Leonardo's portrayal of St. John the Baptist goes beyond mere representation; it captures the essence of the saint's important spirituality and his part as a precursor to the divine. The painting exudes an apparition of mystery and introspection, inviting the viewer to contemplate the depthy spiritual significance and symbolism associated with St. John the Baptist.

The relationship of light and shadow in the painting further demonstrates Leonardo's mastery of chiaroscuro, adding depth and dimension to the figure. The contrast betwixt the illuminated face and the dark background acts to heighten the aura of transcendence and spirituality that surrounds the saint.

Inasmuch we peer upon Leonardo's portrait of St. John the Baptist, we are drawn into a world where art and spirituality converge. The painting captures the timeless essence of a revered figure, inviting us to reflect on our own spiritual quest and the quest for inner enlightenment.

Leonardo da Vinci's portrait of St. John the Baptist holdeth as a confirmation of his artistic brilliance and his ability to infuse his subjects with important humanity and spiritual depth. The painting remains to allure viewers with its ethereal beauty and acts as a confirmation of Leonardo's lasting heritage as a master of the human form.

By use of his brushstrokes, Leonardo immortalized the likeness of St. John the Baptist, forever displaying his significance upon the canvas. His heritage as an artist, inventor, and scholar drives home the important impact that art can have on our understanding of the lived experience and the domains of the divine.

Inasmuch we contemplate Leonardo's portrait of St. John the Baptist, we are encouraged to welcome the power of art to bypass the limitations of time and space, to dive across the nexus of spirituality, and to inquire into the complex dimensions of mankind's soul. His painting acts as a timeless glimmer of the transformative nature of art and its ability to create important truths about life.

82. TOWN PLANNING / PIANIFICAZIONE URBANA

Leonardo had plans for efficient town designs.

Leonardo da Vinci, the visionary artist and polymath, committed his ingenious mind to the development of efficient town designs. By use of his thorough planning and innovative ideas, he strove to create urban environments that would enhance the quality of life for their inhabitants and promote harmonious living.

Leonardo's plans for efficient town designs were rooted in his depthy understanding of mankind's needs, infrastructure, and the principles of aesthetics. He envisioned towns that would optimize space utilization, transportation systems, and public services. His designs incorporated elements such as enmeshed streets, efficient water management, and strategically located public spaces.

In his town designs, Leonardo emphasized the importance of sustainable development and the integration of nature within the urban fabric. His plans featured green spaces, gardens, and tree-lined boulevards, aiming to create a balance betwixt built structures and the natural environment. Leonardo saw the importance of a harmonious relationship betwixt humans and their surroundings.

Leonardo's vision for efficient town designs also considered the social aspect of urban living. He proposed the inclusion of communal spaces, gathering areas, and civic buildings that would nourish an apparition of community and promote social interaction. His plans strove to create an environment where people could thrive, connect, and engage in meaningful relationships.

Inasmuch we inquire into Leonardo's plans for efficient town designs, here we see the lasting importance of urban planning and its impact on our daily lives. Cities and towns shape our experiences, influence our prosperity, and contribute to the overall fabric of society. Leonardo's ideas lead us in to reconsider our approach to urban development and to strive for designs that prioritize sustainability, functionality, and the prosperity of inhabitants.

Leonardo da Vinci's plans for efficient town designs stand as a confirmation of his visionary thinking and his commitment to improving life. His thorough planning, innovative ideas, and forward-thinking concepts inspirit architects, urban planners, and thinkers in the present day.

By use of his designs, Leonardo offered a specter into a future where towns and cities could be designed with efficiency, beauty, and human prosperity in mind. His heritage as an artist, inventor, and scholar drives home the transformative power of design and its potential to shape our lives and communities for the better.

Inasmuch we contemplate Leonardo's plans for efficient town designs, we are encouraged to envision cities and towns that prioritize sustainability, connectivity, and the creation of coruscating, livable spaces. His designs act as a timeless glimmer of the importance of thoughtful urban planning and its potential to create environments that enrich our lives and contribute to a more harmonious society.

83. THE ELEMENTS / GLI ELEMENTI

Studies and sketches about the classical elements - fire, earth, water, and air.

Leonardo da Vinci, the visionary artist and scholar, dived into the study of the classical elements - fire, earth, water, and air - By use of his thorough studies and sketches. His exploration of these fundamental forces of nature strove to uncover their secrets, understand their properties, and map their essence through art.

In his studies and sketches of the classical elements, Leonardo observed and contemplated the complexities of each element's behavior and characteristics. He scrupulously observed the flickering flames of fire, the solidity and stability of earth, the fluidity and movement of water, and the intangible and ethereal nature of air. By use of his acute eye and insightful observations, he strove to understand the essence of these elements that shape our world.

Leonardo's sketches of the classical elements reflect his depthy fascination with the natural world and his desire to comprehend its workings. His drawings procured the dynamic relationship of these elements and the impact they have on the environment and lived experience. With each stroke of his pen, he strove to depict the transformative power, beauty, and complexity inherent in fire, earth, water, and air.

By use of his studies, Leonardo recognized the enmeshment and balance of the classical elements. He understood how fire consumes and transforms, how earth provides a foundation for life, how water nourishes and sustains, and how air permeates all spaces. His sketches portrayed the harmony and interdependence of these elements, offering a specter into the complex nexus of nature.

Inasmuch we inquire into Leonardo's studies and sketches of the classical elements, here we see the timeless significance and universal presence of these fundamental forces. Fire, earth, water, and air have been revered and contemplated by cultures throughout history, symbolizing the essence of existence and the forces that shape our world. Leonardo's sketches lead us in to contemplate the power and beauty of these elements and their important impact on our lives.

Leonardo da Vinci's studies and sketches of the classical elements stand as a confirmation of his unquenchable curiosity and his depthy reverence for the natural world. His thorough observations, technical expertise, and artistic sensibility inspirit and influence our understanding of the elements that surround us.

By use of his sketches, Leonardo immortalized the dynamic nature of the classical elements, forever displaying their significance upon the parchment. His heritage as an artist, inventor, and scholar drives home the important enmeshment of the natural world and our place within it.

Inasmuch we contemplate Leonardo's studies and sketches of the classical elements, we are encouraged to welcome the beauty, power, and mystery of nature. His sketches act as a timeless glimmer of the transformative nature of the elements and their ability to shape our world and ignite our imagination.

84. THE EYE / L'OCCHIO

Detailed studies of the human eye.

Leonardo da Vinci, the renowned artist and acute observer of mankind's anatomy, committed his talents to conducting detailed studies of the human eye. By use of his thorough observations and exquisite sketches, he strove to untwist the mysteries and complexities of this remarkable organ.

Leonardo's studies of the human eye lay bare his steady fascination with its complex structure and the necessary part it plays in the lived experience. With every stroke of his pen, he procured the swift curves, the relationship of light and shadow, and the mesmerizing complexities of this extraordinary sensory organ.

In his quest to understand the human eye, Leonardo scrupulously observed its various components. He studied the shape and curvature of the cornea, the crystalline lens, and the complex connections of veins and arteries that nourish this necessary organ. By use of his drawings, he strove to lay bare the inner workings of the eye, starting with the complex mechanism of the iris to the swift sensitivity of the retina.

Leonardo's studies of the human eye went beyond mere anatomical accuracy; they dived into the domains of perception, vision, and the mysteries of sight. He strove to map not merely the physical attributes of the eye but also its important connection to the human mind and its ability to perceive and interpret the world around us.

By use of his sketches, Leonardo endeavored to create the depth and complexity of the human eye's capabilities. He observed how the eye could focus, dilate, and adapt to varying light conditions. His studies procured the complexities of vision, showcasing the eye's remarkable ability to perceive depth, color, and movement.

Leonardo's thorough attention to detail in his studies of the human eye mirrored his unquenchable curiosity and his undying followings forth of knowledge. His observations and sketches laid the foundation for our understanding of ocular anatomy and vision, contributing to advancements in the fields of optometry and ophthalmology.

Inasmuch we peer upon Leonardo's studies of the human eye, here we see the remarkable complexities of this miraculous organ. The eye acts as a window to the world, allowing us to perceive its beauty, navigate our surroundings, and connect with others. Leonardo's sketches inspirit us to appreciate the wonders of our own vision and the extraordinary gift of sight.

Leonardo da Vinci's studies of the human eye stand as a confirmation of his exceptional skills as both an artist and a scientist. His thorough observations and detailed sketches inspirit and educate, shedding light on the inner workings of this alluring organ.

By use of his sketches, Leonardo immortalized the marvels of the human eye, forever displaying their significance upon the parchment. His heritage as an artist, inventor, and scholar drives home the important complexities of the human body and the unlimited wonders of the natural world.

Inasmuch we contemplate Leonardo's studies of the human eye, we are encouraged to swoon at the beauty and complexity of this precious gift of sight. His sketches act as a timeless glimmer of the remarkable capabilities of the human eye and the endless possibilities that unfold before us with every peer.

85. INVENTIONS / INVENZIONI

Sketches of his various invention concepts.

Leonardo da Vinci, the visionary artist and inventive genius, filled his sketchbooks with a multitude of alluring drawings depicting his various invention concepts. Through these sketches, he brought to life innovative ideas that pushed the bounds of technological possibilities during his time.

Leonardo's sketches of invention concepts reflect his unquenchable curiosity, unlimited imagination, and depthy understanding of mechanics and engineering. With thorough detail and artistic flair, he searched out a wide range of ideas, from flying machines and hydraulic systems to weaponry and architectural innovations.

In his sketches, Leonardo procured the complexities of his invention concepts, showcasing his exceptional ability to merge artistry with scientific exploration. Each stroke of his pen relayed a new vision, offering glimpses into a future where machines and technology would revolutionize human existence.

Amid his sketches of invention concepts, his designs for flying machines stand out as famous examples of his visionary thinking. With a acute understanding of aerodynamics, Leonardo sketched complex contraptions resembling wings and propellers, exploring the possibilities of mankind's flight. These sketches foreshadowed the advancements in aviation that would unfold centuries later.

In addition to his fascination with flight, Leonardo's invention concepts encompassed a wide range of fields. He designed innovative mechanisms for water transportation, showcasing his understanding of hydrodynamics and navigation. His sketches also included ingenious devices for warfare, such as multi-barreled cannons and tank-like vehicles.

Leonardo's sketches of invention concepts not merely demonstrated his technical expertise but also mirrored his depthy concern for the betterment of society. He envisioned machines and systems that aimed to improve the quality of life, enhance efficiency, and promote progress. His designs strove to harness the power of nature, optimize human potential, and shape a more advanced and harmonious world.

Inasmuch we examine Leonardo's sketches of invention concepts, we are allured by the brilliance of his ideas and the breadth of his visionary thinking. His sketches inspirit inventors, engineers, and artists, fueling innovation and pushing the bounds of what is possible.

Leonardo da Vinci's sketches of invention concepts stand as a confirmation of his lasting heritage as an inventor and a firstman of technological advancement. His imaginative ideas and inventive spirit remind us of the power of mankind's creativity and the limitless potential that lies within us.

By use of his sketches, Leonardo immortalized his invention concepts, forever displaying their significance upon the parchment. His heritage as an artist, scientist, and visionary acts as a constant glimmer that innovation and imagination can shape the course of mankind's history.

Inasmuch we inquire into Leonardo's sketches of invention concepts, we are encouraged to welcome our own creative potential, to imagine and dream of a future where new technologies and ideas can reshape the world. His sketches act as a timeless glimmer that innovation knows no bounds and that the human spirit has the power to transform possibilities into reality.

86. ENGINEERING MACHINES / MACCHINE DI INGEGNERIA

Designs of various machinery for engineering projects.

Leonardo da Vinci, the brilliant mind of the Renaissance, left behind a wealth of sketches showcasing his designs for various machinery used in engineering projects. These complex drawings lay bare his important understanding of mechanics and his undying followings forth of innovation in the realm of engineering.

Amid Leonardo's sketches are designs for machinery that spanned a wide range of applications. He envisioned machines for construction and excavation, including cranes, hoists, and pulley systems that could lift heavy loads with ease. His sketches showcased his depthy appreciation for the principles of leverage and mechanical advantage.

In addition to construction machinery, Leonardo's sketches included designs for hydraulic systems, illustrating his grasp of fluid dynamics. He envisioned mechanisms that could harness the power of water to drive mills, pumps, and other engineering devices. His thorough attention to detail and understanding of water flow allowed him to create efficient and effective designs.

Leonardo's sketches also revealed his fascination with transportation and mobility. He designed innovative vehicles, including prototypes of self-propelled carriages and even rudimentary versions of bicycles. His sketches demonstrate his forward-thinking approach to transportation and his desire to improve the ways in which people traveled.

Furthermore, Leonardo's designs for machinery extended to his exploration of renewable energy sources. He sketched ideas for windmills and waterwheels, harnessing the power of nature to generate energy. His visionary approach to sustainable energy foreshadowed modern advancements in renewable technologies.

Each of Leonardo's sketches for machinery reflects his steady commitment to practical problem-solving and his undying followings forth of efficiency and effectiveness. His designs strove to simplify tasks, enhance productivity, and stretch the bounds of engineering knowledge during his time.

The intricacy and precision of Leonardo's sketches demonstrate his mastery of both art and science. His ability to translate his visionary ideas into detailed drawings set him apart as a true polymath of his time. His sketches inspirit engineers and inventors, serving as a confirmation of the power of imagination and innovation in the field of engineering.

Inasmuch we examine Leonardo's designs of machinery, here we see the remarkable depth of his intellect and his ability to bridge the gap betwixt art and engineering. His sketches lead us in to appreciate the beauty and functionality of his designs and to recognize the lasting impact of his contributions to the field of engineering.

Leonardo da Vinci's designs of machinery embody his important understanding of mechanics and his passion for pushing the bounds of mankind's achievement. His sketches act as a glimmer of the indomitable spirit of innovation and the potential for human cleverness to shape the world around us.

By use of his sketches, Leonardo immortalized his designs for machinery, forever displaying their significance upon the parchment. His heritage as an inventor, artist, and engineer acts as a lasting impetus for future generations, encouraging us to dream, create, and stretch the bounds of what is possible in the world of engineering.

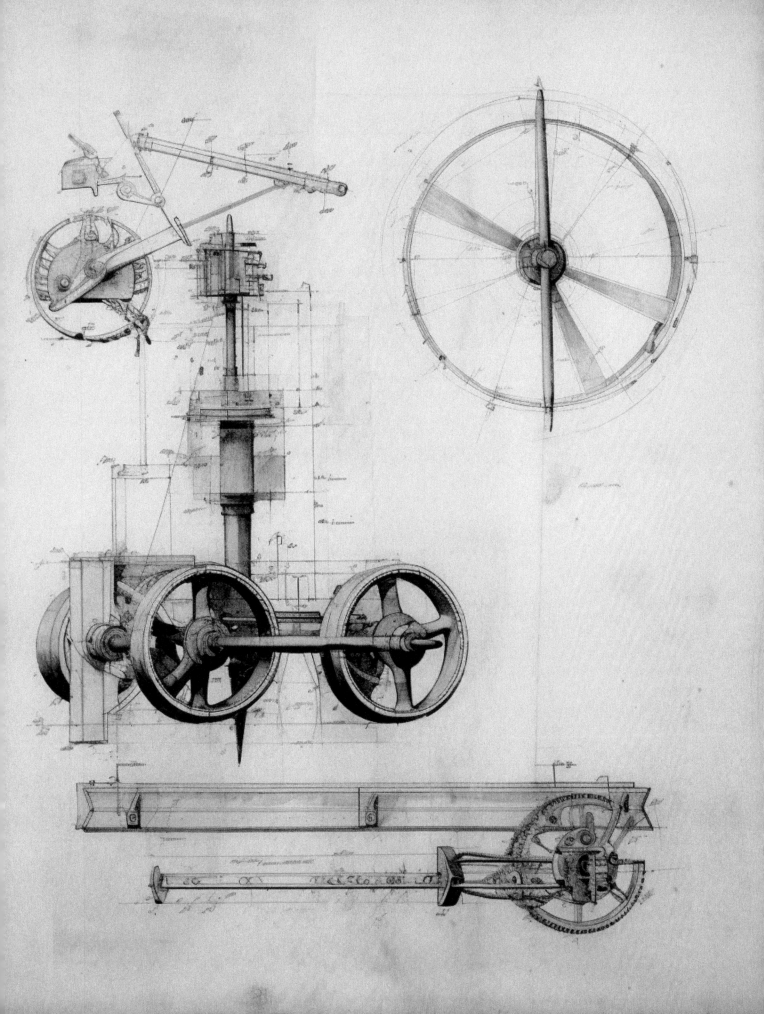

87. MYTHOLOGICAL CREATURES / CREATURE MITOLOGICHE

Sketches of creatures like dragons.

Amid the diverse array of sketches left by Leonardo da Vinci, one can find alluring depictions of mythical creatures, including the majestic and awe-provoking dragons. These sketches offer a specter into Leonardo's imaginative exploration of the fantastical world, where myth and reality intertwine.

In his sketches of dragons, Leonardo's creativity knows no bounds. With his skilled hand and acute eye for detail, he brings these mythical creatures to life on the parchment. His drawings show off the complex scales, the graceful curves of their bodies, and the fierce expressions that embody the essence of these legendary beings.

Leonardo's fascination with dragons reflects his unquenchable curiosity and his ability to bridge the gap betwixt the real and the imaginary. By use of his sketches, he strove to map the essence of these mythical creatures and to inquire into their symbolism and significance in human culture and mythology.

While dragons may exist only in the domains of folklore and imagination, Leonardo's sketches offer a tangible connection to these mythical beasts. His attention to anatomical details and his understanding of natural forms lend an air of realism to his depictions, allowing us to envision these creatures as if they were part of our own world.

Beyond their artistic allure, Leonardo's sketches of dragons act as a confirmation of his mastery of composition and form. His ability to map the dynamic movements and complex features of these creatures flaunts his exceptional skill as an artist. These sketches inspirit awe and wonder, transporting us to a realm where imagination takes flight.

Inasmuch we peer upon Leonardo's sketches of dragons, here we see the power of myth and the lasting fascination with these legendary creatures. They embody our collective imagination and reflect our desires for adventure, mystery, and the unlimited possibilities that lie beyond the confines of our everyday reality.

Leonardo's sketches of dragons not merely entertain and allure, but also lead us in to reflect on the part of mythical creatures in human culture and storytelling. They remind us of the universal human fascination with the unknown and the lasting power of imagination to shape our understanding of the world.

By use of his sketches, Leonardo immortalized the enigmatic allure of dragons, forever displaying their essence upon the parchment. His heritage as an artist and visionary remains to inspirit artists, writers, and dreamers alike, encouraging us to inquire across the nexus of our own imagination and welcome the fantastical wonders that lie within.

Inasmuch we dive into Leonardo's sketches of dragons, we are invited to welcome the magic and wonder of mythical creatures and to celebrate the unlimited creativity that resides within each of us. These sketches stand as a confirmation of Leonardo's lasting heritage and his ability to transport us to worlds beyond our own, where imagination knows no limits and where the fantastical becomes tangible.

88. VIRGIN MARY / VERGINE MARIA

Various sketches and paintings of the Virgin Mary.

Amid the huge collection of sketches and paintings left behind by Leonardo da Vinci, one can find a multitude of depictions of the revered figure of the Virgin Mary. These sketches and paintings show off Leonardo's important reverence for this famous religious figure and his exceptional artistic skill in displaying her grace and beauty.

Leonardo's sketches and paintings of the Virgin Mary exude an apparition of serenity and spiritual depth. By use of his masterful use of light and shadow, he brings forth the ethereal glow that surrounds her, emphasizing her divine nature. His attention to detail and the swift rendering of her features reflect his steady devotion to displaying the essence of the Madonna.

In each sketch and painting, Leonardo explores different aspects of the Virgin Mary's character and part in religious narratives. From the tender depiction of the Madonna and Child, to her serene presence in scenes of the Annunciation or the Assumption, Leonardo's interpretations map the essence of her maternal love, purity, and compassion.

Leonardo's portrayal of the Virgin Mary goes beyond religious iconography; it reveals his depthy appreciation for the beauty of the human form and his mastery of artistic techniques. His use of soft, flowing lines and subtle color transitions infuse his depictions with an apparition of tranquility and grace. Each brushstroke and pencil mark conveys a reverence for both the subject and the act of creation itself.

By use of his sketches and paintings, Leonardo invites viewers to contemplate the divine and to experience an important sense of spirituality. His depictions of the Virgin Mary act as a bridge betwixt the earthly and the divine, inviting viewers to connect with their own faith and sense of wonder.

Inasmuch we admire Leonardo's sketches and paintings of the Virgin Mary, here we see the lasting power of religious art to inspirit and uplift the human spirit. They stand as a confirmation of Leonardo's ability to map the essence of his subjects and to evoke an important emotional response in the viewer.

Leonardo's sketches and paintings of the Virgin Mary be revered as masterpieces of religious art. They remind us of the lasting heritage of the Madonna as a symbol of grace, love, and devotion. By use of his artistry, Leonardo invites us to contemplate the mysteries of faith and to find solace in the presence of the divine.

Inasmuch we contemplate Leonardo's sketches and paintings of the Virgin Mary, we are invited to inquire into our own spiritual quest and to appreciate the beauty and power of religious art. They stand as a confirmation of Leonardo's artistic genius and his ability to map the divine in human form.

Leonardo's depictions of the Virgin Mary remain timeless, continuing to inspirit and resonate with viewers across generations. By use of his art, he has immortalized the beauty, grace, and significance of the Virgin Mary, leaving a lasting heritage that remains to allure and uplift the hearts and souls of those who behold his works.

89. APOSTLES / APOSTOLI

Sketches and studies of the apostles.

Within the large body of work left behind by Leonardo da Vinci, one can see a multitude of sketches and studies committed to the apostles. These thorough drawings and studies show off Leonardo's fascination with these revered figures and his undying followings forth of understanding their character and essence.

Leonardo's sketches and studies of the apostles lay bare his depthy interest in displaying the human form and expressing the complexities of individual personalities. Each sketch is imbued with an apparition of reverence and a desire to unveil the innermost depths of these important figures in Christian tradition.

By use of his masterful use of lines and shading, Leonardo breathes life into the apostles, displaying their unique features and expressions. His attention to detail is apparent in the careful rendering of their faces, hands, and gestures, allowing viewers to specter into their inner thoughts and emotions.

In his studies, Leonardo explores the nuances of each apostle's character, seeking to understand and create their distinct qualities and contributions. From the steadfast faith of Peter to the enigmatic wisdom of John, Leonardo's sketches offer a window into the diverse personalities and roles of the apostles.

While the sketches may remain incomplete, they act as a confirmation of Leonardo's unyielding commitment to displaying the essence of his subjects. His studies of the apostles demonstrate his commitment to understanding human nature and the complexities of character, transcending the bounds of time and space.

Leonardo's sketches and studies of the apostles invite viewers to reflect on the universal themes of faith, devotion, and lived experience. By use of his artistry, he brings these revered figures closer to us, offering an opportunity to connect with their stories and teachings on a deeper level.

Inasmuch we examine Leonardo's sketches and studies of the apostles, here we see the lasting heritage of these figures and their impact on the Christian faith. Leonardo's artistry allows us to contemplate their significance and reflect on the timeless messages they impart to humanity.

Leonardo's sketches and studies of the apostles stand as a confirmation of his artistic genius and his ability to map the essence of his subjects. They act as a bridge betwixt the past and the present, inviting us to dive into the important narratives and teachings associated with these central figures in Christian tradition.

By use of his art, Leonardo immortalized the apostles, forever displaying their essence upon the parchment. His sketches inspirit and allure viewers, offering a specter into life and the lasting power of faith.

Leonardo's sketches and studies of the apostles leave an indelible mark on the annals of art history. They act as a glimmer of his artistic brilliance and his commitment to displaying the complexities of the human spirit. These sketches offer us an opportunity to contemplate the lives and teachings of the apostles, encouraging us to reflect on our own journeys of faith and spiritual growth.

Inasmuch we contemplate Leonardo's sketches and studies of the apostles, here we see the transformative power of art and its ability to connect us with important truths and timeless wisdom. They stand as a confirmation of Leonardo's steady followings forth of understanding and his lasting impact on the art world and beyond.

90. CHRIST / CRISTO

Various sketches and paintings of Christ.

Within the huge collection of sketches and paintings left behind by Leonardo da Vinci, one can see a multitude of depictions of Christ. These sketches and paintings, crafted with thorough detail and important reverence, illuminate Leonardo's exploration of the divine figure of Jesus Christ.

Leonardo's sketches and paintings of Christ bypass mere representation; they strive to map the essence of divinity and humanity intertwined. By use of his artistry, he endeavors to create the spiritual depth and universal significance of Christ's teachings and sacrifice.

In each sketch and painting, Leonardo masterfully portrays the countenance of Christ, embodying both compassion and wisdom. His careful study of facial expressions and subtle nuances reveals his commitment to displaying the multifaceted nature of Christ's character.

By use of his skillful use of light and shadow, Leonardo infuses his depictions of Christ with a divine radiance, symbolizing the illumination that emanates from the Savior. The gentle contours of his face, the serene peer, and the tender gestures speak of the important love and compassion Christ represents.

Leonardo's portrayal of Christ extendeth beyond religious iconography; it dives into the complexities of the lived experience. His artistry strives to bridge the gap betwixt the earthly and the divine, inviting viewers to connect with the teachings of Christ on a deeply personal and spiritual level.

By use of his sketches and paintings, Leonardo invites contemplation and introspection, urging viewers to reflect on the timeless message of Christ's life, teachings, and sacrifice. His depictions act as visual reminders of the transformative power of faith and the unlimited love and grace bestowed upon humanity.

Leonardo's sketches and paintings of Christ resonate with viewers across generations, touching the depths of the human spirit and evoking an apparition of awe and reverence. His artistic interpretations inspirit contemplation, introspection, and a deepening of one's own faith.

Inasmuch we peer upon Leonardo's sketches and paintings of Christ, here we see the lasting power of religious art to inspirit and uplift. They stand as testaments to Leonardo's artistic brilliance and his ability to map the divine essence in human form.

Leonardo's depictions of Christ act as a bridge betwixt the sacred and the secular, inviting us to reflect on the universal themes of love, forgiveness, and redemption. They embody the transformative potential of art to awaken spiritual insights and to nourish a deeper understanding of our own humanity.

By use of his art, Leonardo immortalized the image of Christ, forever displaying the essence of his divine presence upon the canvas. His sketches and paintings inspirit and resonate, offering solace, guidance, and an important sense of connection to the teachings and example of Jesus Christ.

Inasmuch we contemplate Leonardo's sketches and paintings of Christ, here we see the important impact that art can have on our spiritual lives. They stand as lasting testimonies to Leonardo's artistic genius and his steady devotion to displaying the divine in human form.

Leonardo's sketches and paintings of Christ leave an indelible mark on the annals of art history, inviting us to dive into the mysteries of faith and the timeless teachings of Christ. They act as a confirmation of the power of art to inspirit, uplift, and lead us on a transformative quest of the soul.

91. DOGS / CANI

Studies of dogs.

Amid Leonardo da Vinci's huge array of sketches, one can find numerous studies committed to the faithful companionship of dogs. Through these sketches, Leonardo captures the essence of these loyal creatures, exploring their anatomical structure, movement, and unique characteristics.

Leonardo's studies of dogs lay bare his fascination with the natural world and his desire to understand the complexities of living beings. With thorough attention to detail, he captures the various breeds and sizes of dogs, showcasing their diverse forms and features.

In his sketches, Leonardo portrays dogs in different poses and activities, from playful and alert to serene and restful. By use of his acute observation and skilled use of lines, he brings forth their distinctive personalities and expressions, reflecting their innate qualities and behaviors.

Leonardo's studies of dogs go beyond mere representation; they aim to untwist the essence of these creatures, delving into their instincts, movements, and interactions with the world around them. His acute eye for detail allows him to map the beauty and grace of these animals in their most authentic form.

By use of his artistry, Leonardo conveys a depthy appreciation for the companionship and loyalty of dogs, recognizing their significance in human lives. His studies invite viewers to reflect on the bond betwixt humans and animals, celebrating the unconditional love and companionship that dogs offer.

Inasmuch we observe Leonardo's studies of dogs, here we see the complex enmeshment of all living creatures and the wonder of nature's creations. His sketches act as a confirmation of his curiosity and his undying followings forth of understanding the world around him.

Leonardo's studies of dogs resonate with viewers, displaying the timeless appeal of these beloved animals. By use of his art, he immortalizes their spirit and essence, reminding us of the joy, love, and companionship they bring to our lives.

Inasmuch we contemplate Leonardo's studies of dogs, here we see the power of observation and the importance of appreciating the beauty and uniqueness of all living beings. His sketches stand as a tribute to the wonders of the natural world and the harmony that exists within it.

Leonardo's studies of dogs remain a confirmation of his artistic genius and his steady commitment to exploring the complexities of life. They lead us in to deepen our connection with the animal kingdom and to cherish the valuable part that dogs play in our lives.

By use of his art, Leonardo invites us to appreciate the beauty and grace of dogs and to recognize the important impact they have on our existence. His studies of these faithful companions act as a glimmer of the lasting bond betwixt humans and animals, and the enrichment they bring to our lives.

Leonardo's sketches of dogs are a celebration of the remarkable diversity and character found in the canine world. They map the essence of these creatures, immortalizing their beauty and essence upon the pages of his sketchbooks, and provoking us to recognize and treasure the extraordinary presence of dogs in our lives.

92. CLOTHING DESIGNS / DESIGN DI ABITI

Sketches of clothing designs and how they fit on the human body.

Within Leonardo da Vinci's large collection of sketches, one can see a multitude of drawings committed to clothing designs and their relationship to the human body. These sketches show off Leonardo's acute eye for detail, his understanding of form and proportion, and his ability to map the essence of garments and their interaction with the human form.

In his sketches of clothing designs, Leonardo explores the complex relationship betwixt fabric and the human body. With thorough precision, he examines how various garments drape, fold, and conform to different body shapes and movements. By use of his artistry, he seeks to understand the harmonious balance betwixt clothing and the human figure.

Leonardo's sketches demonstrate his depthy appreciation for the art of tailoring and his quest for perfecting the fit and functionality of clothing. He carefully studies the construction of garments, starting with the complex folds and pleats to the placement of seams and fastenings. His attention to detail allows him to map the subtle nuances of how clothing drapes and accentuates the human form.

By use of his sketches, Leonardo explores a wide range of clothing designs, starting with the elaborate attire of the aristocracy to the simple garments of everyday life. He examines the relationship of fabrics, textures, and colors, seeking to create a visual harmony that enhances the beauty and elegance of the wearer.

Leonardo's studies of clothing designs also lay bare his fascination with the cultural and historical context of fashion. He draws impetus from different periods and regions, incorporating elements of various styles and traditions into his sketches. His exploration of clothing acts as a window into the social and cultural dynamics of different eras.

Inasmuch we examine Leonardo's sketches of clothing designs, here we see the important influence that fashion has on our exuberance and identity. His drawings lead us in to reflect on the significance of attire and how it can shape our perception of ourselves and others.

Leonardo's sketches of clothing designs are not merely technical drawings; they are artistic expressions that evoke emotion and map the essence of style. They lead us in to appreciate the craftsmanship and artistry behind the creation of garments and to recognize the transformative power of fashion.

By use of his art, Leonardo celebrates the beauty and diversity of clothing, honoring its ability to enhance and adorn the human form. His sketches inspirit us to welcome the art of dressing and to recognize the inherent creativity and personal expression found in fashion.

Leonardo's sketches of clothing designs stand as a confirmation of his artistic genius and his important understanding of the intimate relationship betwixt clothing and the human body. They remind us of the timeless allure of fashion and its ability to allure and inspirit.

Inasmuch we contemplate Leonardo's sketches of clothing designs, here we see the complex relationship betwixt art and fashion, and the potential for clothing to be a form of exuberance and personal identity. His sketches lead us in to inquire into the world of design, style, and craftsmanship, encouraging us to appreciate the beauty and cleverness found in the art of clothing.

93. SEWING MACHINES / MACCHINE DA CUCIRE

Leonardo da Vinci designed a needle and bobbin system.

Leonardo da Vinci, renowned for his versatile genius, ventured beyond his artistic pursuits to inquire into the realm of engineering and innovation. Amid his wide array of designs and sketches, he conceptualized a needle and bobbin system, showcasing his cleverness and forward-thinking approach.

Leonardo's needle and bobbin system was a confirmation of his curiosity and practical mindset. With a acute understanding of textile production and the complexities of stitching, he strove to improve and streamline the process. By use of his designs, he aimed to create a mechanism that would enhance efficiency and precision in the art of sewing.

In his sketches, Leonardo scrupulously depicted the complex components of the needle and bobbin system. He envisioned a mechanism that would enable smooth and controlled movement, allowing the needle to penetrate fabric with ease while the bobbin held and released thread in a synchronized manner.

Leonardo's designs incorporated innovative features to enhance the functionality of the needle and bobbin system. His attention to detail extended to the material selection, structural integrity, and ergonomics of the apparatus. With his characteristic curiosity and meticulousness, he searched out various possibilities, seeking to create a tool that would revolutionize textile production.

By use of his needle and bobbin system, Leonardo aimed to improve the efficiency and quality of sewing, envisioning a device that would aid craftsmen and seamstresses in their work. His designs mirrored his commitment to merging artistry with practicality, as he recognized the importance of technological advancements in the realm of textile production.

Although Leonardo's needle and bobbin system may not have been realized during his lifetime, his innovative spirit and commitment to improvement paved the way for future developments in the field of sewing and textile manufacturing. His designs inspirit inventors and engineers, fueling advancements in the realm of needlework.

Leonardo da Vinci's needle and bobbin system represents his undying followings forth of knowledge and his steady commitment to innovation. By use of his sketches, he left behind a heritage of creativity and forward-thinking, reminding us of the important impact that his ideas and designs have had on various fields of study.

Inasmuch we reflect upon Leonardo's needle and bobbin system, here we see his remarkable ability to bypass bounds and inquire into diverse disciplines. His designs act as a confirmation of his vision and his desire to improve the world around him, leaving an indelible mark on the domains of art, science, and technology.

Leonardo's needle and bobbin system exemplifies his lasting heritage as a visionary and innovator. It holdeth as a confirmation of his unlimited imagination and his ability to conceive ideas that bypass time. His sketches inspirit and ignite the spirit of exploration, propelling us forward on a quest of discovery and innovation.

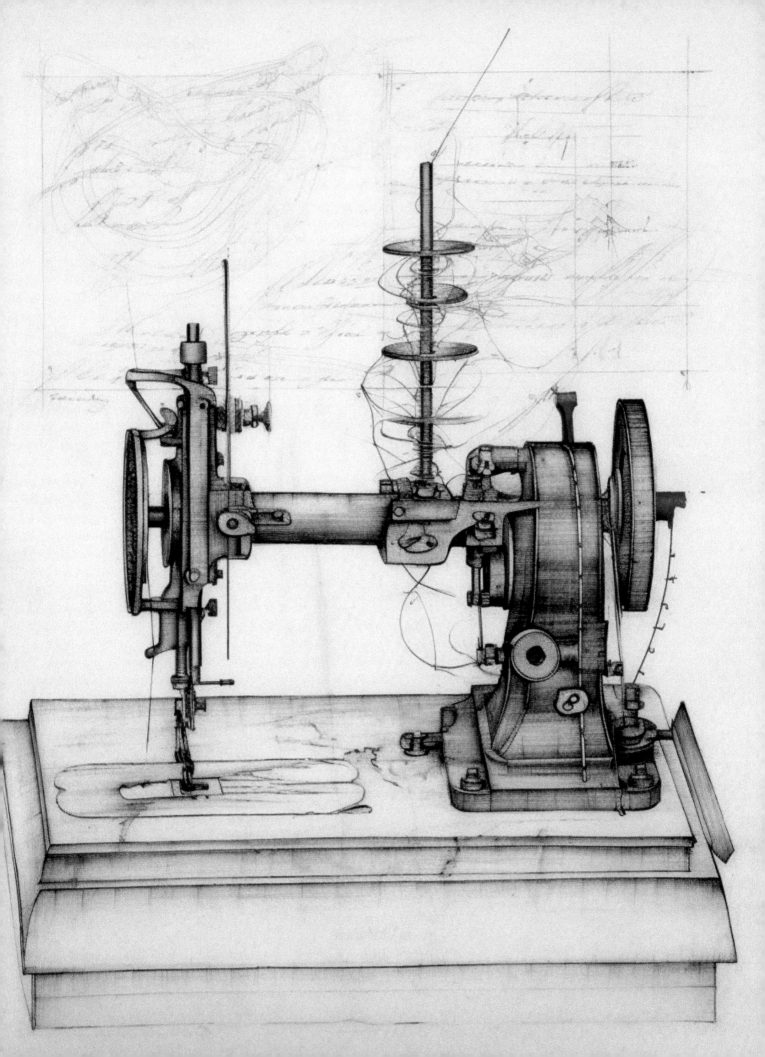

94. SAINT ANNE / SANT'ANNA

He painted "The Virgin and Child with Saint Anne."

"The Virgin and Child with Saint Anne" is a renowned painting that Leonardo da Vinci wisely crafted with his artistic power. In this masterpiece, Leonardo illustrates the tender and important relationship betwixt the Virgin Mary, the child Jesus, and Saint Anne, Mary's mother.

By use of his brushstrokes and attention to detail, Leonardo captures the swift and serene expressions on the faces of the three figures. The Virgin Mary, adorned in her ethereal beauty, cradles the infant Jesus in her arms while Saint Anne, a figure of wisdom and maternal love, gazes upon them with an apparition of reverence and adoration.

The painting flaunts Leonardo's exceptional ability to portray human emotions and relationships with depth and sensitivity. The tender interaction betwixt Mary, Jesus, and Saint Anne conveys an apparition of important love, devotion, and familial connection, inviting viewers to contemplate the sacred bond betwixt mother and child.

Leonardo's artistic genius shows in the composition and arrangement of the figures, as well as the subtle play of light and shadow. He wisely blends colors, textures, and tones to create a harmonious and alluring visual narrative.

"The Virgin and Child with Saint Anne" is a confirmation of Leonardo's mastery of technique and his ability to breathe life into his subjects. The painting captures a snapshot frozen in time, inviting viewers to engage with the spiritual and emotional dimensions conveyed through the figures' expressions and gestures.

Inasmuch we contemplate this masterpiece, here we see the timeless themes of love, faith, and maternal devotion. Leonardo's painting acts as an impetus, evoking an apparition of awe and reverence for the divine and the human connections that shape our lives.

"The Virgin and Child with Saint Anne" holdeth as a confirmation of Leonardo's lasting heritage as one of the greatest artists of all time. It invites us to appreciate the beauty and power of his art, while also encouraging us to reflect on the deeper meanings and significance behind the imagery.

By use of his masterful brushwork, Leonardo invites us into a world of beauty, grace, and spirituality. "The Virgin and Child with Saint Anne" remains a confirmation of his extraordinary talent and his ability to map the essence of mankind's emotions and the divine in his art.

Inasmuch we admire this masterpiece, here we see the important impact that Leonardo da Vinci has had on the world of art, leaving an indelible mark By use of his exceptional skill, vision, and steady commitment to his craft.

95. JUDAS / GIUDA

He painted Judas in "The Last Supper."

As seen in Leonardo da Vinci's famous painting "The Last Supper," he illustrates the important time when Jesus shares his final meal with his disciples before his crucifixion. Amid the figures present at the table is Judas Iscariot, the disciple who would ultimately betray Jesus.

Leonardo's thorough brushstrokes and attention to detail bring each figure to life, displaying their distinct expressions, gestures, and emotions. Judas, positioned amid the disciples, is portrayed with an apparition of inner turmoil and conflict, his face displaying a mix of apprehension, guilt, and trepidation.

By use of his masterful use of light and shadow, Leonardo adds depth and complexity to the portrayal of Judas. The relationship of light and darkness on his face reflects the internal struggle he faces, torn betwixt his loyalty to Jesus and his impending act of betrayal.

While the focus of the painting is on the gathering of Jesus and his disciples, including Judas in "The Last Supper" acts as a poignant glimmer of the complexity of mankind's nature and the presence of both faith and betrayal within the lived experience.

Leonardo's inclusion of Judas in the composition acts to emphasize the important significance of Jesus' sacrifice and the challenges faced by those who followed him. It prompts viewers to contemplate the themes of redemption, forgiveness, and the frailties of mankind's nature.

"The Last Supper" is a confirmation of Leonardo's artistic brilliance, showcasing his ability to map the subtleties of mankind's emotion and the complex dynamics of an important time in history. His painting remains to inspirit and allure viewers, inviting them to engage with the important spiritual and narrative elements depicted.

Inasmuch we peer upon "The Last Supper," here we see the timeless story it portrays and the impact it has had on art and culture throughout the centuries. Leonardo's masterful depiction of Judas acts as a glimmer of the complexities of mankind's character and the universal themes of faith, loyalty, and betrayal.

"The Last Supper" holdeth as a confirmation of Leonardo da Vinci's lasting artistic heritage, a confirmation of his ability to map the depths of mankind's emotion and the timeless narratives that resonate with audiences.

96. MILITARY STRATEGY / STRATEGIA MILITARE

Maps and diagrams for military strategy.

Leonardo da Vinci, a master of various disciplines, dived into the realm of military strategy By use of his detailed maps and diagrams. Recognizing the importance of strategic planning in warfare, he scrupulously crafted visual representations to aid in understanding and executing military campaigns.

Leonardo's maps showcased his exceptional understanding of terrain, geography, and the complexities of battle. Through careful observation and analysis, he strove to provide commanders and strategists with a comprehensive overview of the battlefield, including key details such as topography, natural obstacles, and strategic positions.

His diagrams went beyond conventional maps, offering insights into military tactics, fortifications, and troop movements. He searched out various strategies, incorporating elements such as siege engines, defensive structures, and deployment formations. Leonardo's diagrams provided a visual guide for commanders, enabling them to devise effective strategies and anticipate the actions of their adversaries.

The precision and attention to detail evident in Leonardo's maps and diagrams mirrored his commitment to untwisting the complexities of warfare. He scrupulously studied historical battles, analyzed the strengths and weaknesses of different military forces, and strove to develop innovative approaches to gain a strategic advantage.

Leonardo's military maps and diagrams were not merely static representations but dynamic tools for strategic planning. He envisioned the fluidity of warfare and incorporated elements of mobility, flexibility, and adaptability into his designs. His approach emphasized the importance of situational awareness and the ability to adjust tactics based on the ever-changing conditions of the battlefield.

While many of Leonardo's military maps and diagrams were created as conceptual designs, they demonstrated his visionary thinking and his important understanding of military principles. His insights inspirit military strategists and historians, serving as a foundation for the development of modern military tactics and operational planning.

Leonardo da Vinci's maps and diagrams for military strategy remain a confirmation of his analytical mind, creative thinking, and undying followings forth of knowledge. His contributions to the field of military science exemplify the breadth and depth of his genius, as he applied his artistic skills and intellectual curiosity to the challenges of warfare.

Inasmuch we examine Leonardo's maps and diagrams, we recognize the lasting significance of his work in shaping the way we understand and approach military strategy. His visual representations offer valuable insights into the complexities of warfare, reminding us of the importance of thorough planning, innovation, and adaptability in achieving success on the battlefield.

Leonardo's maps and diagrams stand as a confirmation of his heritage as a visionary thinker and an influential figure in both the domains of art and military science. They act as a timeless glimmer of the power of knowledge, innovation, and strategic thinking in shaping the course of history.

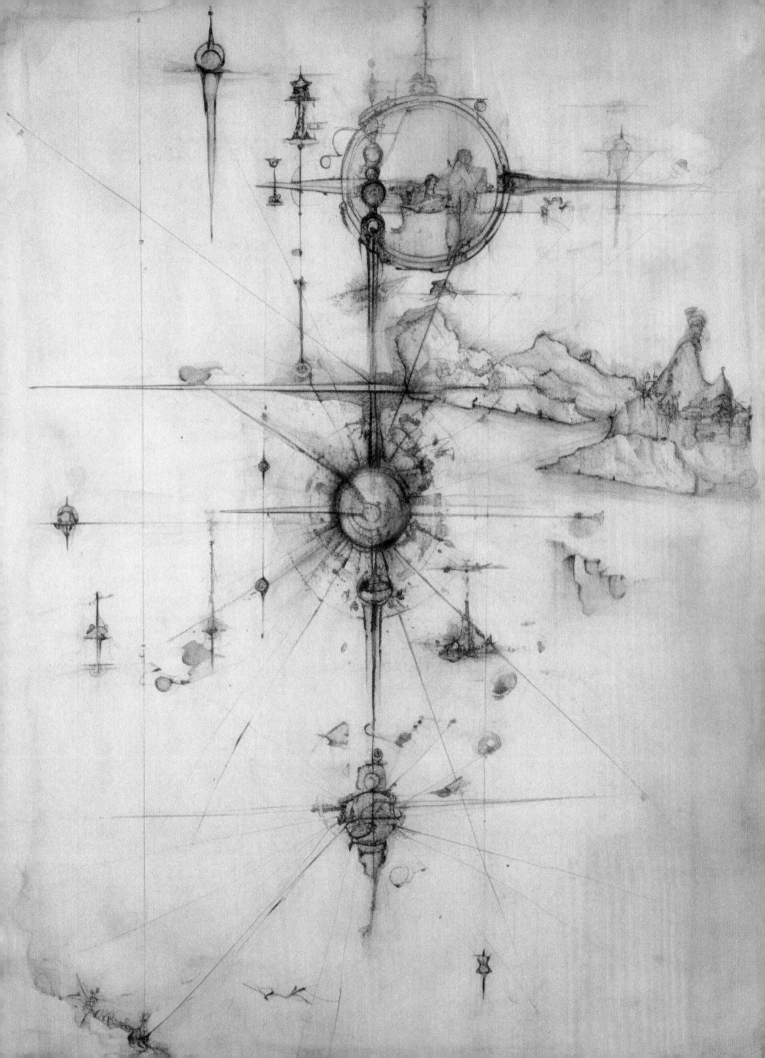

97. GLASS MAKING / PRODUZIONE DEL VETRO

Notes and sketches on glass making techniques.

Leonardo da Vinci's passion for knowledge and exploration led him to dive into various fields of study, including the complex art of glassmaking. By use of his thorough notes and sketches, he strove to uncover the secrets of this ancient craft and understand the techniques involved in shaping and manipulating glass.

Leonardo's fascination with glass extended beyond its aesthetic beauty. He strove to untwist the scientific principles behind its creation and the secrets of its composition. His thorough observations and detailed sketches procured the complex processes involved in transforming raw materials into exquisite glass objects.

In his notes, Leonardo documented various glassmaking techniques, including the preparation of the raw materials, the melting and shaping processes, and the methods of adding color and texture to the glass. He studied the properties of different types of glass, investigating their refractive qualities and exploring ways to enhance their clarity and brilliance.

Leonardo's sketches vividly portrayed the complex tools and equipment used in the glassmaking process, starting with the furnaces and blowpipes to the molds and shaping tools. His acute eye for detail and understanding of craftsmanship were evident in his depictions, displaying the swift and precise movements required to shape and manipulate molten glass.

By use of his studies, Leonardo not merely strove to uncover the technical aspects of glassmaking but also to stretch the bounds of the craft. He experimented with innovative ideas, exploring new ways to mold and shape glass, and even delving into the potential applications of glass in various fields, such as architecture and optics.

Leonardo's notes and sketches on glassmaking techniques stand as a confirmation of his unquenchable curiosity and his desire to lay bare the secrets of the natural world. His thorough observations and artistic renderings offer valuable insights into the art and science of glassmaking, providing a specter into the craftsmanship and cleverness of artisans of his time.

While Leonardo's direct impact on the advancement of glassmaking may be difficult to quantify, his documentation and exploration of the craft contributed to the collective knowledge and understanding of the field. His commitment to thorough observation and his followings forth of knowledge inspirit and inform contemporary glass artists and craftsmen.

Inasmuch we examine Leonardo's notes and sketches on glassmaking techniques, here we see his undying followings forth of knowledge and his ability to seamlessly blend art and science. His exploration of the secrets of glassmaking acts as a confirmation of his multifaceted genius and his lasting heritage as one of history's greatest polymaths.

Leonardo's studies on glassmaking techniques reflect his steady commitment to untwisting the mysteries of the natural world and his important impact on the fields of art, science, and craftsmanship. His inquisitive mind and artistic vision inspirit and guide generations of artists, scientists, and innovators who follow in his footsteps.

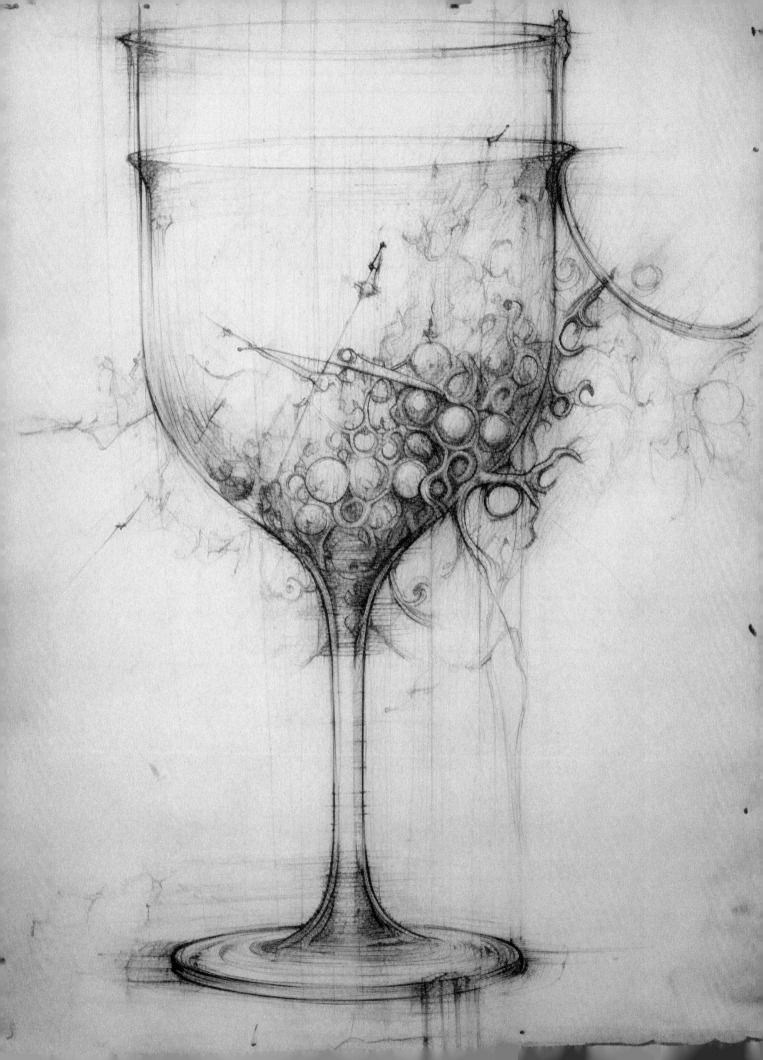

98. MONUMENTS / MONUMENTI

Designs for monumental structures.

Leonardo da Vinci's imaginative mind and visionary spirit extended beyond the domains of art and science to include the design of monumental structures. By use of his sketches and designs, he searched out grand architectural concepts that aimed to leave a lasting impact on the built environment.

Leonardo's designs for monumental structures showcased his innovative thinking, pushing the bounds of what was considered possible during his time. He envisioned structures that not merely acted practical purposes but also encouraged awe and admiration, leaving an important mark on the territory.

His sketches and designs revealed a depthy understanding of structural engineering and aesthetics. Leonardo carefully considered factors such as scale, proportion, and harmony, seeking to create harmonious compositions that seamlessly blended with their surroundings. His attention to detail and thorough study of architectural principles ensured that his designs not merely allured the eye but also stood the test of time.

Leonardo's designs for monumental structures encompassed a wide range of projects, from grand cathedrals to imposing fortresses. Each design mirrored his unique artistic vision and his desire to create structures that would endure as symbols of mankind's achievement and innovation.

In his sketches, Leonardo searched out various architectural styles, incorporating elements from classical antiquity as well as innovative concepts of his own. His designs incorporated soaring arches, complex facades, and elaborate decorative details, all contributing to the grandeur and splendor of the envisioned structures.

While many of Leonardo's designs for monumental structures remained unrealized, they acted as a confirmation of his unlimited imagination and his desire to stretch the bounds of architectural possibilities. His visionary approach to design remains to inspirit architects and designers to this day, challenging them to think beyond convention and create structures that leave a lasting impression.

Inasmuch we dive into Leonardo's designs for monumental structures, here we see his important impact on the field of architecture and his ability to bridge the gap betwixt artistry and engineering. His sketches act as a source of impetus, encouraging us to dream big and inquire into new possibilities in the realm of architectural design.

Leonardo da Vinci's designs for monumental structures not merely mirrored his mastery of artistic expression but also demonstrated his depthy understanding of the principles of engineering and aesthetics. His heritage as a visionary architect remains to influence the field, provoking architects and designers to create structures that are not merely functional but also awe-provoking, leaving an indelible mark on the world around us.

Inasmuch we swoon at Leonardo's designs for monumental structures, here we see the power of architecture to shape our environment and evoke an apparition of wonder and admiration. His lasting contributions act as a glimmer of the transformative potential of mankind's creativity and the important impact that visionary design can have on the world we inhabit.

99. FLOOD PREVENTION / PREVENZIONE DELL'INONDAZIONE

Designs for flood prevention structures and techniques.

Leonardo da Vinci, a master of innovation and cleverness, also searched out the realm of flood prevention By use of his designs and sketches. Recognizing the destructive power of floods and the need for effective flood control measures, he strove to devise innovative structures and techniques to mitigate the devastating impact of overflowing rivers and torrential rains.

Leonardo's designs for flood prevention structures showcased his depthy understanding of hydraulic engineering and his commitment to protecting communities from the ravages of flooding. His sketches depicted a range of innovative ideas, including dams, levees, and canal systems, designed to divert, control, and manage the flow of water during periods of excessive rainfall or rising river levels.

In his sketches, Leonardo scrupulously procured the complex details of his flood prevention designs. He studied the topography of the land, the natural flow patterns of rivers, and the potential vulnerabilities of settlements located in flood-prone areas. His designs integrated these factors, aiming to create a comprehensive and sustainable approach to flood management.

Leonardo's flood prevention designs often included elements of channeling and redirecting water, such as sluice gates and diversion channels. He searched out the use of reservoirs and basins to store excess water during flood events, effectively reducing the risk of inundation downstream. His sketches also incorporated innovative concepts like movable barriers and flood walls that could adapt to changing water levels.

While many of Leonardo's flood prevention designs remained conceptual, his visionary thinking and scientific approach laid the foundation for future advancements in the field. His insights into hydraulic engineering and his focus on sustainable flood management principles inspirit modern flood control strategies and technologies.

Inasmuch we examine Leonardo's designs for flood prevention structures and techniques, we recognize the importance of his contributions in safeguarding communities and protecting lives and property from the devastating impact of floods. His visionary approach to engineering and his commitment to finding practical solutions to complex problems act as a guiding light for contemporary flood control efforts.

Leonardo da Vinci's sketches and designs for flood prevention structures and techniques underscore his multidisciplinary genius and his steady commitment to improving the prosperity of society. His heritage as an innovator and problem solver lives on, provoking engineers, scientists, and policymakers to develop sustainable and effective flood prevention strategies that can withstand the challenges of a changing climate.

Inasmuch we confront the increasing risks and challenges associated with flooding, Leonardo's designs act as a glimmer of the power of mankind's cleverness and the potential for creative solutions. His visionary thinking remains to influence the field of flood prevention, provoking us to think beyond conventional approaches and develop innovative strategies to protect our communities from the destructive forces of nature.

100. OPTICAL ILLUSIONS / ILLUSIONI OTTICHE

Studies of how the eye perceives optical illusions.

Leonardo da Vinci's unquenchable curiosity and acute observation extended to the fascinating realm of optical illusions. By use of his thorough studies and sketches, he strove to untwist the mysteries of how the human eye perceives and interprets these intriguing visual phenomena.

Leonardo's studies of optical illusions revealed his depthy fascination with the complex workings of the human visual system. He scrupulously examined various optical illusions, exploring the ways in which our eyes can be deceived and our perceptions can be manipulated. His sketches procured the complex patterns, shapes, and color combinations that give rise to these alluring illusions.

In his followings forth of understanding optical illusions, Leonardo observed the relationship betwixt light, color, form, and perspective. He strove to decipher the mechanisms that cause our brains to perceive things that may not align with reality. His studies encompassed a wide range of illusions, including the famous "impossible objects," ambiguous figures, and perceptual distortions.

Leonardo's sketches of optical illusions often showcased his attention to detail and his ability to accurately depict complex visual phenomena. He searched out the underlying principles of illusion, such as figure-ground relationships, Gestalt principles, and the effects of contrast and shading. His acute observations and artistic renderings offered valuable insights into the mechanisms of visual perception.

By use of his studies, Leonardo not merely strove to understand optical illusions as a scientific phenomenon but also recognized their artistic potential. He experimented with techniques to create illusions in his paintings, employing perspective, foreshortening, and other visual tricks to allure and engage the viewer.

Leonardo's exploration of optical illusions acted as a confirmation of his inquisitive mind and his desire to untwist the mysteries of perception. His studies and sketches contributed to the collective understanding of how our eyes and brains interpret visual stimuli, shedding light on the complexities of mankind's vision.

Inasmuch we dive into Leonardo's studies of optical illusions, here we see the complex relationship betwixt art and science. His insights into visual perception inspirit artists, scientists, and researchers, encouraging them to inquire into the bounds of mankind's vision and challenge our understanding of reality.

Leonardo da Vinci's studies of optical illusions stand as a confirmation of his unquenchable curiosity and his steady followings forth of knowledge. His sketches offer glimpses into the enigmatic nature of visual perception, alluring our minds and stimulating our imaginations. They remind us of the complex relationship betwixt our eyes, our brains, and the world of illusions that surrounds us.

As we reach the end of this revelatory journey through Leonardo's rediscovered sketches, the genius and humanity of this Renaissance polymath shines through. In these pages we have seen the full span of Leonardo's restless intellect, from anatomical studies to grand architecture, from whimsical fables to prescient inventions centuries ahead of their time. But underlying this eclectic brilliance remains his unquenchable curiosity about the natural world and the inner workings of the human mind and soul.

Leonardo approached art and science as interwoven rather than separate endeavors. For him, meticulous observation was the key that unlocked nature's subtle patterns, allowing both artistic creativity and rational inquiry to flower through understanding the cosmic order. As we pore over these sketches, we can imagine Leonardo hunched over each page, his piercing eye recording the minutest details of botanical life or musculature in spare yet evocative strokes, distilling their essence with mimetic fidelity.

Vision was Leonardo's primary sense, the root of his muted colors and sfumato haze when translating three-dimensional forms to a two-dimensional canvas. In these sketches we observe his study of optics and perspective, creatively bending the rules to suggest invisible forces and imbue his scenes with inner dynamism. He wrote, "Perspective is nothing else than seeing a place behind a sheet of glass, smooth and quite transparent, on the surface of which all the things may be marked that are behind the glass." ever experimenting to enhance perceptual verisimilitude and emotive power on the flattened plane.

Yet for all his empirical rigor, Leonardo did not shy away from flights of imagination. Whimsical allegorical sketches reveal his appreciation for mythic beauty and dreamlike metaphor. Studies of natural catastrophes evoke an almost Romantic grandeur and terror at nature's overwhelming scale. Dramatic chiaroscuro studies plumb the extremes of light and darkness, prefiguring the Baroque. This interplay of observation and imagination, logos and mythos, embodies the Renaissance Humanist faith in man's creative dignity.

Leonardo valued knowledge for its own sake - "*saper vedere*" - to know how to see. He wanted to comprehend the totality of existence through syncretic connections, encompassing what he called the "science of painting." From the Mona Lisa's inscrutable smile to the sinuous braids of Leda's hair, his artistic genius celebrated the wonder of life and the joy of understanding even as his notebooks reveal the relentless diligence behind such marvels.

As an inventor, Leonardo designed projectiles, musical instruments, mechanical looms, flying machines, hydraulic pumps, and revolving stages. His Tank, Pulley, and Giant Crossbow sketches display his talent for blending form and function. Remarkably inventive, they present imaginative prototypes for technologies centuries ahead of their time. Here we see his commitment to improving human life by mastering nature through skillful design, presaging the engineering ingenuity that would flourish from the Industrial Revolution onwards.

While da Vinculum primarily highlights Leonardo's revelatory art and inventions, we must not overlook his passion for architecture. As evidenced by his luminous red chalk studies for centralized churches, he saw buildings as living organisms mirroring universal proportions. Architecture represented the mathematics undergirding beauty through geometric harmony and rationally-ordered space. Leonardo sought to integrate engineering, design, and metaphysics within sweeping architectural symbioses.

As we close this book, what resonates is Leonardo's ceaseless sense of wonder and joy in the act of creation. Across disciplines and genres, his curiosity about existence shines through. He remarked, "The desire to know is natural to good men," and considered humility key to sustenance of that desire. For Leonardo, creativity arose not in some sudden flash of solitary genius, but rather, through building each discovery upon those before in an open-minded spirit of collaboration with nature herself.

In this sense, Leonardo embodied the Renaissance Humanist faith in man's creative potential. But he also prefigured the mode of systematic inquiry that would characterize modern science. His elegant conjunction of aesthetics, imagination, and empiricism captures both the beauty and power of the human mind growing in wisdom. As we put down these sketches, may we carry forward Leonardo's spirit of diligent creativity aimed at forging new syntheses and raising life to ever more harmonious forms.

This collection has allowed a glimpse into Leonardo's restless, far-roaming intellect. But it also reveals his underlying ethic of compassion and human dignity derived from understanding our interdependence with all existence. Leonardo saw humanity as strands in nature's great web - at once gifted with godlike powers of imagination, yet humbly aware of how much remains unknown. As we stare at a dusty notebook of tireless observations, we catch a glimpse of Leonardo's spirit still searching, still yearning, ever seeking to reveal nature's elusive patterns.

Leonardo's life embodied his own saying, "Learning never exhausts the mind." For this polymath who considered himself "a disciple of experience," learning was a lifelong endeavor driven by an insatiable hunger to comprehend the whole. The sheer scope of disciplines he mastered, from anatomy to zoology, aeronautics to hydraulics, art to architecture, displays a systems-thinking genius who intuited the interconnectedness of knowledge centuries before our current age of synthesis.

He remarked, "The organ of genius is the hand." Through the hand illuminating the eye, intellect and senses were allied in his ceaseless quest to unveil nature's mysteries. We watch Leonardo exercise this genius across every folio, recording endless permutations of the human condition and the natural world with matchless skill and psychological acumen. Light and shadow, geometry and anatomy, emerge through his draftsman's hand as if discovering their ideal forms for the first time. Every sketch testifies to his unending marvel at life's complexity.

Leonardo pursued knowledge as the pathway to virtue and human dignity, writing "Good men by nature desire knowledge." He would be overjoyed to know his sketches now enlighten as a trove of lost wisdom restored for posterity. Like his Vitruvian Man, arms and legs eternally outstretched, these recovered works symbolize the enduring human striving for truth across the ages. Though dimmed for centuries, Leonardo's alchemic brilliance kindles our modern age once more.

In his own life of relentless self-improvement and boundless horizons, Leonardo personifies the soaring Renaissance spirit of transformation that pulled Europe from the Medieval into the light of rediscovered Graeco-Roman ideals. As we release these sketches back into the world, may da Vinculum reawaken something of that recuperative impulse in our own time - the faith in our shared capacity for ceaseless self-creation through the marriage of art and science in wisdom's alchemical crucible.

- Vannevar and Leila W. Mommsen

We would like to thank Cineris Multifacet for helping us publishing this book, and we would even the moreso like to thank you, the reader, for going through it with us. Please leave your honest thoughts as a review and pass the book along to who you think might enjoy it next. Those who share it will be blessed. In the spirit of da Vinci, keep up the inventiveness of life.

Continua con l'inventiva.

ISBN: 979-8-852-81075-5

Printed in Great Britain
by Amazon

27120629R00130